# BEYOND THE SKYLINE

LISE GOLD

*To my amazing wife,*
*my wonderful friends*
*and to my readers!*

*You've given me the confidence to write*
*And to follow my passion*

*#spreadthelove*

"Life in Hong Kong transcends cultural and culinary borders, such that nothing is truly foreign and nothing doesn't belong."

— PETER JON LINDBERG

# 1

Sophie let out a sigh of relief as she saved her last technical drawing of the week. Scrolling through the files on her desktop, she checked the garments for the coming summer season one last time to make sure everything was there. Five dresses, eighteen tops, seven cardigans, ten skirts and ten pairs of leggings. Oh, and the socks. People were really into socks these days. She pulled the lever on her chair and leaned back, resting her feet on a cardboard box underneath her desk. It was getting late now, and she couldn't wait to get out of the office. Her laptop went into sleep mode and she saw her reflection in the black screen. It wasn't pretty. Her eyes were sore and red and her skin looked blotchy. She wiped the mascara stains from underneath her eyes and stretched out, hands behind her head, relieving her back from sitting in the same position for hours on end.

"Oh, for fuck's sake!" A loud curse came from Aiden, one of the new developers, who looked like he was in total panic mode. Sophie turned to him with curious amusement.

"Are you okay?"

He rolled his eyes. "Not really. It's Saturday night and I'm not even on schedule for this week. Are you nearly done?"

Sophie nodded. "You'll get used to it. It's always like this in high season but it only lasts for about two months, so don't give up just yet."

Aiden didn't look too convinced. "Oh yeah? Well, I certainly hope so because my life has been alarmingly repetitive lately." He stared at Sophie like a wounded animal. "Do you have any idea what it's been like for me since I started?"

Sophie nodded. "I think I have an idea."

Aiden slammed his palm on his desk. "Well, I'm going to tell you anyway because I need to get this off my chest." He sighed. "I get up early, exhausted. I go to work, leave late and pick up a takeaway on my way home before working some more from my bed. No social life, no movies, dinners or anything fun. And here I am again, on a Saturday for God's sake! I mean, what's wrong with me? It's only you and me in the office. Where's everyone else? We should be out partying right now." He sighed. "I promised my girlfriend I'd take her to a concert tonight and I don't even know if I'm going to make it."

Sophie couldn't help but giggle. "Relax, Aiden. It will all be over next week. I've been here for years and it never changes, so either get used to it or look for another career." Aiden shot her an annoyed look and Sophie chuckled. She didn't care. They were both in the same predicament but she had stopped feeling sorry for herself a long time ago. In fact, she felt great. The monotone pattern that became the core of her existence each year during high season was about to be broken. The work was done, and finally, the moment had come when she could allow herself to relax a little bit. She turned her music up and felt a spark of excitement as she watched the drawings printing onto thick, shiny paper. 'Happy' was playing through the speakers on her desk and that seemed pretty appropriate right now. The range looked good and she was pleased with how it had all come together yet again.

Usually, she did this with her colleague Maggie. They would stay late, order pizza and make a celebration out of their last night in temporary fashion slavery. Then they would go to the pub. That had been their ritual for as long as Sophie had been in the role, but Maggie wasn't there today and Sophie found herself missing their banter and the dancing, their guilty secret when they were alone in the office. She checked her phone again, but there were no updates from Maggie, apart from her last text message.

'*Sorry I'm letting you down. Will explain everything over drinks tonight. Meet me at the Black Horse, 9 pm. Can't stay late.*'

Sophie shook it off and took a step back, admiring her work.

"Done," she said out loud. Downtime never lasted long but she tried to make the most of it. She still had a business trip to Hong Kong scheduled in, but that would be relaxing compared to the chaos of the past month. After that, she would be in paradise. Two weeks in Thailand with nothing but the sun, the sea and a couple of books. Her face lit up at the prospect. She tidied up after herself, switched off the lights and gathered her things, before turning to her only colleague left in the office.

"Bye, Aiden. Have a lovely weekend." Aiden didn't reply. He was too busy kicking the printer.

The light in one of the storage rooms next to the elevator was still on and Sophie stuck her head around the corner. A worn-out looking intern was sitting on the floor, labelling sample boxes. They were piled five-high and there wasn't much room for her to move around.

"Are you almost done?" Sophie asked. The girl turned around, putting on a brave smile.

"Couple more hours to go," she said. "These need to be sent to New York on Monday for a conference so I'd rather just get it over with."

Sophie nodded. "I'm sorry you're stuck with all the tedious chores. I have to go and meet someone. Otherwise, I'd have helped you." That wasn't entirely true. Even if she hadn't agreed to meet Maggie, she seriously doubted she would have stayed to label boxes on a Saturday night. But it did feel wrong to leave her there, so she gave the girl her most compassionate look. "Take it easy, yeah? It's okay to tell them you weren't able to finish it all. I'll vouch for you. I'm sure there will be someone who can help you out on Monday."

The girl shook her head. "Thanks, but I think I'll just finish this while I'm here."

Sophie leaned against the doorpost and crossed her arms. "I used to do this too, you know... we've all been there." She hesitated. "I'm Sophie by the way."

"I know," the girl said. "You're the senior designer, right? Aren't you about to take over as design manager during Debbie's maternity leave?" She held out a hand. "I'm Kendra. Intern. Or maybe I should say pushover?" They both laughed.

"Yes, it looks like I'll be taking over," Sophie said. "But I can so relate to you. You know, I worked for free for a year and a half."

Kendra's eyes widened. "No way. You're joking, right? At least I get paid."

Sophie shook her head. "No, I'm not joking. I worked the

longest days out of everyone; doing all the shitty jobs that no one else could be bothered to do." She gestured to the pile of boxes. "But let me tell you something. It might seem like a big deal right now but the world is not going to end if you don't finish this job tonight. Nobody is going to fire you, and I know this sounds harsh but they might not even notice." She winked and turned around. "So go home, Kendra and enjoy what's left of your weekend."

The chaos of London welcomed her as soon as she exited the building onto the main road. Sophie contemplated taking the tube but decided against it and hailed a cab. She felt like rewarding herself.

"King's Road please," she said to the cabbie. She pulled her hair out of her face to tie it into a knot at the back of her head and then remembered it wasn't long enough anymore. She regretted cutting it off. Without her hair, she somehow felt powerless and each time she remembered it, a slight panic crept up, reminding her it would take at least two years to grow it all back. Like most haircuts, tattoos and other bodily decorations she had ever attempted, it had seemed like such a good idea at the time. A fairy on her ankle and a Tasmanian devil on her right shoulder reminded her of that every single day. There was also a significant hole in the skin under her navel, which was the result of an infected DIY job from when she was fourteen. She glanced in the rear view mirror and adjusted the short locks behind her ears before putting on some lip balm. Then she looked down and inspected her clothes for coffee stains but the day had been kind to her and there was only a small ink stain on her left sleeve. Her faded jeans with trainers and the old sweatshirt she was wearing would have to do for now. They passed her parents' Victorian four-bedroom corner house and Sophie chuckled at the thought of her prim mother's disapproving look, should she see her like this. The front garden looked immaculate as always, with rose bushes in full bloom and a perfectly trimmed hedge that followed the building around the corner. Behind this was the generous annex that functioned as her father's practice, shielded from the street.

Getting out of the cab in Chelsea, Sophie inhaled the smell of fish and chips from the takeaway on the high street. It was the old familiar scent that always made her feel hungry on her way home from work. She crossed the road and waved at her parents' neighbours who were just leaving Partridge's with their weekly shopping. It was a lovely, mild evening in May and the bars were full of people, drinking and catching up on their week. She passed The Old Dog and smiled at the locals outside, who were gathered in groups on the pavement, each with a pint in one hand and a cigarette in the other. Behind them, the hanging baskets, which decorated the façade of the pub, were in full bloom, painting the perfect picture of West London. Sophie breathed in the fresh air and allowed herself to feel part of it all for the first time in weeks. Tonight, she was one of them. She took a shortcut and crossed the gardens of the Saatchi Gallery, stepping over the flower beds. She almost crashed into someone as she turned the last corner for the pub.

"Sophie, my darling! How are you?" Sophie nodded politely at her father's oldest and most loyal customer.

"Oh, hello Deidre." She knelt down to greet the senior lady's poodle. "Hi, Toby! Look at you. Such a handsome boy, aren't you?" The small dog jumped up and down, delighted to see her. Then she turned her attention back to the old lady in the red coat and the bright red lipstick.

"You look lovely as always, Deidre." In truth, Deidre's face looked like it had been torn off and sewn back on several times. Sophie studied the taut skin at her temple, where it stretched over her skull like a condom.

"Thank you, my dear. I'm glad you say that because I've been trying to get an appointment with your father for the past three weeks for a bit of 'maintenance work,' shall we say? Unfortunately, he couldn't fit me in until June, so I've been feeling a touch self-conscious lately."

Sophie shook her head. "No need, you look great. My father's been terribly busy lately. Not that he's complaining of course. But you know, summer is coming, and everyone wants a make-over." She scratched the poodle behind his ears and his little stumpy tail started wagging at full speed. "Would you like me to take Toby to the park tomorrow? I can pick him up at ten if you're home?" She shot Toby an excited look. "Would you like that, Toby?"

Deidre smiled. "That would be wonderful. Thank you, dear. Toby loves to run around you see, but I can't keep up with him on my old legs."

Sophie stood up and pushed the heavy door to The Black Horse. "No worries. I'm going for a run anyway so I might as well take him with me."

She grimaced when she entered the pub. It smelled of beer-soaked carpet and old frying oil. She greeted the bartender and some of the familiar faces, before ordering a beer for herself and a cider for Maggie. She then made her way through the back door and took a seat at the only available table in the beer garden.

"Bloody hell Sophie, you're looking rough. Hard week?" Maggie materialized from out of nowhere, carrying the same order. She was dressed casually in jeans and an army jacket but as always, her hair was styled with precision, each strand of her black bob perfectly in place. "Double cheers," she said. "I was waiting for you over there in the back." She put their drinks on the table and sat down with a big grin. "I'm early, you're early. What's happening to the world?"

They clinked glasses; then each took a long drink. Maggie pulled her sorriest face, crossing her hands in front of her chest.

"Okay, so I'm sorry I wasn't there to help you today. It's... complicated," she said, with an apologetic smile.

Sophie eyed her up and down in mock-accusation. "What's your excuse, then? Big news? You left me in the shit today and if I didn't love you so much, I wouldn't be here right now. So tell me. What the hell is going on?" She reached over the table to take Maggie's hand, searching for a ring.

Maggie laughed. "No, it's not like that. I'm not getting married, although it would have been perfect timing." She shot Sophie a mysterious look.

"Pregnant?" Sophie guessed.

Maggie shook her head. "God no, please." She took another large sip of her cider, removed her coat and folded it over the bench as if playing for time. At last, she spoke.

"Okay, well you know Dan is from New York, right?"

Sophie nodded. "Yes, that would be hard to miss." It had certainly not gone unnoticed that Maggie's boyfriend was from New York. His accent, his cocky attitude, the way he dressed. Everything about him screamed New York. Sophie really liked him though. He was different from the other men she knew and she kind of understood Maggie's attraction to him.

"Well," Maggie continued. "I don't quite know how to tell you this, so I'm just going to say it. We're moving to New York!" She pulled a smug face, ignoring Sophie's shocked expression. "Isn't it amazing? New York of all places! I got a job at Ralph Lauren and they're in the process of arranging a work visa for me as we speak." Sophie's jaw dropped. She was, quite literally, gobsmacked. Maggie shrugged. "Dan had to go back because of his contract and I thought I'd just try to apply for a couple of random jobs because I honestly couldn't live without him and somehow it just worked out. Ralph Lauren, Sophie! It feels so unreal!" Sophie couldn't tell if she was shivering from the thought of losing her favourite colleague and friend, or whether it was just the evening breeze. But she managed to keep it together and flew across the table to give Maggie a long hug.

"Why didn't you tell me you were applying, you selfish cow? That's amazing. I mean... Oh my god, it's huge!"

Maggie nodded and smiled, her eyes filling with tears. "I know, I'm sorry. I just didn't think anyone would hire me with all the visa fuss and all that. I only applied about two months ago and I didn't even tell Dan. It's all gone so fast. I had a chat with them and they called me back yesterday. That's why I was at home, waiting for their phone call. I was half expecting them to tell me I wasn't going through to the second interview but then they told me I had the job if I wanted it. I still can't believe it."

Sophie was crying too now. "I'm so proud of you," she said. "Really, I am. And I'm incredibly happy for you to have this opportunity to spend time in New York with the love of your life. But from a selfish point of view, I don't want you to go. You know that, right?"

Maggie wiped the tears from her cheeks. "I know. I'm going to miss you too," she sniffed. "But the flights are cheap and it's the perfect place for you to spend a long weekend whenever you want." Maggie paused, resting her chin in the palm of her hand.

"If everything goes smoothly with the visa, I'll be starting next month. I'll have to hand in my notice on

Monday for contractual reasons; otherwise, I could get into trouble. I just wanted you to know first. It's been so hard keeping it quiet but I didn't want to jinx it. You know how superstitious I am."

Sophie tried to force a smile but anyone could have seen that she was disappointed. "You never told me you wanted to leave. I understand that you want to be with Dan but you could have talked to me about it. We tell each other everything, right?"

Maggie took Sophie's hand and squeezed it. "I'm sorry," she said. "You're right. I should have told you first. I'm not sure if I wanted it to be real. I mean, I love London just as much as you do. But now it is... I can't let an opportunity like this slip by." Maggie searched for her cigarettes in her bag and lit one. "I'm terrified, Sophie," she said, before taking a long drag. "I'm scared of starting all over again and I'm afraid of failing. But I'm also super excited at the same time and right now, I need you to be happy for me. Can you do that?"

Sophie wiped her cheeks too. "Of course I can be happy for you," she sniffed. "It's amazing. You're going to have such a great time there. Maybe even a great life, who knows? I won't expect you to come back anytime soon and I'm okay with that. We can still talk and visit each other, right?" She sighed. "You'll only be six hours away."

"Hell yeah." Maggie's eyes widened. "Maybe I could find you a nice American boyfriend and we can all live happily ever after? You have to let me try, at least. Dan has lots of single friends over there. Americans love the English ladies, apparently." She laughed, almost spilling her drink.

"Seriously Sophie, I wish I could take you with me. I'm so nervous about moving to a city where I don't know anyone. I don't want to seem like a clingy girlfriend so I'll have to let Dan do his thing and I know that's going to be hard." She leaned forward. "Did you know that moving abroad together is one of the biggest risks for a relationship?"

Sophie shook her head. "Don't worry. You two will be fine. But I'll be coming over as soon as I can. You need to be prepared for that, okay? Now, let's get one thing straight. You are not leaving early tonight. I don't care how much you have to arrange. This might be the last Saturday we'll be here together, and you need a night to remember so you can miss me when you're gone."

Maggie laughed at her desperate plea and gave in. "All right. Whatever you want, Sophie. But you're buying."

## 2

Sophie was slouched in the chair opposite her manager's desk but corrected herself when Debbie walked in. She had tried really hard to be happy for Maggie but her efforts hadn't been successful. She missed her already. Besides that, she was worried about the prospect of doing both their fittings in one week. They would never be able to find a replacement for Maggie in such a short space of time, and even if they did, it would cost her even more of her precious time to get the newbie up to speed. The first thing she had found on her desk when she sat down that morning was a post-it note from Debbie requesting that she come and speak to her as soon as she got in. Sophie was an hour late, as usual on a Monday morning, and suspected Maggie had already informed her of the news. Debbie walked over to her desk and took a seat, and Sophie noticed the deep frown between her eyebrows. She knew from experience that it only appeared when she was either angry or stressed. Debbie moved back and forth in her chair, trying to find a way to sit comfortably behind her desk without her belly being in the way. She was getting bigger now. Her baby bump was at least the size of a basketball, and Sophie could see the outline of her belly button through the thin fabric of her beige t-shirt, which certainly didn't enhance her complexion at this stage in her pregnancy. She was sweating too. There were small drops above her upper lip and marks had already begun to form underneath her armpits. Sophie felt sorry for her. It wasn't the best situation to leave a business behind in, a key member of staff down, and months of maternity leave stretching before her. But Debbie, perhaps not as fragile as she looked right now, took charge and got straight to the point.

"Sophie, I need to talk to you about a situation we need to solve together." Sophie nodded, aware of what was coming.

"As you might know, considering you're a good friend of Maggie's, she handed in her notice this morning."

Sophie sighed. "Yes, I know. But she only told me Saturday night. And yes, I also know we've got a problem, and at such short notice, I'm not sure what to do about it."

Debbie was slowly impaling her mouse mat with her pen as she was talking. It seemed like a severe nervous tick, but Sophie managed to refrain from commenting on it. Debbie finally spotted the holes in the mat and put the pen away, folding her hands in front of her.

"Obviously Maggie can't come into work anymore. She's coming in to pick up her personal belongings tomorrow, and I would appreciate it if you could pack everything up for her. It's against company policy for her to be here as she's going to another designer label. Which means we're now officially understaffed." She paused. "I've thought about offering her role to one of the junior designers, but I don't think any of them are quite up to the job, so we're going to have to replace her with someone of her own level." She rummaged through a pile of paperwork and handed Sophie a CV.

"This girl sent me an open application letter for the position of senior designer a couple of weeks ago. Her name is Mel Johnson, and she's very passionate about working here. She's got five years of experience and has been promoted within all of her roles so far. I know Maggie has eleven years of experience but different people develop in different ways. Her references are excellent. I'm going to give her a probation period of three months, and if she's interested in the offer, I'll send her to Hong Kong with you. If it doesn't work out, we'll have to get a freelancer for the time being." She regarded Sophie, who looked over the CV with very little interest as if she had already dismissed the designer.

"Sophie, I need you to work with me here. There's no other option at the moment and this girl seems highly capable. You need to teach her everything you know as fast as you can. If she's as good as she claims, we'll be up to speed in no time. I'm going to give her a ring now and if she accepts, we'll talk about the details later. It will benefit you to have someone stable here when you take over during my maternity leave. I'm sure you agree with me on that?"

Sophie relaxed, suddenly remembering her upcoming promotion and the fact that she wouldn't be able to sulk anymore when she stepped into Debbie's shoes. She straightened her back and gave her a reassuring look.

"Of course. We'll make it work, I promise. I'm just a bit upset about Maggie leaving, as you can probably imagine. But you're right. I'll prepare Maggie's files and make sure everything is ready and clear for when the new girl starts. I just hope she's good."

That landed her an approving smile from Debbie. "Good girl. I'm counting on you."

## 3

"For the love of God! Enough work drama. I'm sure your new colleague will be fine. Now, more importantly, did you hear that Millie had some work done on her nose? Apparently, she hasn't left her apartment for two weeks, and someone I know saw her walking around with a bandage in the middle of her face." Cat grinned proudly as if obtaining the information had been an actual accomplishment.

Sophie rolled her eyes, amused by her oldest friend's unhealthy obsession with gossip.

"Cat, leave her alone. You know the reason she hasn't told you is that you 'yakyakyak' too much." She made a talking sign with both her hands next to her face. "And as much as I love your juicy theories, you can't make assumptions. Maybe she just fell and broke her nose?" Cat tried to keep a straight face, but they both burst out in laughter. Sophie and Cat had their weekly catch up. It was a sacred meeting that they only cancelled when one of them was abroad.

"So, what's up with you, my lady?" Sophie asked after their second Martini.

Cat sighed. "Nothing. My life's just boring. It's one big boring nothing. Ben wants to have kids, and I've been secretly taking the pill to make sure that doesn't happen. I'm not ready yet."

Sophie frowned at Cat's statement. "Ben wants to have kids? I didn't take him for the broody type."

Cat raised a hand. "I know, right? I mean, can you imagine? My life is eventless enough as it is. There will be nothing left of me if I have to stay at home with a baby twenty-four-seven. I'll lose my Monday nights with you - the one night in the week I can have a drink with a friend. The only reason I'm here is that Ben is playing volleyball and he'll probably call me in an hour to check what time I'll be coming home. I'll even have to say goodbye to my Tuesday night bridge club, however boring that may be. Monday and Tuesday. That's my weekend. Isn't that sad?" She pulled a sorry face. Cat was an expert at pulling faces, perfected by years of practice, with the sole goal of gaining sympathy from her audience. "Hey, it's better than nothing I suppose."

Sophie stared at her in disbelief. "Cat, you're a lady of leisure. Do you realize how many people would kill to be in your position? You can do whatever you want. There's no need to be bored. You can take up any sports or hobbies; do volunteer work, study, look for a job... You can go on holiday anytime you want. Visit cities, take some language courses. As far as the baby plans go, just tell Ben you don't want to have kids right now. And if you don't ever want them, you should let him know that too. Tell him that you want to go out more and that you refuse to schedule your social life around his calendar. Because that's stupid. I'm sure he'll understand."

Cat shrugged. "I know. When you put it like that, I sound like a spoilt brat. But Ben wants me to be home when he comes out of work and I don't have many people to go on holiday with. Ben doesn't have time to take trips with me, and anyway, he hasn't been much fun lately." She sighed. "Maybe I should just get a job. Right now I feel like I have to justify myself to him about everything. Especially about the fact that I'm sitting at home all day doing nothing. And if I don't want to be a mum anytime soon then what the hell is my purpose in life?"

Sophie poked her. "Chin up, Cat. I'm not saying your first world problems aren't important. I'm just saying that you need to be your own person, not just Ben's wife. You do know it's okay to change your mind, right? You don't have to stay with him if it's not working out, no matter how much money your parents spent on the wedding or how much security his wealth gives you. I know you can take care of yourself if you have to."

Cat waved at the waiter and pointed at her empty glass. "Maybe you're right," she said. "I'm not leading my own life. I'm leading Ben's life. It's just not the fairy tale I expected it to be, Sophie. I was so in love with him when we first met. I thought we would have fun together, travel and see the world. He was fun, wasn't he?" Sophie nodded but didn't necessarily agree. To Sophie, Ben had always been the person who had stolen Cat away from her. Her Cat. She blinked to suppress the painful memory of their wedding day. Seeing Cat there at the altar had been hard. She had looked so beautiful in her lace vintage dress, surrounded by candles...

But Cat wasn't hers and she never had been. She turned her gaze back to her friend, who was clearly on a mission to pour her heart out.

"He's become so serious since he started this new job and I think spending time with me has become an obligation to him, like it's something he does to prove to himself that we have a healthy marriage." She shifted on her barstool, scanning the crowd to make sure their conversation was private. "I looked in his diary the other day and it actually said 'spend time with Cat' between seven and ten pm every Wednesday and Thursday night. Then I started flicking through the whole damn thing and found that he had filled in all our weekends for the coming three months with dinners, family visits and social obligations. It made me feel sick." Sophie gave Cat a comforting smile and put an arm around her shoulder. Cat sighed, looking up at her.

"I think I want a divorce. I thought I wanted this but I don't. I don't even know who I am anymore. I feel like I'm slowly losing myself." She took a sip of her drink and stared at nothing in particular. "I'm an onion, Sophie."

Sophie tried to suppress a giggle. "I'm not sure what you mean Cat. What's an onion?"

"You know, an onion. The thing you cook with. I feel like an onion that's being peeled away, layer by layer. I've been trying so hard to be perfect that I've shed all the questionable things about me that made me who I am." She looked down and watched a lock of dark hair fall into her drink. "And in the end, all what's left is a bitter core that no one likes." Sophie took the strand of hair and tucked it back behind Cat's ear, leaving a drop of Martini to run down her neck.

"He's turned me into an onion and I'm afraid that if I don't leave him I'll become the left over crap that you put in a cheap curry just because it's there."

"Calm down, Cat," Sophie said, reaching for the bowl of peanuts on their table. "You're not an onion and you'll never be one. If you want to leave Ben, I'll support you. You can live with me for a while - or for as long as you want. But if you decide to stay with him, you two need to have a serious talk. Let him know what you want and what you need for this marriage to work."

Cat looked up at her and nodded slowly. "Thanks Sophie. You're wise, as always, but I think I'm just going to stick my head in the sand for a little bit longer. I don't think I can handle any conflict just yet." She cast Sophie a sad smile. "It's funny, isn't it? How all of our friends are married or in relationships but very few of them seem genuinely happy. Don't you find that strange?"

Sophie shrugged at Cat's words. "I don't know. I suppose a lot of the settled girls in our circles chose to be with someone who could provide for them—someone with social status or a comfortable future—not someone they were head over heels in love with. It's surprising that it still happens in this day and age. That's the strange thing if you ask me. I could never do it."

Cat nodded absently, stirring the olive through her Martini. "So how's your love life, Sophie?" she asked, more out of habit than out of curiosity. Everyone knew that Sophie didn't have a love life.

"Nothing new to report," Sophie mumbled, licking the salt from the peanuts off her fingers. "If I meet someone interesting enough to talk about, you'll be the first to know."

Cat crossed her arms and leaned in over the table. "Why won't you let me set you up? Isn't it about time that you settled down? Aren't you lonely? You've been single for almost a year now. I know at least three good looking, successful men that would line up to go on a date with you."

Sophie looked at her with a hint of annoyance. "Cat, I wish you would just stop going on about the bloody subject every single time we have a drink together. I've told you before and I'll tell you again. I'm happy and I don't need a man in my life. What good would it do me anyway? You weren't exactly selling the concept five minutes ago."

Cat pursed her lips. She picked up some peanuts, rolled then between her thumb and two fingers and threw them back in the glass with a sour look on her face. "Yeah. I guess you're right. But you never even have one-night stands anymore. How can you not want the excitement? The thrill? I would kill for a bit of spice in my sex-life. Sometimes I wonder if he still finds me attractive. I don't think he does, actually. Not like when we first started dating." She pursed her lips. "Maybe he's right. Maybe I've become old and unattractive and boring. Can't blame him."

"You idiot," Sophie said in a low voice, trying to keep their conversation private from the crowd around them. She took Cat's hand. "You are not old or unattractive or boring. Look at yourself. Do you have any idea how beautiful you are? Your wonderful thick dark hair and those deep blue eyes... It's the most magical combination one could ever wish for. And you have freckles. Perfect freckles. People would kill for those, you know?"

Cat didn't say anything. She just smiled sadly, her eyes watery from the alcohol. Then she raised her glass and bowed her head. "I love you, Sophie."

## 4

"There's my darling daughter," Eleanor Scott chirped. She air-kissed Sophie on the cheeks before rushing her inside. Sophie studied her mother as she followed her inside. She looked like a weather presenter from one of the conservative channels today. Her camel-coloured dress, pearl earrings and straight dark bob were the result of a recent visit to a style guru, whom she'd paid a fortune to tell her how to best present herself.

"Just in time. Deborah and Mark are already here and guess what? They've brought Aldo along. Isn't that great? You remember Aldo, don't you?" Sophie's face couldn't have hidden her disappointment if she'd had a gun to her temple. Of course she remembered Aldo. He had been trying to impress her ever since they were twelve, when their parents first became friends. As they ran in the same circles, they would often see each other at parties or in pubs and as much as she tried to avoid him, he always managed to corner her somewhere and push a glass of Champagne into her hands, which meant that Sophie felt obliged to listen to his pompous bragging for the duration of her drink. Sophie was convinced the only reason he hadn't abandoned his pursuit yet was because of her complete lack of interest. Which was obviously hard for him to stomach. Although his eyes were relatively small in relation to his face, Aldo was considered a charmer and he was always on the hunt for the prettiest girls in London. He had broken many hearts and had even dated some of her friends. They were usually replaced after two to three weeks by someone skinnier, wealthier or more interesting. He had not been missed when he disappeared for a couple of years to continue his quest on the campus of Cambridge University. He was now a private investor, just like his father, and made no secret of his wealth. No, Sophie was certainly not a fan of Aldo, and the fact that she would have to sit through lunch with him brought her mood down straight away.

"Mum, you're not trying to set me up again, are you? Because if you are, I can spare you the effort. I don't like Aldo. Not even a little bit." Her mother pouted her plump lips. She always did that when she disagreed but with the new set of fillers it was better if she didn't. The duck face could be disturbing to people who didn't see it coming.

"Don't be so negative, Sophie. He's an eligible bachelor with a prosperous future ahead of him, not to mention he's good looking. Many girls would give their right arm for a chance to date him. I don't see why you have to be so cross with me all the time." She gave Sophie's outfit, especially the beanie, a disapproving glance but didn't comment on it. Sophie wore trainers, tights, a leather miniskirt and an oversized black cable-knit sweater. She had stopped dressing to her mother's tastes a long time ago. She took off her beanie and shook her hair back into place before suddenly realizing that her mother hadn't seen her new haircut yet.

A gasp escaped her mother's mouth. "Sophie, what have you done to yourself?" Eleanor whispered, an expression of horror creeping across her face. Sophie laughed. Her mother looked at her as if she'd just grown a moustache.

"Chill out mother, it's only hair. It's not like I got a tattoo on my face." Eleanor clearly didn't find it funny. She took a step forward and reached out to touch Sophie's hair. She studied the front and the back, examining the length that was still left of it.

"Don't worry my love, we can fix this. I'll schedule you in for some extensions. Would you like that? There must be someone who can help you. Oh dear. What were you thinking?"

"No Mum, it doesn't need fixing. I like my hair like this. Just leave it." Sophie sighed. She still wasn't sure if her new haircut had been a form of rebellion against her mother or if she had done it because she wanted a change, but it no longer mattered. It was too late to do anything about it now. Eleanor shook her head again, then looked at the door leading into the living room.

"Well, I suppose now is not the right time to talk about it. We have guests waiting so hurry up. I'm serving the starter in twenty minutes but we're having a Bellini first." Sophie rolled her eyes and followed her mother into the dining room where she was greeted by her parents' pushy friends and their evil son, who regarded her through his beady little eyes. Deborah threw herself onto Sophie and squeezed her shoulders and arms as if she were checking for defects.

"Look at you, all trendy with your short hair. How is everything in the wonderful world of fashion?" Sophie tried to answer but Deborah talked over her immediately. "You remember Aldo, right? You two used to get along like a house on fire when you were kids. Aldo is working as a private investor now. He's doing really well for himself." She winked at Sophie, who nodded politely at Aldo and Mark.

"How are you?" she said. Then she turned to her father. "Hi Dad."

Her father smiled at her from behind his cigar. "Glad you're here, Sophie. Unfortunately your brother couldn't make it today. He had to go to the office. Some kind of emergency with a client." Sophie grinned. *Or an emergency hangover,* she thought. She reluctantly took a seat next to Aldo, which they had kept free for the special occasion. This was going to be awkward. She braced herself for an afternoon of polite conversation in front of two mothers who were desperately trying to detect any sparks flying around. Aldo turned to her with a smug look on his face.

"Well, well. You look exquisite as always. How's life treating you, Sophie?"

Sophie forced a smile and took a large gulp of her cocktail. "Great, thanks. Nothing new really, just working hard as usual. Last time we spoke was a couple of months ago, right? At the opening of that new club in Mayfair?" If Aldo was uncomfortable, he didn't let it show. That night, Sophie had walked into an entertaining situation where a girl had just thrown a drink in his face right in front of the bar. Aldo had stormed out, embarrassed by his friends' laughter and mocking comments.

"Yes that's right," he said. "Great place. I've been back two or three times but I try to get my well-deserved rest on the weekends nowadays. I'm travelling a lot for work and as comfortable as the standards of flights and hotel rooms are, it can be quite tiring."

Deborah beamed proudly, as if her son had just invented a whole new sort of wheel.

"Always business class and five star, our Aldo. New York, Moscow, Monaco, you name it. Actually, he's leaving for Hong Kong next week." Sophie's stomach dropped. Could this get any worse? She tried to meet her mother's eyes, begging her to keep quiet, but it was too late. Eleanor was already clapping her hands in excitement.

"I can't believe the coincidence!" she shrieked. "Sophie is going there next week too, aren't you Sophie? You two could meet up for dinner on the other side of the world. How cosmopolitan are our kids, Deborah?" Deborah threw her hands in the air in sheer delight and smiled broadly, looking from Sophie to her mother and then back to Aldo.

"Perfect," she said. "Show Sophie what a gentleman you are and take her out to a nice restaurant, will you Aldo?"

Aldo nodded and looked just as pleased as his mother. "Certainly mother," he said. "How about Friday night, Sophie? Will you still be around?" Sophie's mind was doing overtime, looking for excuses to turn down the offer.

"Actually," she stammered, "I'm meeting my new colleague at the airport. She's travelling with me and I don't want to leave her on her own. I'm so sorry. I would love to but it's her first trip and it wouldn't be decent."

"No problem," Aldo insisted. "Bring her along. The more the merrier. I'll bring a friend too. Dinner on me for everyone. How about that?" Sophie leaned back and sighed. She had lost the battle and there was nothing more she could do.

"That would be great, thank you." Sophie was furious. They were a cunning pair, her mother and Deborah. There was no doubt they had planned this together during their weekly shopping trip. She dragged herself through lunch, trying to help her mother in the kitchen as much as possible so she wouldn't fall victim to the predatory creep next to her.

She wasn't sure if her mother's permanent grin was the result of her extensive surgery or the tiny spark of hope that her daughter would finally start dating a respectable man.

"I'm really pleased you two are getting along," Eleanor said when Sophie was helping her carve the lamb. "You're not getting any younger, you know? Now is the right time to make decisions about your future. You're still fertile but who knows in a couple of years?"

Sophie shook her head. "I'm twenty-nine, Mum. That's really young. I've known him for seventeen years and I still don't like him. Having babies with him is the last thing on my mind, okay? You really need to stop interfering with my life."

Her mother ignored her protest. "Just give him a chance," she said. "You never know how you'll be feeling about the situation in two weeks' time. Now be a darling and bring the vegetables out, will you? They're getting cold."

## 5

"Are you sure you're going to be okay, Mum?" Mel Johnson shifted another pillow behind her mother's back on the couch in her living room. Isabella was wrapped up in a blanket, reading a book. Next to her was a large mug of hot chocolate, topped off with a dollop of whipped cream. Her long grey hair was braided and secured at the back of her head as it had been for as long as Mel could remember. She looked up at Mel and smiled.

"Stop worrying about me, Melzinha. Go and enjoy your new job. Be the best like you always are. I'm so proud of you. You know that, don't you?" Mel kissed her mother on the forehead.

"I know, Mum. You tell me that every day. But your back is so bad at the moment, and I won't be around to take care of you next week. I wish you would let me hire some help while I'm away." Isabella shook her head and pointed at Mel's suitcase.

"Just go, Melzinha. How many times do I have to tell you that it's a waste of money? I can still walk and cook." She held up the Kindle in her hand. "While you're away, I'm going to rest and read and look for a ground floor flat, so you won't have to put up with me for much longer."

Mel sighed. "You don't have to look for a new place. You're not a burden. I like to take care of you, and I like having you around." She walked into the kitchen and came back with her mother's mobile. "Here. Keep this with you at all times, just in case something happens. I don't want you to fall and not be able to call for help." Her mother reluctantly took the device and placed it on the coffee table next to her. "Promise to call me every day, okay? I want to know that you're alright. And don't even think about going for a walk or driving if you're having a bad day."

Isabella laughed, exposing the wrinkles around her eyes. "Trust me; you don't want your nosey old mother around when you finally decide to bring a girl home. And speaking of girls, isn't it about time you met someone you're serious about? I don't want you to be alone for the rest of your life."

"I'm not looking for a girlfriend, Mum. I have my new job to focus on now, so I'm not even going to think about dating until I get through my first three months."

"I know." Isabella sighed. "I just want you to be happy. You're beautiful and special, and you have so much to give, Melzinha." She raised an eyebrow. "And I don't want to be waiting around for grandchildren forever. I had three children by the time I was your age."

Mel gave her mother a playful push. "Stop the girlfriend and the baby talk, Mum. I like my life the way it is. Besides, I never said I wanted to start a family. Those were your words, and I've been hearing them a little too often lately. Go pester Don and Erik instead - at least they're settled."

Isabella giggled. "Okay. Fine, fine." She studied Mel's hair. "Shake that out before you leave, it looks flat."

## 6

It was busy at Heathrow airport, but then weekends were always busy. Sophie made her way through the crowd, looking for the business class check in. There was a queue there too. She had thought of coming early and checking in so she could hide in a bar somewhere. She liked the idea of having a bit of time to herself before spending the rest of the week with someone she barely knew. But then that wouldn't be a nice thing to do, and her parents hadn't raised her like that. Sophie looked around for a girl with long, dark, wavy hair, as described by her manager. She couldn't even remember her surname. Was it Mel Johnson? Johnston? She had her work number just in case. Maggie's old work number. A rather nervous looking woman was waiting in line for check-in. Her dark hair was curly but only shoulder length. She was scanning the area as if she were looking for someone. Sophie walked up to her and tapped her on the back.

"Hi, excuse me, are you Mel by any chance?" She asked.

The woman turned around and looked at her in confusion. "Me?" She put her hand on her chest. "No, I' m not.

Sorry." Before Sophie could apologize, she heard a husky voice coming from behind her, followed by a slap on her shoulder.

"That would be me." Sophie turned around, startled. There she was. The new designer. The girl who could never replace Maggie, even though she just had. Sophie felt her jaw drop when their eyes met, and she tried to hide her surprise with a polite smile. Mel was beautiful. She had thick dark brown curls, draped over her shoulders, and her eyes were a striking pale green. She smiled, showing off a neat row of perfect white teeth. Sophie couldn't work out her heritage. South-American maybe? The caramel skin and full lips gave her a sensual attitude, but her dimples were cute and made her look younger than her twenty-eight years. Sophie swallowed hard.

"Hi, I'm Sophie. Pleased to meet you, Mel."

"Likewise." Mel shook her hand firmly, and they walked up to the check-in desk together.

"Would you like adjoining seats?" The ground stewardess asked. Sophie hesitated, frustrated with the straightforwardness of the question she knew to be perfectly normal. She liked to be alone on flights unless she was with Maggie.

"Yes please," Mel answered before Sophie had the chance to say anything. "A two-seater would be great if you have one available." She turned to Sophie with a beaming smile. "Perfect. You can brief me on the coming week and tell me anything I need to know before I start. And I don't snore, or at least not that I know of."


"SO HAVE you been to Hong Kong before?" Sophie asked after they had settled down in their seats. She took her shoes off and put them in the compartment in front of her. Then she removed the blanket from the packaging, wrapped it around her, and stretched her legs out on the footstool while downing the glass of Champagne that had been waiting on the side table next to her. It was always better to get comfortable straight away. Sophie had travelled a lot over the years as a designer and had developed a set of predictable habits, which she refused to steer away from.

"No, I've never been there," Mel said. "I'm excited actually. Going somewhere new is nice. I've always worked with Italian factories, and in my last role, I used to go to India a lot. This trip couldn't have come at a better time. It's a great way to start a new job, getting right to the source of everything. I can't wait to get to the office and meet everyone. It's so much easier when you can put a face to the person you're speaking with over the phone, don't you think?" She focused on removing her own shoes, not waiting for an answer. "Do you know Hong Kong well?"

Sophie nodded. "Yeah, I do. I've been going there for seven years now, and I've also spent four months in Hong Kong and China a couple of years back when we were setting up our new factory. It's one of my favourite cities."

Mel nudged her. "Great. You can show me around after work. I bet you know all the cool places and the best restaurants."

"Sure. I'll be your guide for the week." Sophie tried to sound enthusiastic, but her voice fell flat. "Just don't expect too much, I get jet-lagged and might be wiped out by nine o'clock." She really wanted to go to sleep so she wouldn't have to socialize but it seemed rude to do so. She mentally scrolled through the list she had memorized in the taxi in case they wouldn't have anything to talk about, but all she could come up with was a lame statement, lifted from the front of Mel's CV. "So you've been a designer for five years?"

"Yes, I have. Five years next month. I know I'm not as experienced as my predecessor but I promise you I can do this. Debbie believes I can, I'm sure she's discussed my CV with you?"

Sophie frowned. "She did discuss it with me, but she'd already made up her mind about you, so it's not like I had a lot of say in the decision." She shook her head. "I'm so sorry. That came out wrong and totally sounded like I don't want you here..."

Mel raised both her hands to stop her from saying more. "It's okay. Really, it is. You must be worried that I'm not experienced enough or good enough for this job, that I might be a burden to you, or that you'll have to mentor me for months until I can function on my own." She shot Sophie a challenging look. "I understand. And that's fine because I'm going to prove you wrong. I'm good at what I do. Now let's be friends, shall we?" She put her hand on Sophie's, which was resting in her lap. Sophie was taken aback by her mature approach and regarded her with a mixture of regret and curiosity.

*Shit! Now she's the bigger person. That's just wrong. It's all so wrong.* This wasn't the way she had planned their first meeting to go. She felt a hint of shame and tried to hide it with a smile.

"I'm sorry," she said. "You're right. Maybe I was judging you and I shouldn't. Let's get to know each other and try to have fun." She looked down at the hand, still resting on her own. This girl was unusually tactile in her ways. Mel pulled her hand back to accept the glass of wine the flight attendant brought over.

"I ordered you one as well while you were in the toilet.

Hope you don't mind." She winked. "I'll drink them both if you don't."

Sophie smiled and took the glass. "Thanks. I could really do with another drink. Cheers."

Mel stretched out her legs and got more comfortable in her seat. "My kind of girl," she said. "Now tell me about yourself. Where do you live? Are you married? Do you have kids? How's the job?"

"You've got a lot of questions." Sophie shrugged and took a sip of her wine. "But there's not much to tell, I'm afraid. I've been a designer for seven years, and I've worked mostly with Chinese factories but some in Turkey too. This is my third job, and I've always done knitwear. I'm not necessarily passionate about knitwear; it just turned out that way. I'm twenty-nine, single, no kids. I live in London, South Kensington. I studied product design... That's it." She laughed, surprising herself. "God, I sound boring."

Mel laughed too. "I doubt that you're boring." She looked at Sophie intently. "You're very pretty, did you know that?" Sophie blushed and shifted in her seat. It happened every time someone gave her a compliment. Was Mel trying to flatter her into a friendship? She looked ahead and smiled awkwardly, avoiding her beautiful neighbour's gaze.

"I'm not sure I agree with that today." She ran a hand through her hair. It still felt like a wig. "But thank you, I guess." She turned her attention back to Mel. "You're very pretty yourself, Mel. But I'm sure you hear that all the time." Sophie meant it. Mel's eyes were amazing. The way the green of her irises radiated and became lighter at the edges made her eyes seem almost otherworldly. "Where are you from originally?"

Mel batted her eyelashes and grinned. "Thank you for the compliment. My mother is from Brazil, but I was born in

London. Not quite South Kensington though. I grew up in Brixton. I still live there, actually." She tilted her head. "Bet you've never been there, huh?"

Sophie shook her head, refusing to give in to Mel's sudden provocation. "No, I haven't. Do you like living there?"

"Yeah I do," Mel said. "It's my home. It's always been my home. My ground floor flat is around the corner from where I grew up and next to the village market. It used to be quite rough around there, but now they've opened all kinds of restaurants and bars, so it's really cool, actually. I bought it a couple of years ago. Great investment."

Sophie was impressed with the fact that Mel had managed to purchase a house at such a young age. This was London after all. She didn't dare mention the fact that she too owned her own flat, but that her parents had paid for it.

"Did you buy it on your own?" She asked.

"Yep," Mel said. "I've never had any help from anyone, and I'm proud of that. I've worked my ass off to pay my way through university and to be able to buy my own place." She raised an eyebrow and cocked her head. "And I'll work my ass off for anything else that I want. Believe me. I'm the best person in the world to work with. I don't cut corners." Sophie laughed.

"Well, that's good to know. But I do cut corners. Sometimes, not always. So you'll just have to grind your teeth and live with that." She took the menu the attendant handed her and browsed over the selection of starters. If she wasn't mistaken, she was starting to have a good time.

"Do you have a boyfriend?" She asked, looking up from the menu. Mel shook her head and grinned, her dimples deepening.

"Absolutely not. Never had one. Actually, my ex-girlfriend and I just broke up last month." She shrugged and hastily added: "But I'm okay with it. I mean, I'm not a mess or anything. We were just too different; it would never have worked out." Sophie tried to hide her surprise. Mel didn't seem like the kind of girl who was into girls. But what did she know? Sophie didn't have any gay friends in her inner circle. Most of her friends were married or engaged or pregnant with their first child.

"I'm sorry," she said. "Were you together for long?"

Mel shook her head. "It's okay. We were together for a year but the past four months have just been a big blur of one argument after another. There was no fun in it anymore." She leaned back, rearranging her pillow behind her neck. "In the end, we were living separate lives. I didn't know what she was up to; she didn't know what I was doing... It didn't make sense anymore." She lowered her voice and whispered. "We didn't even have sex in the last four months. That's crazy, don't you think?"

Sophie burst into laughter. She would have usually found the subject too intimate to talk about with someone she barely knew, but the Champagne and the wine had already gone to her head.

"You think that's crazy? Are you serious? What if I told you I haven't had sex in a year?"

Mel's eyes widened. "No. I don't believe that. Why would you even do that to yourself?" She poked Sophie in the shoulder and leaned into her. "A pretty girl like you should have no problem getting laid, right?"

Sophie blushed again and looked down at her menu. "I'm just not that bothered," she said. "I'm quite happy on my own." Sophie herself had lowered her voice too as if they were exchanging secrets. She couldn't believe she was opening up to a stranger, but it felt right, somehow. Besides, it couldn't really hurt, could it? It was just an innocent conversation.

"My mother on the other hand," she continued, "is not okay with it. She's been desperately trying to set me up for the past couple of years. It's the most annoying thing. Last week, she lured me over for Sunday lunch, and I arrived to find myself sitting next to their friend's son, Aldo. The guy's a total creep, but his parents were there too, and they practically cornered me until I finally agreed to go for dinner with him and his friend. He's in Hong Kong this week too. I told him I'd bring you along if you wanted to come." She rolled her eyes and shook her head. "Of course, you're more than welcome to, but I totally understand if you have better things to do. I know I'm not making it sound very appealing, but I'm just being honest here."

Mel laughed at Sophie's discomfort. "No way. Dinner with a creep? Maybe even two? Sounds tempting. Who would say no to that? Besides, it'll be fun watching someone desperately trying to win you over all night, only to be blown off at the end of it. Great entertainment, right?" She gave Sophie a reassuring smile. "Don't worry; I'll come along. I can always fake food poisoning to get you out of there if you want me to. I never understood the whole concept of setting people up when they already know each other. If there's no instant connection, chances are minimal there will ever be one."

Sophie was stunned by how well they seemed to be getting along. Mel was easy to talk to and without realizing it, she had already told her far more than she normally would.

"So, what about your family?" sophie asked. "Are your parents still together?"

"Not exactly," Mel said. "My father passed away a couple of years ago."

Sophie flinched. "I'm so sorry. Were you two close?"

"I don't know. Not close, I suppose, but I loved him. He was a good man and I know he loved me too, but the generation gap was too big. He never really got me and we didn't talk very much. He was just someone who was always there, around the house, you know?" She noticed Sophie's confusion and continued.

"My mother came here from Brazil when she was twenty-one. She left her family and everything she had behind to work as a cleaner in a hotel in London. She met my father after a couple of weeks. Not in the hotel, though. They met in a pub. My father liked to drink and he spent most of his evenings at his local. I would say he was probably a functioning alcoholic. He was also fifty-two. Dirty old Englishman, basically. He left his wife for her. He didn't have children then, or not that I know of. My mother was young and poor and lonely. It probably seemed like a reasonable solution at the time. They had me a year later and after that my two younger brothers." She glanced at Sophie. "Sorry, I don't usually hang my dirty laundry out, but you asked." Sophie shook her head, gesturing for her to continue.

"My mother stayed with him until he died of a heart attack. She's traditional in that way. I always expected her to leave him at some point. Even at a young age, I understood that that was a very realistic scenario. But she never did. She was always loyal to him, despite his heavy drinking and gambling problems. It was a strange arrangement. My mother never seemed unhappy, just determined to make a good home for her family." She smiled. "I'm proud of her. If it weren't for my mother, my life would have been a whole lot harder right now. That is if I'd been born at all. I would probably be living in Rio, working as a waitress or a cleaner. Not that there's anything wrong with that, but I'm happy I'm here." Mel nodded, indicating she was done talking. "So that's my story."

"That's quite a story," Sophie said quietly. "Your mother must be a strong woman. It's a courageous thing to move to the other side of the world at such a young age."

"She is. Now let's see..." Mel studied the menu, clearly trying to change the subject. "I'm going to go with the courageous decision of having the Mezze for my starter. What do you think?"

## 7

The long flight had been pleasant, and they had eaten, laughed and talked for hours on end until they both fell asleep. Mel's presence hadn't been weird or uncomfortable at all. On the contrary, Sophie had enjoyed every moment of it and couldn't believe how rested she felt when they arrived at their hotel. The grand lobby was crowded with people in business attire. They were either checking in or out or were gathered around the tables with files and laptops, looking as corporate as one possibly could. Their dark suits were a stark contrast to the opulence of the large marbled reception area with glass chandeliers, velvet sofas and a wide ornamental staircase, which led to the dining area and terrace. Hotel porters in crisp white uniforms were running around with coats and luggage tags, collecting bags and leading guests to their rooms. In the far corner, a Chinese woman in a black sequined evening gown was playing classical music on a grand piano. The scent from the air freshener, used throughout the hotel was familiar to Sophie, although she had never been able to work out what the main ingredient was. She smiled. It felt like home here.

"Wow. Nice place", Mel said after they had checked in. She looked genuinely impressed. "Is this where you always stay?"

Sophie nodded. "There's a gym and an outdoor pool on the roof. It opens at seven in the morning. I love to have a swim before I start work. Want to go up and have a look? They'll take our bags up to our rooms." She gestured to the bellboys who were already stacking their suitcases onto a trolley. Mel nodded eagerly and followed Sophie to the elevator to explore their home for the week.

THE SUN HAD ALREADY BEGUN to set when they finally sat down to have dinner. Sophie had asked for her favourite outdoor table, and they had a great view over the harbour and Central. She loved how the warm wind felt on her skin, welcoming her back after six long months.

"I love it," Mel said. "This trip is already way better than what I'm used to. And this dinner..." She grinned. "This dinner is already way better than any of the dates I've ever been on."

Sophie raised an eyebrow. "Were they that bad?"

Mel shrugged. "The dates or my business trips?"

"Both."

Mel held up a finger as if she was about to make an announcement. "Well, first of all, I've never been taken out for a fancy dinner. My dates have always been more casual. You know, like the pub or a movie. Not that it bothers me, I'm not a high maintenance kind of girl." She giggled. "But still... this is great. Even though it's not a date, of course." They both laughed, and Mel gazed out over the water. The reflection from the illuminated sky-scrapers on the other side of the harbour cast a colourful glow over the dark ripples of the water, creating a surreal-looking dreamscape.

"It's impressive. I don't think I've ever seen anything like it. And then there are the candles, the wine..." Mel pointed at the basket in between them. "And this bread. Oh my god, how good it this bread?" She tore off another piece of rosemary flatbread and soaked it in the olive oil. "And as far as my business trips went," she continued after swallowing her mouthful of bread, "the hotels certainly weren't as fancy as this one, and I usually had to work over the weekends. On a couple of occasions, I even worked three weeks on end without downtime. Hong Kong almost feels like a holiday compared to my previous trips." She lifted her wine glass and clinked it against Sophie's.

"Well, I guess I've always been quite lucky that way," Sophie smiled, trying to lighten the mood. "Hong Kong is a great place. We'll have Wednesday morning off so I can show you around if you like? Maybe take a trip to Lantau or Stanley, or go to the beach? And I know some great markets that are open until midnight. Unless you want some time to yourself," she hastily added. "You might not want to be stuck with me all week."

"No, no. Not at all," Mel said, waving a hand. "I'm so happy that you know your way around. And it'll be fun, right? I feel like we get along."

Sophie waited for the waiter to top up their wine. "I'm sorry if I made you feel unwelcome," She said, shaking her head. "It was childish of me to compare you to Maggie. That's not a fair start for anyone. But I promise you I'm not a terrible person and I'll help you as much as I can until you've settled into your job."

"That's okay," Mel said. "I kind of understand. Where is she going anyway?"

Sophie sighed. "She's moving to New York next month. Ralph Lauren. Her boyfriend is American, so I doubt she'll ever come back if everything goes to plan. They'll probably get married soon and live the American dream with two babies, a puppy and weekends in the Hamptons, or whatever it is they do over there."

Mel leaned in and put a hand on Sophie's arm. "Well I guess this is a new start for the both of us then, so let's make it a good one." She smiled at Sophie and held her gaze with her intense green eyes. Sophie felt that awkward feeling in her stomach again. It happened every time Mel looked at her in that way. Mel was stunning, and perhaps it was her ravishing beauty that made her slightly nervous. Sophie had found herself staring at her on more than one occasion during their flight, and she was starting to worry that she was coming across as a weirdo. Because for some reason, it mattered to her what Mel thought of her now. She wanted Mel to like her, and she wanted them to get along. She quickly redirected her gaze towards the harbour and went to twirl a non-existent lock of hair around her finger.

"You do that a lot," Mel noticed. "Did you recently cut it?"

"Yeah", Sophie said. "Not quite used to it yet. I feel like I've lost a part of myself, you know?"

Mel inclined her head. "I know how it feels. I shaved my head once, but unfortunately, it wasn't a good look for me."

Sophie gasped and almost choked on an olive. "You? Shaved your head?" Mel's thick curly long locks were so defining that she couldn't imagine her without them. Without thinking, she reached out and let her fingers run through the silky hair surrounding Mel's face.

"I know," Mel said. "Never again. I like short hair though. I think it looks hot. It just doesn't work for me, so I'll have to live with this for the rest of my life." Sophie realized her hand was still in Mel's hair and quickly pulled it back.

"I love your hair," Sophie said. "I've been staring at it since I met you, wondering if it was real." Mel looked down and smiled, rolling up the sleeves of her oversized white shirt.

"Thanks," she said. Sophie could have sworn she was blushing, but she couldn't be sure, as their table was only dimly lit by a couple of candles and the fairy lights in the palm trees above them. Their food arrived and Mel attacked her steak as if she was on a battlefield.

"Sorry if I eat like a pig," she laughed. "I'm starving. Must be the time difference."

"Me too," Sophie mumbled through a mouthful of sea bass. "I'll take you out for some great Cantonese food this week, but I was just too tired to go anywhere tonight." A headache was threatening to kick in, and she knew it would get worse if she didn't go to bed soon, even though she wouldn't be able to sleep for a while. "We've got a busy week ahead. Tomorrow, we'll be in the office, which is a ten-minute walk from here. It's that tall building with the green neon lights," she said, pointing at a skyscraper. "You might feel as if you're working in the dark, but I'll help you out as much as I can. After Maggie resigned, she was immediately dismissed from the office, so she didn't exactly have the chance to leave notes behind. We'll both have to improvise a little bit, but I'm sure it will be fine. Then there's the end-of-season office lunch, which is an important tradition to the employees here. It's going to be a long one, but it's good that you'll get to talk to everyone and get to know the people you'll be working with. Tuesday we're going to one of the factories in China and Wednesday we've got a late start. Two pm, I think. We have to wait for the new prototypes to come in from China, so there's no point in us being there. Thursday we've got another factory visit with fittings in China and on Friday we're going for some inspirational shopping to get ideas for the new season. Maybe we could visit some pop-up stores and galleries?" Mel nodded eagerly, her mouth full, and Sophie giggled at the sight of her while she continued.

"And let's not forget about our double date on Friday night. I can't say I'm looking forward to it, but it should be interesting."

Mel laughed at Sophie's deadpan expression. "Sounds peachy. You seem to have a plan, so I'll just follow you around like an obedient puppy." After they had finished the bottle of wine, Sophie started yawning.

"I'm sorry for being so boring," she apologized. "But I think I need to go to bed." To her surprise, Mel stood up from the table and gave her a hug.

"Thank you," she said. "You've made me feel a lot less nervous about this week, and I'm excited to get started tomorrow."

"You're welcome," Sophie stammered. "I had a good time tonight." Her body seemed to react in strange ways whenever Mel's skin touched hers. The old familiar picture of Cat's face so close to hers flashed through her mind, and she shrugged it off. *Don't think about it. This is different. Everything is different now.* She walked away from the table and hurried to her room. She felt cold and sweaty at the same time and was dying for a shower. No point fretting over it. She was probably just jet-lagged and giddy with exhaustion. That was all.

## 8

"Did you sleep well?" Sophie asked when Mel sat down at the breakfast table on the terrace. Mel wore a sleeveless denim shirt and a frilly skirt that bounced around her bare legs when she walked.

"Like a baby," she said, throwing a pile of newspapers on the chair next to her. She looked sleepy. "You?"

Sophie yawned. "Me too. Woke up at six but it was kind of nice. I got a coffee and went for a walk. It's so great to be back." Mel's eyes widened.

"You should have woken me up. I don't want to miss anything." She put a hand in front of her mouth and looked around at the other tables. "I'm sorry. It's only eight in the morning, and I'm screaming already. I'm way too over-excited." Mel pointed at the glass doors that lead to the breakfast buffet. "Is that our breakfast?"

Sophie laughed. "I'll wake you up tomorrow morning, but I can promise you that you won't feel so great then. The time difference hasn't caught up with you yet. And yes, that's our breakfast. I'll watch your bag if you want to go first." Mel seemed pleased with that. A big grin spread across her face, bringing out her dimples. She put her canvas bag next to Sophie's chair.

"Thanks. I'm starving. I was wondering if it was an early wedding banquet when I passed it on my way out. It looks so indulgent. They have lobster, Sophie. For breakfast!" She got up, and Sophie forced herself to focus on her mobile while Mel skipped towards the dining room, her hips shaking with every step. There was something positive and upbeat about Mel that made Sophie smile whenever she opened her mouth to speak. She stirred her coffee and quickly scrolled through her emails. There was nothing urgent, so she opened one of the newspapers Mel had deposited on the chair earlier, searching for something light to read, only to realize after a while that the one she'd picked up was Chinese.

"Anything interesting?" Mel asked. She put down a plate of fresh fruit, a bowl of noodles, a green tea cake and a bowl of congee, topped off with deep-fried fish skin. Sophie shot her an amused look, staring at the display of food on the table.

"Well, I'm afraid I wouldn't know as the newspapers you brought with you are all in Chinese." She pointed at the congee. "Are you feeling adventurous today?"

Mel smiled. "Of course I'm feeling adventurous. I need to try this. All the Chinese people inside are eating it so how can I not?" She lowered her voice. "I'm a sucker when it comes to new foods. I have to put everything in my mouth that I haven't tried before. You should know this about me." She took one of the newspapers from Sophie and held it up in front of her. "Even this is fascinating to me. It's one big mystery, and I'm determined to figure out what the big story of today is." She laughed. "I don't care if you think I'm a loser."

Sophie stood up and nudged her. "I don't think you're a loser. But I also don't think you'll be able to finish all of that without getting sick. If you manage, I'm going to seriously question your mortality."

"SO YOU'RE NOT FEELING sick yet?" Sophie enquired. Mel shook her head. She didn't seem the slightest bit affected by her enormous breakfast. They exited the footbridge that spiralled over the motorway and entered a no-traffic zone. The mirrored facades of the modern high-rise buildings reflected the bright morning light and people were seeking shade on wooden benches underneath large trees or drinking coffee on the terrace, lined with red parasols. It was busy, but no one seemed in a hurry.

"What a beautiful day." Mel sighed. "Oh look at all those cute little cartoons. They're everywhere." She pointed at a shop front with an illustration of two bunnies under a rainbow, surrounded by dollar signs. "This looks fun."

"That's actually a bank," Sophie grinned. "But we can go there later if you want. They open at midday."

Mel laughed. "Okay, so what about that one, the one with the thing that looks like a poo?"

The sign above the shop front was questionable, indeed. Sophie had to agree with that. It was a poo-shaped thing with eyes and a big, happy smile. It even had dimples; she noticed as she approached the window.

"Ah, I think I know what this is. But it's new, so I can't be too sure. See those chairs there? They look like dentist chairs." Mel nodded, pressing her face against the window. She covered her forehead with her hands to block out the bright morning light. "Well," Sophie continued, "it kind of looks like a beauty salon, so I guess the poo thing is actually a placenta, which would make this shop a placenta beauty clinic."

Mel looked puzzled. "What do you mean? Do they make you eat placenta?"

"No," Sophie laughed. "They use creams and serums made out of placentas. It's quite big here. Apparently, it regenerates the skin and enhances the release of stem cells, making your skin look younger and smoother." She turned to Mel. "But I've never tried it; it's quite expensive."

They walked on and passed numerous bakeries and coffee shops until they reached the large square in front of the office entrance, decorated with palm trees and fountains.

As soon as they arrived at the office, they were both greeted with tea and welcome hugs from all the staff. Sophie glanced around the industrial L-shaped space with its low ceilings and at least fifty cubicles lined up in neat rows, running through the names of the employees in her mind. She knew them all, including the receptionist and the cleaner. The polite formalities only lasted for about twenty minutes though. The crowded room seemed even smaller than usual now that word of Maggie's leaving had gotten around, and her developers wanted to know exactly what was going on. They had so many urgent questions and were milling around her, trying to get a word in edgeways. Sophie suddenly remembered she was the one in charge now. She got up on a chair and waved her hands for everyone to listen.

"Hi, everyone! It's so nice to see you all again. I've missed you guys, and we'll take you all out for lunch today, so we can catch up. I hope you can all make it. First of all, please let me introduce you to Mel. She's our new designer. Unfortunately, Maggie decided to leave the company, and I'm personally quite upset by that, as I'm sure many of you are too. She sends her love to all of you, and she's very sorry she wasn't able to say goodbye." Sophie paused for a moment to emphasize the sincerity of her words. "Thankfully, we have found a great replacement for her in Mel. It's her first day at work today so take it easy on her and don't scare her away, okay? Now, let's set up two offices. One for me and one for Mel. We can use the two meeting rooms next to reception if they're available. Can we do that?" The floor manager nodded. "Great. We'll gather in fifteen minutes in separate groups. Everyone okay with that?" The staff nodded, relieved that someone was taking charge. Everyone went to work moving chairs, tables, and laptops. Mel winked at Sophie as they lifted a table together.

"Thanks," she said. "I love you already."


IT WAS A HECTIC DAY. As expected, the lunch took forever. They couldn't really afford to lose the time but it was a courtesy to the staff, and it was the right thing to do. They had been working hard for the last couple of months to get their samples ready, so Sophie didn't rush to get the orders out. Gathered around the larger-than-life round table at the dim sum restaurant opposite the office, she noticed how good Mel was with people. They all seemed to love her and laugh at her jokes. She was completely relaxed around them. And most of all, she was incredibly respectful and had clearly looked up the etiquette for Cantonese dining before she came. She knew how to use her chopsticks; she drank her tea, tapped two fingers to thank the server for the refill, turned the table after serving herself, tried all the dishes and was unfalteringly polite. Sophie watched Mel nibble on a chicken foot. She tore the skin off the bones with her teeth, then swallowed it, promptly followed by a large gulp of tea.

"Not bad," she laughed, turning the table for her neighbours to get stuck into them. Everyone was clapping and cheering. Sophie smiled at her. She had gone through the challenge of chicken feet twice, but she would never admit that she actually quite liked them from the start, because the staff needed their entertainment. Sophie sometimes wondered if it was some sort of initiation ritual for Westerners arriving in Hong Kong for the first time. Whatever it was, Mel was doing fine. She didn't need to save her or entertain her or keep her busy in any way. Sophie had checked on her a couple of times that morning during the meetings, but Mel seemed to be comfortable making decisions and quite confident with the product. It left her feeling both reassured and intrigued. Mel was chatty and loud, asking question after question. When they asked her if she had a boyfriend, she answered honestly.

"No I don't, and I prefer girls." The ladies next to her giggled and pointed at Suki, the Japanese receptionist. Suki was the bravest of the bunch, and they were poking her, encouraging her to say something. Suki laughed.

"They say Candy from the night shop opposite the office likes girls too. They say maybe you can take her."

Mel chuckled. "Take her, huh?" She shook her head. "I'm quite happy by myself, thank you. But I'm sure Candy is really sweet. I hope she finds a cute girlfriend." That comment led to even more laughter. Sophie's eyes met Mel's for a couple of seconds. They lingered on hers and seemed to challenge her, saying; 'Hey, I can do this, watch me.' Another burst of laughter brought her back to the table.

Remembering that Debbie wasn't there, she got up and gave her rehearsed speech, congratulating Ken on his new baby, Apple and Diamond on their recent promotions and Suki on her engagement.

"THAT WAS FUN," Mel laughed when they finally left the office. They took a detour and passed restaurants, bars, a basketball court and a park where groups of seniors gathered to perform tai chi. It was nine pm and already dark.

"Fun?" Sophie sauntered behind the crowd of office workers who were making their way to the tube station. "I expected you to be stressed and tired today. But instead, you seem chilled."

"Well, I am. Your colleagues are great. Our colleagues. They're lovely and professional and honest. I'm so happy I came to work here. I am tired though; you were right about that."

Sophie glanced at her and decided to be honest. "You surprised me," she said.

"What do you mean?"

"Well, you're great. You know, with people." Sophie shrugged. "You're good with them. I admire you in that way."

Mel laughed and waved it off with a casual gesture. "People are just people. My mother always told me 'treat people the way you want to be treated, and you'll have nothing to worry about.'"

"I know," Sophie said. "But still, I wasn't like this the first time I came here. I felt alien and taken aback by the smallest of things."

"Well, if that was the case, you've come a long way." Mel took her phone out of her bag and started snapping pictures of the buildings and signs that Sophie had passed at least a hundred times before. It was fun to be with someone who saw everything for the first time, still fascinated by the fountains on the square in front of the office, the tiny night shops, and the food stalls. For Sophie, it was like seeing Hong Kong through new eyes again, appreciating everything that was so different from back home. She waved at the lady in the 7-Eleven where she always bought her magazines and smiled at a group of busking teenagers. She felt a funny sense of pride and a need to show Mel around, but she also felt exhausted. Mel clearly felt the same as she yawned and rolled her shoulders.

"Hey, I don't know about you, but I feel jet-lagged, and I could do with some food. And as much as I'd like to explore the city, I don't think my body could handle it tonight." Mel gave Sophie an apologetic look. "Shall we get some room service in my room?"

Sophie couldn't have been more surprised with her joyous reaction. Usually, she would have gone to her own room, happy to be alone. Now, she wanted to spend time with her new colleague. Mel was like a drug, someone who gave her joy and energy. Maggie had been great to travel with, but Sophie was pretty sure she hadn't felt this before.

"Sure," she heard herself say. "Sounds great." They crossed another network of footbridges over the motorway and passed through a shopping mall that housed a mixture of funny beauty clinics and toy stores. The air was warm and humid, promising rain later that night. Sophie broke the silence.

"I feel like pizza and a movie. You?" Mel chuckled.

"Perfect. I love pizza. So what kind of movies do you like?"

"Honestly," Sophie grinned, "I'll watch anything, but I

really like horror movies, especially Japanese ones." Mel broke out in hysterical laughter, and Sophie frowned, laughing along with her.

"Why is that so funny? Have you never watched one?" Mel shook her head, trying to catch her breath.

"God, it's too warm to laugh right now. And no, I've never watched a Japanese horror movie. I don't know why I find the idea so funny; it just seems really random coming from someone like you. I thought you'd prefer white girl movies like...I don't know...Notting Hill or something like that."

Sophie pretended to be offended and raised an eyebrow. "Well, as a matter of fact, I don't. And I think you should give horror movies a try if you haven't already. You might like them." She bounced the question back at Mel. "So what kind of movies do you watch? Wait, let me guess. I bet you binge watch soppy Disney movies and sing along to all the songs. Am I right?" Mel giggled and punched her in the side.

"I do not like Disney movies. I'm actually quite insulted you think that's my kind of thing. No," she announced, spreading her arms and spinning around. "I like dance movies." She ended the spin with two waving jazz hands, and now it was Sophie's turn to laugh.

"Yeah? You like those? The 'follow your dreams' movies? Oh my God Mel, I can't believe you fall for that crap."

"It's not about following your dreams," Mel protested. "I like dancing myself, so I love to watch other people dance."

Sophie tried to ignore the visuals that were now taking over her headspace of Mel dancing. *Stop it. Stop trying to picture her like that.* She took a deep breath.

"Okay, I have a proposal. How about you watch a horror movie with me and then I'll put myself through the torture of watching a dance movie with you? Or the other way around, whatever you want."

AN HOUR LATER, they were on Mel's bed, sharing a giant pizza. A bottle of red wine rested between them. Sophie had insisted on dimming the lights and turning up the volume.

"It has to be dark, or you won't get the full experience needed to appreciate this masterpiece," she said wide-eyed, scrolling through the pay-per-movie channel, looking for Ringu. Mel didn't look convinced but went along with it anyway, pouring them both a second glass of wine.

"Bring it on, woman. I'm not scared. Nothing scares me!" Sophie wondered again why she wasn't in her own bed, enjoying some time alone with a book and a cup of tea. Just the way she liked it. *Maybe because I like this more?* She watched Mel's eyes grow bigger by the minute as the movie played, and laughed when she eventually put her pizza aside and slipped under the covers, pulling them up over her nose.

"I don't think I can take this anymore," she said in a tiny voice as the spooky video tape scene that had made the movie famous played on screen. She moved closer to Sophie and leaned into her. "Get under the duvet, dude. How am I supposed to cover my face if you're sitting on top of it?"

Sophie hesitantly moved underneath the covers too, by now very aware of the lack of space between them. She could feel Mel's body heat radiating beside her, so close. She tried to watch the movie, but her concentration span was broken. She moved away, just a little bit, afraid that Mel could hear her pounding heartbeat over the sound of the movie. She knew this was ridiculous, but it beat so violently, she could feel it in her throat. Mel had changed into a pair of grey sports shorts and a white vest top, and ever since she'd returned from the bathroom, Sophie had not been able to keep her eyes off her. *What is going on with me? Why am I so aware of my own body? And why is this making me so nervous?* Sophie was brutally torn away from her train of thoughts when Mel screamed and swung her arms around her waist, burying her face under the sheets against Sophie's chest. In a reflex, Sophie put her arm around Mel, protecting her from the ghost that was about to crawl out of the T.V. Then she laughed.

"Do you want me to switch it off?" she asked, teasing. "If I didn't know better, I'd almost think that you were...scared?"

Mel stuck her head above the sheets and shot her a grin. "I'm not scared. I was just cold." She smiled. "Okay, maybe it's creeping me out a little bit. I mean, this movie has ruined me now. If I don't watch the end, I won't be able to sleep, and if I do watch the end, I'll be up all night too." She sighed and sat back up straight, leaning against the pillows, still covering her face with her hands.

"It's okay; you can look now, Sophie said when the subtitles came up on the screen. "I'm sorry I put you through this, but I thought you could handle it. Clearly, you couldn't."

Mel hit her playfully with one of the pillows and Sophie fended her off by throwing her on her back. She held Mel down with both hands until she realized what she was doing. It wasn't a normal situation between two adults who worked together and had only just met. They both knew that. It wasn't a normal situation in general. They were technically too old to watch a movie in bed together. Sophie moved away slowly, pretending she needed the bathroom. Standing in front of the mirror, she splashed some cold water on her face and glared back at her flustered reflection.

*I need to leave.* This wasn't friendly banter anymore, but it wasn't flirting either. It was something in the middle, something that balanced on the dangerously thin line that couldn't be crossed. She wiped her face on the towel and got a faint waft of Mel's sweet perfume. Without thinking, she buried her face in it, inhaling deeply. *I have to go back to my room. Now.* But even as she thought this, she stayed there for just a little bit longer.

"Are you okay? You look a bit flustered," Mel said when Sophie came back from the bathroom. She was lying on her stomach, cupping her chin in the palm of her hand. Her feet were tapping restlessly behind her on the mattress.

Sophie rubbed her face. "I'm okay. Just tired. Think I need some sleep. Can we watch your movie next time? I'm not making up excuses here," she added, grinning. Standing next to the bed, she looked down at Mel, unconsciously focusing on her lips.

Mel nodded. "Sure. I think I need some sleep too. That is, if I'm not too terrified to close my eyes." Their laughter suddenly sounded too loud and strangely artificial as it echoed through the room. Sophie shuffled on the spot, waving clumsily with two hands before she turned to the door.

"Well, goodnight then. See you tomorrow."

## 9

B y the time they sat down for their meeting in the factory the next day, everything was back to normal. Breakfast had not been uncomfortable, but Sophie had noticed that Mel was more reserved than before. Although she was sweet and polite, there wasn't the physical interaction they'd had the day before. The little touches, the closeness, the winking. Sophie hadn't slept very much. She'd been thinking and thinking and then over-thinking some more. One minute she'd tried hard not to think about Mel, the other she'd desperately tried to recall every second of their evening. In the end, she had given up, exhausted and confused. Now they were on opposite sides of the table with a pile of garments in between them. It was freezing in the air-conditioned office, and Sophie was shivering, cursing herself for not bringing a jacket. Mel was cold too. She could tell by the goose bumps that covered her arms each time she reached for a garment on Sophie's side of the pile. Sophie had changed at least five times that morning but not a single time had she thought about layering up. First, it had been jeans and a t-shirt, her stan-

dard outfit for a factory visit. It always worked for her
before, but this morning it had bothered her. Then she had
changed into a skirt with an over the shoulder top, which
she quickly disposed of. Too girly. She wanted to wear
something cool. Something more casual. In the end, she
wore a pair of blue denim jeans, chunky leather sandals,
and a black vest top. Mel however, was looking girlier than
before with a tiny little ditsy floral ruffle dress. It was cute.
Really cute. Not to mention how it showed off her legs each
time she walked around the table. Sophie swallowed hard
when Mel put her feet up on the chair next to her, leaning
back and rolling her shoulders with an arrogant noncha-
lance. She looked picture perfect sitting there. As if Mel
could sense that she was thinking about her, she turned her
attention to Sophie while drawing new seams, darts and
other notes on a silk blouse.

"So, did you sleep after that movie? Because I didn't."
Her husky voice sounded sexy in the quiet room.

"Of course I did," Sophie lied, looking up from the jersey
dress she was measuring. If only Mel knew that it hadn't
been the movie that had kept her awake.

Mel giggled. "Well don't get too excited. Our next movie
night will be dance movie night, in case you forgot and I'm
going to make you sit through the whole two-and-a-half
hours. No breaks."

"Can't wait," Sophie laughed. But the truth was, she
really couldn't wait to spend another evening in bed with
Mel. She watched her work methodically, as she stood up
and put the blouse on the mannequin. A textile pen was
tucked behind her ear, and a roll of seaming tape decorated
her wrist. It dawned upon Sophie that for once, she wasn't
bored at a factory visit. She had something far more interesting to focus on besides her garments, and it felt like a

welcome change. Whenever Mel would look at her, she'd quickly bow her head, pretending to be consumed in her notebook.

"Miss Johnson?" Lemon, the stern director's assistant who had let them in, stuck her head around the corner. "The factory team would like to meet you. Do you mind if they come in?"

"Of course not! That would be lovely," Mel said. "Please call me Mel."

Lemon nodded and read from a piece of paper. "At Ho Manufacturing, we pride ourselves on excellent working relationships. It is important for our employees to know the people they work for. It enables them to produce quality garments with passion and flair." Her voice sounded monotone as if she had no idea what she was saying. Sophie pursed her lips together and looked at Mel, who was trying her hardest to keep a straight face too.

"Passion and flair. I like that," Mel said.

Lemon nodded in agreement. "Yes. Passion and flair. I'll be right back."

Mel chuckled. "Is she always this serious?"

"Yeah." Sophie sighed. "I made it my mission to make her smile years ago, but I've never managed. Maybe you should take on the challenge." The door opened again, and seven women entered the room. Sophie waved at them.

"Hi, guys, nice to see you again!" They waved back, smiling.

Mel stood up, and Sophie watched her in amusement as she held out a hand to greet Idy, who went in for a hug. It resulted in an awkward clash, in which Mel ended up holding Idy's limp wrist while their heads collided. If either of them was in pain, they didn't let it show. Sophie tried not to laugh as Mel pulled herself together and decided to give the next person whom she was introduced to a hug instead. However, Fairy, who had already observed the first faux pas, held out her hand last minute, punching it into Mel's breast. Mel yelped, jumping back.

"Now that's what I call an intimate introduction." She glanced nervously at the other people in the room.

"Hi, I'm George," a younger girl with pink hair said. "Print technician." She held her arms out wide, indicating that she was going to hug Mel.

"Nice to meet you, George. I love your hair." Mel seemed relieved to have some clarity but, with George being only half her height, she had to bend down so far that she almost lost her balance in the process. Sophie had seen this happen many times, but it never failed to amuse her. When the painfully confusing ritual was over, and everyone had left the room, she finally allowed herself to laugh. Tears were running down her cheeks, and she was unable to stop. Mel laughed too.

"You could have warned me about that," she giggled.

Sophie tried to catch her breath. "Now what would be the fun in that?" She shook her head. "Physical interaction should be prohibited when being introduced to people from other cultures. It's just too confusing for everyone. We're trying to do it their way; they're trying to do it our way." She pointed at her face. "I once had a black eye from a nose poke." Mel burst out into laughter again. "I'm not joking, Mel. I even had someone kiss me on my neck once. Now that was confusing." Her eyes wandered down to Mel's chest. "How's your boob? Does it hurt?" Mel shook her head, still laughing and Sophie walked around the table to put an arm around her shoulder. "Don't worry; it gets easier. Next time, just wave."

## 10

It was dark when the driver stopped at the entrance to the hotel. Mel struggled to get out of the car with all her bags and files.

"Oh that's nice," Mel said, facing the fountain that functioned as a seating area for the taxi stand. Sophie closed her eyes and sighed as the wind blew cool mist into her face. It felt great after a long drive and a two-hour wait at the border. "I wouldn't mind jumping in there to soak for a while."

Mel nodded towards the roof. "I'm going for a swim upstairs. Do you want to join me? If you're not bored of me yet, that is?"

"I was going to ask you the same thing, but I figured you would be sick of me by now." They both laughed at Sophie's statement before Mel gave her a playful push with her shoulder.

"No way. How could I turn down a hot chick in a bikini?" Sophie blushed. Although it was intended as a joke, she sensed that Mel regretted saying it because she looked away and shook her head as if cursing herself.

. . .

SOPHIE RUSHED to beat Mel to it. She didn't want to be the last one walking into the pool area half naked. She had quickly thrown on a black bikini and wrapped herself up in a cosy hotel robe before going up to the roof garden in her flip flops. But Mel was already there when Sophie arrived, sitting on the edge of the pool with her feet in the cool water. She was facing the skyline, staring into the night. The purple glow of the pool lights illuminated her face. Sophie walked over to her and gazed in the same direction. Mel didn't look at her when she spoke.

"I love it here. Don't you? All I can see is chaos. So many people, so much traffic, so much movement, it's like they never sleep. But up here it's quiet. You can see life moving below you like a nest of ants on fire, but you can't hear them." She slid the robe off her shoulders, revealing a low cut white swimsuit and slowly lowered herself into the water. "Come in, it's nice." she swam to the other end of the pool, beckoning for Sophie to join her. Sophie dived in and shivered as her body hit the water. She quickly got used to the change of temperature and dipped her head in the water, wetting her hair. It felt good after a day in the humid and polluted air of the factory. They both leaned on the edge of the infinity pool, looking down on the hustle and bustle of Hong Kong. Large cargo ships shared the waterways with ferries, yachts and the iconic dragon boats. Behind the boats was Hong Kong Island, lit up like a funfair.

"I wouldn't mind staying a week longer," Sophie said quietly. "I'm having fun." She turned her head to Mel and rested it on her forearms. She couldn't have imagined a more perfect way to end the day if she'd tried. The roof garden was deserted and, apart from a loved up Japanese couple on the sun loungers in the back, they had the pool all to themselves.

"Tell me something I don't know about you," Mel said, her green eyes piercing right through Sophie. Water was dripping from her hair, tracing her forehead, nose, and lips. She licked them slowly, sending Sophie into a sudden frenzy of excitement. Was she doing that on purpose?

"Like what?" Sophie asked, fighting to keep her voice steady.

"I don't know. Anything. What's your biggest fear?"

Sophie laughed. "Heavy subject, Mel. Are you sure you want to go there?"

Mel smiled. "Yeah, I'm sure. Tell me."

"God, I don't know." Sophie paused, looking up at the sky for an answer. "I suppose my biggest fear, apart from the obvious things like dying or getting sick or losing people I love, would be turning out like some of my friends."

Mel cocked her head. "Why is that?"

"Well..." Sophie frowned. "We all come from families with money. Families where expectations are high. Most of my friends have great degrees from renowned universities and speak at least two languages. They're wealthy and good-looking." She laughed. "Apart from me. I wouldn't call myself wealthy on my designer salary. Anyway, that's not the point. The point is when it comes to relationships and significant life choices, they've all settled. Take my friend Cat, for example. She used to be so much fun until she decided to marry her boyfriend. She stopped working as a broker because she could. Now she's twenty-nine and in a passionless relationship where everything evolves around material things. She's bored out of her mind, and the only person she can be herself around is me. Her husband and family expect her to have children soon and although she's not ready, she doesn't want to disappoint them either."

"That's sad," Mel said. "You don't strike me as the type to settle for less, though."

Sophie shrugged. "I know. And I hope I never will. It's just the pressure. It's driving me crazy. Everywhere I go, people either ask me if I'm dating or they're trying to set me up. I'm happy alone, but apparently, that's not good enough." She rolled her eyes. "I'm dreading the dinner on Friday, and I would have definitely cancelled if you weren't coming along."

Mel winked and moved closer. "But I am coming."

Sophie blushed. "Yes, you are and thank you for that. But now it's your turn. What's your biggest fear, Mel? Besides the obvious?"

Mel dipped her hair in the water and combed it back with her fingers. "Falling for a straight girl." They both laughed.

"What do you mean?" Sophie asked. "Is that your thing? Straight girls?" She made quote marks in the air.

"Yeah, that's my thing, unfortunately, and it always ends badly. The last one wasn't straight though. I thought I'd broaden my horizons with my ex and try it the mature way, but I wasn't madly in love with her." Mel turned on her back, looking up at the sky. "I want something real, something all consuming. I want to drown in her eyes, swim in her skin, and I want to love her so much that it hurts when she's not around." She paused and grinned sheepishly. "I know it sounds stupid, but I also know it exists."

Sophie would normally have laughed at such a statement. But she didn't. "I can see that," she said, lowering her voice.

"I'm glad you can see that," Mel said in an amused tone.

"You didn't seem like you were remotely interested in romance when we spoke about it the last time." She arched an eyebrow as if she was on to Sophie. "Has something changed your mind?"

Sophie shook her head, trying to keep her cool. Mel seemed to be hinting at something and it made her feel so nervous that she could feel her hands shaking under the water. She took a deep breath. At least she was in a pool. There would be no sweat marks under her armpits, and the rash that would soon spread to her neck wouldn't be visible in the dark.

"No," Sophie stammered. "Maybe I haven't experienced romance or found that one true love, but I still want to believe there's someone out there who will blow my mind. Just like everyone else, I guess, right? I just don't know what I want."

"Right," Mel said, smiling. "I've got the feeling you'll find out soon enough. Anyway, I'd better get myself to bed if we're doing this early morning tourist thing tomorrow. Call my room if I'm not there, okay?" Sophie's gaze followed Mel, who stepped out of the pool with the grace of a goddess. She looked like a dream in the dimly lit surroundings, her hips moving sensually as she walked. Before putting on her robe, she squeezed the water out of her hair. It ran down her back, tracing her bottom and her legs. Sophie forced herself to look away, to act like she was perfectly fine spending some more time on her own in the pool. She leaned into the ceramic tiles again and turned her attention back to the skyline.

## 11

"Hi Mum, how are you? How's your back?" Mel had her phone on loudspeaker while she was painting her toenails.

"I'm good, Melzinha. Cherry came over for a coffee today. You know, my friend from the community centre. She brought me some lovely flowers. How is Hong Kong? And how is the job going?

"It's great," Mel said, shifting her concentration to her left foot. "I'm glad to hear you had some company. Hong Kong is incredible, although I haven't seen much yet. It's busy, and I'm tired, but the job is going well. I haven't had any significant issues, so I think I'll get used to it pretty quick. Sophie, my new colleague, is nice too, so that's a bonus. We just went for a swim." She hesitated for a moment. "I think you would like her." Her mother was quiet on the other side of the line. "Mum? Are you still there?"

"Yes, I'm here, sweetie." She laughed. "Just listening to your lovely voice. So you two are getting along? That's nice. And is she...?"

"Is she what, Mum?" Mel rolled her eyes.

"Well... does she like girls?"

Mel sighed. "Mum, you have to stop doing this. No, she's not gay. And even if she was, she's not my type, and we work together." She took a deep breath. "I just said she was nice. I didn't say I'm going to marry her and have babies so you can be a grandmother."

"Calm down Melzinha," Isabella laughed. "I will stop pestering you about babies if you get me a nice souvenir, okay? I was thinking maybe a kimono or a handbag? Cherry told me they have this fake market where you can buy branded bags for a fraction of the price. And if you can find me a nice silk kimono, I can wear that in the hospital when I'm in for my operation. At least I'll look good for the doctors."

Mel smiled as she screwed the top back on to her nail polish bottle and studied her feet. "That sounds like a good deal. I'll bring you a snazzy handbag and a beautiful kimono - a small price if it gets you to stop talking about babies for at least another two years." They both laughed. Mel stood up, looking for her moisturizer. It had been a long time since she had gone through the trouble of looking after herself to the extent that she was now. There was no point in kidding herself; she knew Sophie was the only reason for her sudden attention to her appearance. She studied herself in the long mirror on the closet door, draping her hair over her shoulders. She wasn't quite sure what to think of herself, and that was a first.

"Oh, and one more thing," Isabella said. "Cherry asked if you could bring her a little something back too."

Mel groaned. "Sure. Typical Cherry, always fishing for presents. What does she want this time?"

"Well..." Isabella paused. "She asked me if you could

bring her a fluffy pink Hello Kitty toilet seat. Only if you happen to stumble upon one."

Mel took a sip from her tea while her mother spoke and almost choked on it. "Are you serious? She wants me to bring a toilet seat back for her? How does she imagine I would just stumble upon a fluffy toilet seat while I'm working? And how does she expect me to bring it back? Sitting on it?"

Isabella laughed. "I told her it was too much to ask, but I'm just passing on the request."

"Hell yeah. That's too much to ask; you can tell her that. And her husband, what's his name again?"

"Bernie."

"Right, Bernie. What is she going to do when Bernie refuses to put the seat up, and he pisses all over the pink fluff?"

Isabella laughed even harder now. "Alright, alright. Forget about the toilet seat. What's the hotel like?" her mother asked, changing the subject.

"Oh Mum, you'd love it. I've got a lovely room with an office, a king-size bed, a Jacuzzi and a toilet that talks to me in the morning. And the view is fantastic. I'm looking over the Hong Kong harbour. And there's a spa, a garden and a pool on the rooftop. It's great."

"Sounds like you've hit the jackpot with this company." Isabella sighed. "I'm so happy for you, Melzinha."

Mel moved back to the bed, looking for her tweezers in her toiletry bag. "Hopefully you'll be able to travel again soon, Mum. When your back gets better, we can go to Brazil together to visit your sister."

"Yes, I've been thinking about that," Isabella said. "That would be wonderful." She paused. "I'm not going to keep you any longer. I'm sure you're tired. It's just good to hear your voice."

"Take care, Mum. I need to get some clothes together for tomorrow morning. We're leaving early to go to Lantau Island for a bit of sightseeing." She could picture her mother smiling at the other end of the phone.

"You go and have fun, Melzinha. I'm going to finish my book now and make myself some lunch. I love you, sweetie and I'm glad you're fine. Be careful out there." Her mother had hung up before Mel had the chance to reply. She rummaged through her suitcase and found the bottle of moisturizer, which she applied with care. She stared at her reflection for the second time, turned to the side and held in her stomach. Then she put the clothes she would wear the next day on the chair by her desk before crawling under the crisp white sheets.

*Stop thinking about her.*

## 12

"This better be worth it," Mel said in a coarse voice. She rubbed the sleepy expression from her face and took a sip of the black coffee she had taken earlier from the breakfast buffet. It was seven in the morning. "If I weren't so excited about playing the tourist, I would have stayed in bed." They were making their way through the tube station during the early rush hour. It was a task that seemed impossible to complete without getting their eyes stabbed out by one of the many parasols waving around, or without passing out from heat stroke.

"Don't let go of my hand," Sophie commanded, dragging Mel along the busy corridor leading to the platform. She told herself it was purely practical. It was crowded with people, and they would lose each other if they didn't stick together. Even so, she was shocked by the effect that their physical contact had on her body. A restless stir settled deep down in her core. She led them through the crowd into the tube. People were pouring in and out at the same time. "It's every man for himself here," She shouted over the noise. "Don't be afraid to push; you won't offend anyone." When the doors finally closed, they found themselves squashed in between students and office-goers like sardines in a tin. Sophie felt Mel's breasts pressed against her back through the thin fabric of her t-shirt. A tingle spread through her lower belly. *Damn it*, she thought. *Control yourself!* She looked down at her hand, still holding Mel's and wondered if she should let go or not.

"Please don't let go," Mel said as if she could read her thoughts. "I don't want you to get dragged out when the door opens at the next station. I'll never be able to find you again." She held on firmer to Sophie's hand and slid her other arm around Sophie's waist to protect her from the people trying to get in and out. The embrace came unexpected, and Sophie wasn't prepared for the sudden need she felt to turn around and press her lips against Mel's. She closed her eyes and held her breath as the fingers tightened around her. Each time the train halted, Mel's fingertips spread and pressed into her abdomen, preventing her from falling over. Sophie felt her heart race. She hoped Mel wouldn't notice, being so close to her. She struggled to keep her breathing under control, wondering why the hell standing in a crowded tube with Mel was so sexy? Was that what it was? And why was Mel holding her like that? Was she enjoying it too?

"Two more stops and it will get better," she said, turning to Mel. "As soon as we get out of the city centre, we'll change trains and should be able to sit down." Mel smiled, her face close to Sophie's.

"I don't mind. It's quite an experience." She bit her bottom lip, staring at Sophie's mouth as if lusting after it. When their eyes met, Sophie didn't look away. Mel held her gaze too, challenging her, daring her to give in to whatever it was that was happening between them. The train came to an abrupt stop, and more people tried to squeeze their way into the carriage. Sophie gave up her inner battle. She leaned back against Mel to give herself some more space and tried to relax, but the warm breath on her neck made her shiver with excitement. All she could think about was the mouth that was only inches from her skin. Mel tightened her grip on both her hand and her waist, and it felt amazing. They didn't speak, and when, two minutes later, the majority of the people finally got off, Sophie felt reluctant to move. Eventually, she released herself from Mel's grip and sat down in one of the seats at the back of the carriage. Her legs were trembling, and her hands were shaking from the closeness that had awoken a desire in her she didn't know she had. Mel followed and took the seat next to her. She sat back but leaned towards her and hooked her arm through Sophie's as if she missed the contact too. Without saying much, they continued the journey with only the odd remark or giggle when passing something peculiar. Mel stroked Sophie's palm with her fingertip, and playfully traced the veins on her wrist. It felt thrilling, electrifying and sensationally good. How could Mel touch her so casually? As if it was nothing, when it was all Sophie had been able to think about for the past couple of days. She could feel Mel's eyes on her when she gazed out of the window but didn't dare to turn her head. Something had changed the energy between them in those five crowded minutes between TST and Austin station and they both knew it. At the Nam Cheong stopover, Sophie reached out for Mel's hand again, even though it wasn't as busy there. Her body reacted like it had become addicted to her touch; craving her and claiming a little bit more each time an opportunity presented itself. A silent gasp escaped her mouth when Mel changed her grip and entwined their fingers on the steep escalators.

They squinted as they came out, adjusting to the bright light that welcomed them to Lantau Island.

"Okay, so now what?" Mel said, taking in the rather uninspiring looking square, surrounded by parking lots and an outlet shopping mall.

"Don't worry; it gets better. Are you scared of heights?" Sophie asked.

Mel shook her head. "I don't think so, but I've never tested it either."

Sophie pointed to the Starbucks next to the mall. "Great. Let's get another coffee and take a cable car."

HALF AN HOUR later they were looking down at the mouth of the Pearl River and the lush mountains underneath their feet. The glass bottom in the cable car was slightly uncomfortable at first, but as soon as they got used to the height, they relaxed and moved from the bench on to the floor, silently sliding over the island's tropical forests, villages, and temples as they rose. The Giant Buddha towered prominently above the mountains as if reigning over the island.

"This is incredible," Mel sighed. "I can't believe I was thinking of staying in bed this morning; this is so worth it." She smiled at Sophie and leaned back against the glass wall. "I haven't seen much of the world, you know. When I was younger, we couldn't afford to go on holiday, and when I went to University, I worked day and night to pay my way through that. My job has always been the only way for me to see the world, and I love travelling. I don't care if I have to work hard, as long as I get a little bit of time in between to explore the culture and the food and soak it all up. It's still special to me."

"But you could start travelling now?" Sophie suggested.

"I know. And I will. But even though I've had a decent job for the past couple of years, I haven't had anyone to travel with. My friends are always broke, and my mother isn't that mobile at the moment. She has a bad back, a slipped disk. I could go on my own, but I guess I'm too scared." Mel shrugged. "I know that sounds silly, but I'm quite timid on my own. I'd probably lock myself up in my hotel room." She laughed. "Don't you find it daunting to be on your own?"

"No, not at all," Sophie said. "I have to admit; I was nervous when I went on holiday by myself for the first time. But after two days, I got used to it and gave in to the solitude. Just relaxing with my books and doing absolutely nothing for two weeks... I loved it. The downside is that I don't do much exploring when I'm alone. I tend to stay in the resort, apart from the occasional shopping trip to a market or maybe a restaurant visit. That's okay though. I see it as two weeks of ultimate relaxation and recharging, which is exactly what I need after a busy season. I'm really looking forward to going away next week. Me, my books and a bikini. Chilling on the beach and swimming in the sea."

Mel sighed. "Wow, that sounds amazing. I'm jealous." She laughed. "If I hadn't just started this job, I'd beg you to take me with you."

Sophie nudged her. "Well, maybe you should come along next time. That is if we haven't killed each other by then."

The cable car stopped at Ngong Ping Village, and they followed the signs to the Po Lim Monastery. The village was quiet, but the restaurants were already open for breakfast. White buildings, built in traditional Chinese style, dominated the main street on either side. They carried rows of red lanterns that were hanging down from the gabled roofs.

The tiny red and yellow temples in between drew people inside with the aroma of incense.

"I love it," Mel said, squeezing Sophie's arm while she looked around. "It's like entering another world here." Sophie smiled at Mel's face that lit up when they approached the Po Lin Monastery. When Mel looked up, her lips parted at the sight of the enormous Buddha, towering thirty-four meters above them. It was impressive, standing underneath it, looking up at the glorious bronze statue that shimmered in the morning sun.

"Wow," she said. "Just wow."

Sophie grinned. "I'm so glad you like it. It's worth getting up early for, right? It gets really busy here during the day with both tourists and locals who come to pray and worship." As they came closer to the temple, the air became thick with the sweet smell of the incense offerings. They passed a vegetarian restaurant adjacent to the monastery where the staff were busy setting up the tables for the day. The monks in the al fresco kitchen were preparing food, with steaming pans and woks, spreading a welcoming scent throughout the premises. Mel and Sophie walked around a group of cows that were blocking the main path, not remotely bothered by the passers-by, and headed down to a small temple, surrounded by citrus trees, orchids, and bougainvillea. They walked through the main courtyard, facing the temple gateway. The rectangular open space was full of statues, surrounded by flowers and offerings.

"From what I've been told," Sophie said, "these deities protect the entrance of the Monastery."

"I regret not doing any research before I came here," Mel said. "I love knowing facts about places I visit." She looked at Sophie. "So, what else do you know, tour guide?"

Sophie shook her head. "Not much, I'm afraid. But I do

know that the characters painted on the main roof over there, mean precious lotus. The lotus is a sign of purity in Buddhism. If you look up at the Giant Buddha," she continued, pointing upwards, "You can see that he sits on a throne of lotus too, holding his hand up in a blessing. This place started out as a small monastery, founded by three monks. Then it grew to be a key place of pilgrimage to worship Buddha." She shrugged. "I'm sorry I can't tell you more, as much as I'd like to impress you with my knowledge."

Mel winked at her and nudged her playfully. "You don't need to impress me, Sophie. You've already done that over and over again."

They entered the monastery. Mel hooked her arm into Sophie's as they walked into the great hall and looked up at the high ceilings, lavishly decorated with paintings and lanterns in bright blue, gold, yellow and red. Sophie placed a finger on her lips when a group of monks walked in. They wore brown and yellow robes and silently followed each other through the door, young and old, their heads bowed.

"We have to be quiet now," she whispered. "I think they're about to do a ceremony."

They directed their attention to the monks, who started chanting in a low hum. Then it became louder as they sat down. It seemed effortless, the way they hummed in a trance-like state, completely attuned to one another, seemingly oblivious to their audience. Mel appeared to be captivated by the display. She looked beautiful and humbled, the way she cocked her head each time the humming became louder. Sophie had to remind herself not to stare at her while they stood there side by side, watching the ceremony until the chanting subsided.

.   .   .

AN HOUR LATER, they finally reached the top of the stairs leading to the Giant Buddha. Out of breath, Mel dropped down on one of the steps, looking out over the village and the monastery.

"It's beautiful," she said. "Come and sit here. Let's chill out for a bit." She pointed at the step below her, between her legs. Sophie sat down and immediately felt the rush of being close to her again. It felt wrong but also so good at the same time. What was this weird intimate friendship that was blossoming between them? They connected on a level she didn't think was possible for two people who had only just met. She leaned back, rested her elbows on Mel's knees and looked out into the same direction. The hills seemed to go on forever, only broken here and there by the roofs of temples, peeking out above the trees. She sighed.

"I haven't been here in seven years. I'm glad we came." Mel wrapped her arms around Sophie's neck and rested her chin on her head.

"Thank you. Again," she whispered. Sophie held her breath. She was scared to move or to say anything that would break the spell of that very moment in which everything seemed perfect. So she just sat there in silence until it was time to head back to the office and the chaos of production issues that awaited them.

"Have you had many girlfriends?" Sophie asked on their way down.

Mel laughed. "Define many."

"I don't know." Sophie shrugged. "Just tell me about it, I'm curious." Mel took her arm and hooked her own in, pulling Sophie closer. It was a simple thing that a lot of her friends did all the time, but with Mel it sent her body into overdrive, elevating her senses to a point where she had to concentrate on the simplest of actions like breathing and walking. She could feel Mel's hair tickling her neck and shoulders and shivered as she took in her scent. It was a dark, musky perfume that smelled just as divine as she was.

"Well, let's see," Mel said, digging through her past. "I met my first love when I was thirteen. Her name was Nita, and she was in my class at school. She was a bit of a tomboy, but I guess we didn't know that word back then. I was fascinated by her, and when she first kissed me, I knew why. We were inseparable while it lasted, which wasn't very long. After a couple of months, she moved to the US with her parents, and I was heartbroken." She laughed, thinking about it. "Then there was no one for a couple of years because I was convinced she was the only one for me. I kept on writing her letters, but her parents had found a couple of them in her bedroom and called my parents, asking them to stop me from contacting her. My parents were shocked. They always thought we were just pen pals. My father found it hard to accept at first. He was a lot older, after all, and couldn't really grasp the concept of me being with a girl. But as the years progressed, he got used to the idea and eventually gave up fighting it. My mother didn't even flinch. She said I could be whoever I wanted to be and date whomever I wanted to date. It sounds weird, but she probably thought it was a blessing, preventing me from getting pregnant at a young age." She laughed. "But now, her liberal ideas are kind of backfiring. She insists I find a girlfriend, get married and have lots of babies so she can have grandchildren. She never gets that pushy with my brothers, even though they're both in a steady relationship."

"Wow, that's so sweet," Sophie said. "My parents would go crazy if I ever came home with a woman. It wouldn't exactly fit into their perfect little world."

Mel glanced at her. "That bad, huh?"

"Yeah," Sophie sighed. "As I told you, they have a clear idea of what their children should do for a living and who they should end up marrying. Social status, occupation, career prospects, age, capital... I'm not even going to bore you with it right now because it's too ridiculous for words." She laughed. "Anyway, so what happened next, after your pen pal Nita?"

Mel narrowed her eyes, trying to remember the girls she had dated in her teenage years.

"Well, after that, there were a whole string of girls. I can't remember all of their names. Sabine, Alex, Rachel, Miranda... I serial dated from when I was fifteen until I was about twenty-five." She grinned. "Most of them were straight girls, so they all left me eventually. I had a lot of one-night stands too, as soon as I got my own place. That was fun in the first couple of months, as you can probably imagine."

"Then I dated Becks for a year. She's the one I just broke up with." She smiled bitterly. "It's not like I've always been in relationships. I've been single a lot too, especially when I got into the whole one-night stand phase. But I don't want that anymore. It just seems so pointless now. Maybe I've grown up, who knows?"

"That's impressive," Sophie said. "I wish I could tell you I've had the same adventurous past but unfortunately my love life has been quite boring." She paused. "No, let me rephrase that. Really boring. I've dated but only been in two long-term relationships, and by that, I mean that they lasted roughly a year. I just get bored of them. I don't want any relationship to get too serious either because I know it won't last forever and that will only make it harder down the line. It's just not for me."

Mel gave her a questioning look. "How do you know it

won't last forever? Because you don't want it to?"

Sophie thought about that before she answered, weighing her words carefully.

"Maybe. If I stay with them, I have to take them home at some point, and that's when they'll get sucked up in family gatherings, Christmas celebrations, birthdays, drama and of course my mother bugging me about marriage and children. I've never liked someone enough to deal with the seriousness of it all."

"Okay, I get that," Mel said. "So, have you ever slept with a girl?" Sophie was startled by the question but tried to hide her shock. "I'm sorry," Mel apologized. "I suppose you haven't. But it's not a crazy question. A lot of straight women experiment at some point." She smiled suggestively. "Maybe you don't know what you're missing? You certainly sound like you could do with a bit of adventure."

Sophie was lost for words, and that didn't happen to her very often. "Eh...no, I haven't," she stammered. "It never even crossed my mind." She thought about Cat, contemplating whether to tell Mel or not. She had never told anyone about that. Mel regarded her in silence, waiting for her to speak. Sophie took a deep breath, and suddenly, the words came out as if she had no control over what she decided to share.

"I was in love with my best friend when I was fifteen," she said. "Catherine. Cat. That's what I call her. We're still friends now, but she doesn't know about my crush. Nobody knows, apart from you, now. It passed after a couple of years, and I haven't felt anything like it since." Mel frowned.

"A couple of years is a long time to get over someone. That must have been one serious crush. So do you mean you haven't felt anything as strong for anyone else since? Or do you mean you haven't felt anything for a woman since?"

"No, a woman. I've never been in love with a woman since I had the crush on her." Sophie knew that wasn't entirely true. What she had felt for Cat was way stronger than what she had felt for any of her past boyfriends, but she would take that secret with her to her grave.

"It just happened one day. I fell in love with her, and I can't explain how or when exactly it started. God, why am I telling you this?" Sophie rolled her eyes; her cheeks flushed and rosy.

"Because it's important," Mel said matter-of-factly. "So you never told her, and you just forgot about it?"

Sophie nodded. She looked down, avoiding eye contact. "I don't know. I've never explored it, and I don't really feel the need to." Mel put an arm around her and pulled her in close as they walked towards the bus that would take them back to the MTR station. Sophie leaned in. The embrace felt so good. So right. Why Mel? Why couldn't it just be a man? Or any other woman for that matter? As long as it wasn't Mel, her colleague and soon-to-be subordinate.

"Well, if that's how you feel," Mel sighed. "I'm not going to judge you for being a coward." She laughed and poked Sophie in the side, indicating she was joking. "But if I may give you some advice, I think you need to at least explore your feelings at some point. Before you know it, you'll be married with two kids, living in suburbia and you'll look at your chubby husband in bed one night, wondering what the hell happened to your needs and desires. I'm just saying." Sophie laughed now too, grateful for the light-hearted direction Mel had steered their conversation into.

"And on that note," Mel continued. "I'm looking forward to meeting your future husband on Friday. Aldo, right? That's a stupid name by the way."

## 13

The afternoon seemed to last forever. Each time Sophie tried to shut her computer down, another urgent issue came up. When she finally walked into Mel's office with her bag packed it was ten o'clock. The whole floor was deserted, apart from the security guard, who was watching a Chinese soap opera behind the reception desk. The janitor had switched off most of the lights, leaving the space looking rather creepy with the only sound coming from the air conditioning unit on the wall, which hummed like an electronic bees nest. Mel was fully engrossed in a drawing and didn't see her walk in. So far, she seemed to know exactly what she was doing. She was smart, efficient, good at problem-solving and a great designer. The fact that she had demonstrated all that, only within a couple of days, had impressed Sophie. She had been wrong about Mel. Sophie knew that now. And on top of all that, Mel was beautiful and the most confusing creature she had ever encountered.

"Are you ready to leave soon?" she asked. Mel looked up,

smiling. She lifted her headphones off her head and hung them around her neck.

"Hey there, pretty lady. You bet I am. I've only got one more adjustment to do. Can you wait, let's say, ten minutes?"

"Sure," Sophie said. "I'm starving; I'll call around to see if there are any tables available." Her cheeks were glowing from the comment Mel had just made, and she quickly turned back around the corner, searching for her phone in her bag. *Pretty lady.* Was that flirting? Was Mel seriously openly flirting with her? A tiny smile tugged at the corners of her mouth. She tried to straighten her face back into position while she scrolled through the list of restaurants on her phone.

SEATED at a window table on the third floor of a shopping mall, Sophie and Mel threw a selection of ingredients into the boiling spicy broth and dove into the condiments that had been served alongside the tofu, vegetables and fresh fish. It was busy at the hot pot restaurant, and the last available table next to them had just been taken by a rowdy bunch of Korean businessmen who ordered beer by the bucket load. The food looked fresh and delicious, and they stirred the broth impatiently. Sophie pulled a face when the portion of oysters arrived that Mel had ordered.

"Really? You like those?"

"Uh huh," Mel giggled. "I like them very, very much indeed. I've always liked oysters. Now, why do you think that is?" She smiled and wiggled her eyebrows. "No seriously, I only had them once or twice as a child, but I took an instant liking to them." She dressed one with ginger and lemon juice and slurped it out of the shell, licking her lips suggestively. Her eyes met Sophie's and this time there was no doubt about it. She was flirting with her. Sophie felt a fiery heat deep down in her belly and tried her hardest to ignore it.

"Honestly Sophie, you don't know what you're missing. Oysters are like..." She dropped the shell and took another one, this time with chili. "Well, they're like a woman's private parts when she's really, really turned on by my incredibly skilled..."

"Spare me the details please," Sophie begged, holding her hands up before they both cracked up laughing.

"Okay, so about your favourite subject," Sophie said, throwing some more tofu into the pot. "Why is it so great? I mean, sex with a woman. What's the big deal?"

Mel looked confused. "It isn't a big deal, Sophie. Different people like different things. I love oysters, and you like ... well... bananas? Or perhaps cucumbers?" She grinned. "Sex is great, and I happen to like sex with women. What's so mysterious about that? Do you not enjoy sex with men? Because that's your thing, right? " Sophie shrugged, suddenly uncomfortable with the turn the conversation was taking.

"I don't know... I guess so."

"See, that's where you're wrong," Mel laughed. She pointed an accusing finger at her, wiggling it up and down. "Because that did not sound one bit convincing to me. This morning, you practically confessed to me that your one big love was a woman and if you're not that bothered about men, I know I'm on to something here." She sang the last part of the sentence in a teasing tone. "Just wait till some lucky lady gets her hands on you, then you'll be screaming your lungs out in pleasure."

Sophie giggled and looked down at her plate. It was a topic she hadn't dared to touch upon with anyone, but it seemed easy tonight, like she and Mel could talk about anything. She felt mildly embarrassed, but there was also a certain curiosity lurking around the corner. Mel had opened her mind up to things she hadn't even considered in the past. The idea of being with a woman didn't seem so ridiculous anymore. Only she didn't want it to be just any lucky lady. She wanted it to be Mel. She sat back and watched her devour the last oyster, closing her eyes in delightful bliss when she swallowed it down. When Mel caught her staring, she winked playfully and blew her a kiss. Sophie raised her teacup in front of her mouth to hide her grin.

"So, do you want to come to the market tomorrow?" She asked, trying to sound casual.

Mel nodded. "Absolutely. Shopping and food are two things I'm up for anytime, day or night. I'll have to get some souvenirs for my mum. And some of this tea if we can find it, it's divine." She refilled her cup and inhaled deeply before sipping the jasmine blend.

IT WAS A WARM, humid and unusually busy evening along the waterfront. Sophie had suggested they walk instead of taking a taxi back to the hotel. Besides the prospect of a comforting breeze, she wanted the evening to last just a little bit longer. She couldn't remember the last time she had had such a good time with another person, not even with Maggie. Being around Mel made her feel dreamy, as if Mel painted the world in bright colours, everywhere they went. Mel's charming energy made her happy, and that was a feeling she wanted to savour for as long as she could.

"Come on, let's take a picture together," Mel shouted over her shoulder as she skipped towards the railing along the water's edge. A large dragon boat decorated with thousands of red fairy lights passed through the harbour. Mel took her phone out of her bag and put an arm around Sophie's neck, pulling her in close.

"Smile Sophie. This is the perfect Hong Kong skyline picture right here."

Sophie smiled, then turned her head and planted a kiss on Mel's cheek. An action that surprised both Mel and herself. It wasn't something she had intended to do, but the smooth skin right next to her face had been too tempting not to kiss.

Mel turned her head towards her and grinned. "I don't think it worked," she lied. "Try that again and hold it for five seconds so that I can get a decent picture, you tease."

Sophie's heart was beating out of her chest, yet she couldn't help but laugh at Mel's joke. When the camera was hovering above their faces for the second time, she turned again and lightly brushed her lips against Mel's cheek, more aware of the contact this time. She closed her eyes, and for a split second, she thought Mel might turn her way and kiss her on the mouth. But Mel didn't kiss her, and as swiftly as it came, the moment had passed. Sophie pulled herself together and pushed the enticing vision of Mel's lips on hers to the background. Mel showed her the picture with one arm still around Sophie's neck, their fingers entwined in front of Sophie's chest.

"Oh my God, that's hot!" Mel laughed. Sophie pulled the phone closer so she could see the picture better. Mel was right. They did look good together. It was a close-up, and the dragon boat was nowhere to be seen, but its red lights were glowing around their silhouettes like an aura. Sophie's lips were parted against Mel's skin, and Mel had a smug look on her face, smiling into the camera.

"Well fuck me," Mel said. "If I didn't know better, I

would think you had a huge lady crush on me. Can I please use this as bragging material to my friends?"

Sophie chuckled. "Anytime," she giggled, looking down now. She was terrified to lose herself again if their eyes met, so she focused on her manicured toes in the open sandals and her bare legs that needed a fresh shave.

"Come on, let's go," Mel said, as if sensing her discomfort. They turned and walked back towards the hotel, still holding each other, neither of them wanting to let go.

# 14

---

Sophie couldn't manage to fall asleep. She had left the TV on, dimmed the lights and had drunk a small bottle of whiskey from the minibar before slipping underneath the covers. She was naked, and the cotton sheets felt great against her skin. Usually, this was a recipe for a good night of at least eight hours, but at two am she was still staring at the ceiling, replaying her flirty interactions with Mel over and over in her mind. She felt physically exhausted from the excitement, but her thoughts kept her wide awake. Was she overthinking things? Was Mel attracted to her? Why couldn't she stop thinking about her? Why couldn't she stop picturing them naked in bed together? Sophie imagined Mel was flirty by nature, but she had seen a lot more than just a playful gesture. Mel confused her. She seemed determined and serious about her job, yet she had embraced every opportunity to be physical with her and Sophie couldn't deny that she'd enjoyed it. It was the way she took her hand when they crossed the road and the way she looked at her mouth when Sophie spoke. And then there was the kiss by the harbour and the awkward silence in the elevator after they got back as if both of them were hoping for an invitation from the other but neither of them was brave enough to take the first step. Sophie didn't think she could take the torture much longer. She had to know what it felt like to be with Mel. With a woman... No, she corrected herself. With Mel. Only with Mel. Perhaps this business trip was the best thing that had ever happened to her. Or the worst - she had yet to find out. The lust that Mel had stirred up inside of her made her feel like a different person. She felt strong and sensual, finally facing the fact that she was a sexual person with needs and desires that were begging to be released. By now, it was pure passion running through her veins. She had managed to get through her work so far, but if it got any worse, she wouldn't be able to concentrate on the simplest of tasks. She couldn't sleep, and there was no point trying. She picked up her phone and called Maggie.

"Hey lovely!" Maggie's familiar voice made her feel calmer instantly.

"Hey. How's the packing going? Are you busy?" She imagined Maggie in her tiny one-bedroom flat, surrounded by hundreds of boxes, lacking any kind of system or labels.

Maggie sighed. "God, how do you think it's going? Packing is not exactly my strong point, especially when I have to pack up my whole life. It's a mess, Sophie. I can't find anything anymore. I need your help."

Sophie laughed. "I knew you couldn't do it without me. Just drop the whole New York thing and come back to work," she joked.

Maggie laughed. "Is my replacement so terrible?" Sophie hesitated before answering.

"No, not at all. In fact, she's good. And we get along fine, so I would say it's much better than expected. Her name is

Mel, and I'm sorry to say this, but she's got it all. She's great. I was surprised myself."

Maggie was silent for a few seconds. "Really? Hmm..." She giggled. "Good for you, I suppose. But I was kind of hoping everything would fall apart after I left so they would all talk about how brilliant I was and how much they miss me."

Sophie smiled at that. "Don't worry; I'm sure everyone misses you. I miss you. But no, things are not falling apart. Mel will keep it together; I'm sure of that."

"Well that's too bad," Maggie said. "I guess I'm not irreplaceable after all." She sighed. "So you like her, then?"

"Yeah, I do." Sophie tried her hardest to be politically correct in her answer. "I mean, she's not you," she hastily added. "I've never been more ready to dislike someone in my life but I can't. She's just likable, you know?" She could imagine Maggie rolling her eyes on the other end of the line. "It's not the same without you, though," she said, trying to make up for the harsh truth. She heard Maggie pour a glass of what she assumed to be white wine and shortly after, the clinking of ice cubes. "Wine o'clock already Maggie? Really? What time is it there?

"Mind your own business," Maggie said in a playful tone. She took a sip and swallowed hard. "I'm stressed. I've got all this stuff to pack that I don't need and then I've got to prepare for next week. So let's talk about me now. What do I wear on my first day at work? I need to go shopping for my new job tomorrow, and unfortunately, I can't afford to be on brand."

## 15

"Did you get any sleep at all? You look exhausted," Mel said as she licked her thumb and wiped the mascara from underneath Sophie's left eye.

"Not really. The air con broke," Sophie lied. *Here we go again*, she thought. *I can't think straight anymore. She touches me, and I go weak within seconds. I'm melting like ice-cream. It's getting worse by the day, and there's nothing I can do to stop it.* She wanted to move further away from Mel to create some space but she couldn't. She needed the closeness like a drug. She needed more and more of it to keep herself satisfied or at least sane. They were in the back of the taxi on their way to the factory in China. The journey would take at least three hours, and it was warm in the car.

Mel looked worried. "I called you about ten times. You must have been fast asleep because your ringtone is pretty loud."

Sophie rubbed her temples, fighting the urge to curl up and close her eyes again. "I know," she said. "I never over-sleep. But then again, I was up all night, and I'm not very good like that." She turned to Mel. "Thank you for waking me up and holding the cab."

Mel smiled. "Sweetie, what else was I going to do? I'm the newbie here, remember? Breakfast?" She handed Sophie a cardboard box from the hotel. "I think I got you everything you like. Toast, salmon, avocado and a fresh orange juice." She rummaged through her bag. "Oh, and here's some cold water. That's what you like, right? The waiter even added a tiny ice-pack, in case you're not hungry yet." Sophie looked up at the delicate package.

"Thank you," she said, taking the box. She was genuinely surprised by Mel's gesture. "That's so incredibly sweet of you." She wrinkled her nose. "But I'm not sure if I can eat just yet so I might save it for later."

"Come here," Mel ordered her. "Put your head on my lap and get some sleep. You need it." Sophie shook her head, but there was no arguing with Mel as she pulled her into an embrace, lowering Sophie's head onto her thigh. Sophie closed her eyes. She felt Mel's hands in her hair, stroking her. Soft fingertips parted her hair and tugged the strands behind her ear. She felt them move over her forehead and neck, gently caressing her. If she could have stayed right there all day, she would have been more than happy. The sound of Mel's voice and her touch sent her into a trance of blissful peace, and within five minutes, she was asleep.

THE DAY WAS long and uncomfortably warm, but Sophie felt rested after their three-hour car journey. After their fittings, Mr. Ho, the factory director who had graced them with his presence, had insisted they attend the VIP tour of the premises. Sophie had already been unfortunate enough to go through this twice, but she knew it would be beneficial to

Mel, and so she didn't resist. It was the standard walk-through from the dyeing hall to the shipping hall past the printing room, the coating machines, the garment engineering building and the label and packaging department. Sophie kept a sharp eye out for any workers who seemed to be too young to be there and checked the production lines for any potential issues like the absence of safety gloves and goggles or broken metal detectors at each end of the long row of sewing machines. The brand could get sued if any broken needles were left in the garments and they certainly didn't want to be associated with child labour. She also asked to see the lab reports to ensure no harmful dyes or fixing substances were used during the process. It all seemed fine, apart from one metal detector without a green light. Mr. Ho promised it would be fixed the very same day. They could only understand about ten percent of what he was saying due to his accent and all the background noise of the machines, but they both nodded politely and copied his excitement whenever it felt appropriate. The factory had set up connected basins throughout the buildings to show how they recycled all the water they used during their dying and washing process. The water ran through an open half pipe, out into a pond of Koi Carp in the patio between the buildings to demonstrate how clean their recycled water was.

"Amazing," Mel said, admiring the fish at the edge of the pool. They were beautiful creatures. Most of them were white with bright red marks, and they immediately came to the surface when Mr. Ho took a bag of food out of his pocket.

"They know it's me." Mr. Ho threw in a handful of food. "These are very expensive Koi Carp. They're my greatest possession, and it's my policy that if they cannot live in the recycled water from our factory, we shouldn't be dying fabric or printing at all. I have children, you see. And I worry about them." The big smile he had been showcasing all day had left his face. "This country needs to focus more on the future and less on the here and now. We all need to make money to keep the economy alive, but we also need to think about the land that is the core of our country. It's a serious issue that keeps me up at night." He shook his head. "I gave my staff the challenge to create a water purifying system so ground breaking, that my expensive pets can grow old and be happy here. It's their responsibility to keep them alive by how they run the factory. Koi Carp are very sensitive to their environment, you see. I come here every day and feed them." He pointed at the largest carp, chasing away the smaller ones. "That was my first one," he said. Cost me almost ten thousand dollars. To me, he represents the future of our country. The pollution is so bad in China that we, as business leaders, need to set an example. Otherwise, our children will not have a future here."

Sophie nodded, watching the carp jump. She had seen it many times, but she reminded herself again that it was one of the main reasons she had pursued the job she had now, knowing she wouldn't have to feel guilty about what she did for a living.

"That's why we work with you, Mr. Ho. And I'm personally proud to work with a factory that does everything in its power to give a great example to China's future generations."

Mel knelt down, attracting the fish by hovering her hand over the water. "Thank you for the tour and thank you for your time," she said, looking up at the factory director. "And for reminding us of what's important." She stood up and smiled. "This has made my day, Mr. Ho." Sophie watched Mr. Ho's face light up at Mel's simple statement and was amazed to witness yet again, her positive effect on people.

The cherry on top was a visit to Mr. Ho's office, where they sampled an espresso from his new coffee machine. It was his pride and joy and could only be handled by Lemon, his first assistant, whom they had met during their previous visit. She had clearly been instructed to nod at the right times and to laugh at Mr. Ho's jokes. Even after eight hours, she was no closer to relaxing her face.

"Thank you so much, Lemon," Sophie said sweetly as she accepted the coffee. "You've been so helpful this week. We really appreciate it."

Mel nodded. "It's been inspiring to see how you all work here and you've been incredibly professional."

Lemon clearly liked the sound of the word professional. Her forced smile broke into a more natural one immediately, and she even showed her teeth for a moment.

"Thank you," she said, in a rehearsed tone. "We always strive to meet our customers' expectations and exceed them where we can. Here at Ho Manufacturing, we pride ourselves on short lead times and environmental consciousness. Our employees are granted two extra holidays during Chinese New Year. Unlike most factories, we work in three shifts that never exceed nine hours. Healthy employees are happy employees and a healthy environment is essential for the future of our next generation." She stammered a bit as she spoke the words she probably repeated several times a week, but Mr. Ho seemed satisfied and nodded appreciatively.

"Thank you, Lemon. You can go home now; we are done here."

Sophie and Mel, however, were not done. They had to sit through another hour with the director. In situations like this, Sophie was always tempted to say: "Thank you so much but we've had a long day, and I'm sure you'd like to go home to your wife as well so why don't we skip the polite chit chat and both go and enjoy what's left of the evening." But she couldn't do that. It just wasn't the way things worked in their line of business. Relationships with the factories were essential to their brand in order to keep their lead times short and their prices reasonable so she downed the espresso, gathered her last bit of energy and admired the pictures of his sailboat and his family's last holiday to Europe.

## 16

A fter Sophie and Mel had re-entered Hong Kong, their driver dropped them off at the Ladies' Market. It was too late to get changed first, so they bought a cheap suitcase on wheels to drag their files and laptops along with them as they searched the market for souvenirs to take back home.

"This must be the most crowded place I've ever been to," Mel said. "But I love it." She smiled as she gazed up at thousands of neon signs, sticking out from the buildings that towered above them on either side. Although it was dark outside, the narrow alleyway was lit up like a torch. Music was playing from the stalls where locals and tourists were laughing and haggling. The sea of people was blurred by big clouds of steam, pouring out from the vents of the crowded restaurants behind the stalls, spreading the authentic aroma of traditional Chinese and Cantonese food.

"It's amazing," Mel said. "I feel like we're in a different world." She shook her head and spun around, taking in the three-sixty view of chaos and lights. "First we arrive at this luxurious hotel with an incredible view of the skyline, then you take me to an island where everything is completely calm and spiritual with rich nature and beautiful temples, and now this" She pointed at a stall selling the biggest, most outrageous keyrings they had ever seen.

Sophie laughed. "Welcome to Mongkok. This is a cool neighbourhood, actually. It's gritty and kind of mysterious." She pointed at the high-rise buildings, covered in thousands of satellite dishes and air-conditioning boxes attached to the exterior. They were once white but now dark-grey from the smog and looked like they might fall apart any minute. Clothes were hanging down to dry from extensions on the tiny balconies, soaking up the humid air. "Did you know," she said, "that some of the most interesting places in Hong Kong are in those buildings?"

Mel looked up. "But they're private apartments, right?"

Sophie nodded "Yes. Most of the ones facing the streets are apartments; with London prices I might add. But in the middle, around the atrium, there are music rehearsal studios, karaoke bars, pool bars, handbag dealers, electronic shops, pay-per-hour rooms, arcades and anything else you can possibly think of. It's a labyrinth of entertainment and indulgence and one of Hong Kong's best-kept secrets."

"Wow. It seems like we've got quite some exploring to do," Mel said, eyeing up a souvenir stall with lucky cats. "Take me anywhere you want; I'm game!" She waved at the shopkeeper for help.

Mel bought a handbag and a kimono for her mother and soup bowls with chopsticks for herself. They also found a tea shop where she stocked up on Jasmine tea and an intriguing selection of flower teas, presented in a beautiful wooden box. Although they were tired, they had fun haggling and made a competition out of who could get the best bargain.

"I'm in heaven," Mel said, kissing Sophie on the cheek. "You're the best traveling companion I've ever had." Sophie bought some vintage prints of Shanghai movie stars from the thirties to frame on her wall.

"Just one more thing," Sophie said when they got to the end of the market. "I need to get a handbag for Cat. She led them across the road, into a department store that specialized in electronic products. Mel followed her up the escalators and through the narrow corridors where phone dealers and games specialists clamoured for their attention.

"I'm not sure if this is the right place to find a handbag, Sophie." Mel was out of breath by the time they had arrived on the top floor.

"Trust me. If it's still here, it's the best place," Sophie said as she opened the emergency exit, leading into a dark and dirty corridor. "They tend to move around, in case they get caught." She stopped in front of door number eight hundred and twenty and knocked.

Mel nudged her. "Are we safe? I don't want to be chopped into pieces today." The door opened before Sophie had a chance to answer and an old Chinese lady rushed them inside before closing the door behind them. Mel gasped at the sight of thousands of designer handbags, stuffed into cardboard boxes that were piled up to the ceiling.

"See?" Sophie grinned. "Best place to buy a handbag." She searched on her phone for a picture of the bag she was looking for. The old lady took her phone and brought it close to her face, squinting. Then she nodded and started rooting through the boxes until she found one.

"Nice one," she said, showcasing a toothless grin.

"It certainly is." Sophie smiled. Nice and cheap, right?" The lady nodded and showed her a number on her calculator, upon which Sophie shook her head, laughing. She typed another number into the calculator, and the lady pulled a furious face, balling her fist at Sophie. Mel seemed genuinely entertained by their emotional haggling game. Eventually, they agreed somewhere in the middle and shook hands.

Mel regarded Sophie with interest as she took the wrapped up bag from the sales lady and thanked her in Cantonese.

"So that's for your friend Cat?" she asked, trying to sound indifferent.

"Yes, it is. I've been getting her bags for years. Why?" Mel shot her a cynical look.

"I don't know... Is it because you still like her, maybe?"

Sophie shook her head and laughed. "No, it's not like that. As I've already told you, that died out a long time ago." She paused for a moment and looked at Mel, who seemed to be playing a game with her.

"Why?" She asked. "Does it bother you?" The words were out before she had time to think them over and Sophie felt her cheeks flush.

Mel smiled in silence, then answered her question with another question. "Why? Do you want me to be bothered?"

Sophie looked down at the bag in her hands. This was a game, and she could play it too. "If you're jealous, I'll buy you one too. Which one would you like?"

The sales lady jumped in between them within a split second, presenting a range of twelve different designs, dangling from her arm. "Yes, jealous lady, pick one. Pick two. This one will buy for you," she said, pointing at Sophie. "Sugermama. Rich lady."

At that moment, they both burst into laughter with Sophie almost losing her balance in the overstocked room.

"I'm good, thank you," Mel said, waving her hand at the lady who kept shoving bags into her face. Then she took Sophie's hand and dragged her out of the apartment. "Just take me out for dinner on the company credit card, and I'll be happy." She smiled mischievously. "And for the record," she added. "Maybe I was a little bit jealous."

THEY WERE SEATED at a table so small and low that their knees were touching as they faced each other, looking at the pictures on the menu. Staff members were running around, shouting out order numbers in the long, narrow restaurant. To their side was an open kitchen, where skilled chefs were hand rolling out wrappers, then filling, boiling, steaming or pan-frying sweet and savoury dumplings like they had done it since the day they were born. Sophie and Mel seemed to be the only non-locals in the rowdy crowd, crammed in between noisy students and stall owners, winding down after a long day. Sophie was conscious of the contact, constantly shifting on her stool. Their flirty banter at the handbag store had set the tone for another interesting evening, and now she wasn't quite sure how to behave.

"I'm afraid I have no idea what to order here," Mel announced. "So you choose. I'll eat anything as long as it's not something super weird like testicles or pig's nose." She raised a finger. "No, wait. I take that back. I'm prepared to try that too if you recommend it."

Sophie giggled and pointed out her selection to the waiter who also brought them two large, cold beers in Hello Kitty bottle covers. They cheered, and Mel held up her bottle, cocking her head with a comical grin.

"You know what they say," Mel said. "Seven years of bad sex if you don't look each other in the eyes. And for me, that would be a tragedy." She raised her eyebrows. "Although you wouldn't know, would you Sophie?" She leaned forward, resting her elbows on the table. Sophie chuckled, slightly uncomfortable.

"Stop talking about things you don't understand," Sophie said. "Wait till you try the pork and truffle dumplings. It'll be an orgasm in your mouth, so you won't have to worry about other people's sex lives."

They were both famished, and Sophie didn't realize she had over-ordered until the steam baskets were placed on their table and were stacked so high that they had to peek around the towers to see each other. The waiter gave her a look as to say: You greedy tourists, let's see if you can finish this order. But Mel's appetite was untameable. Eating everything in sight like she had all week, she managed to work her way down the first four levels, praising every single dish with such passion that Sophie almost felt proud of her selection.

"How on earth can you eat so much and stay so slim?" she asked. "I mean, do you always eat for three? Or four? Are you even human?"

"I'm not slim," Mel mumbled around a mouthful. "My bum is rather big but I love my bum, and I'm lucky to have my mother's metabolism." She swallowed and took a sip of her beer. "I can eat anything I want, and I'll always look the same. At least so far anyway. And I love food so thank God for that." She looked up at the sky in a dramatic manner and picked another parcel out of the basket, struggling to hold the slippery dough with the chopsticks before she dipped it into the vinegar. "I swear Sophie; this might be the best meal I've ever had. I'm starting to think you're an ordering genius. After this, you can order for me anytime." They had another couple of beers while they finished off whatever they were capable of eating and discussed the events of the day, laughing at the memory of Mr. Ho's holiday presentation.

"I'm so glad you're nice and normal," Sophie said. "Seriously, I'm pleased and relieved you are who you are. And now that we've got these first couple of days over with, I know it will never be awkward travelling with you, and I can look forward to our future trips together."

Mel kicked her leg playfully under the table. "Me too," she said. "And just so you know, I'm aware of your little secret."

Sophie raised an eyebrow. "What do you mean, what secret?"

Mel laughed. "Oh come on Sophie. I know that you'll be my manager soon. Debbie told me, so no point beating around the bush. Let's talk about this." She straightened her back and raised her head, the way she did when she was talking business. Sophie smiled and found it so sexy that she had to look away for a second while Mel continued.

"You don't seem like the kind of person to bring this subject up yourself because you're modest. Besides that, you're not the typical leader-type who believes in hierarchy and distance." She leaned in again and put a hand over Sophie's, resting on the table. "And that's not an insult, that's a compliment."

Sophie looked at the hand covering her own and every useful phrase she had ever learned from her management training and team building workshops faded into a big blur. Mel's hand felt delightful, and she sighed quietly.

"Thank you," she said. "You're right, I didn't bring it up, and I have no idea why. I'm still getting used to the idea, I guess. You must have noticed the enormous bump on Debbie, but I didn't know she'd told you it would be me

replacing her. It hasn't even officially been confirmed yet."
She shrugged. "But yes, it looks like I'll be taking over from
her and I'm sorry I didn't tell you." Sophie shifted on her
stool.

"Well, that's great for you, and I totally respect that," Mel
said. "After so many years of hard work you deserve a
promotion more than anyone. I'm happy for you."

Sophie could see that she meant it and felt relieved that
the word was out. There was no reason in particular that she
hadn't brought it up in the first place. She had meant to, but
as time progressed, things just seemed to get more and more
complicated between them, and she was now at the point
that she couldn't be around Mel anymore without lusting
after her, so it had just seemed wrong to discuss the matter.
*I'm a bad manager already. Why do I find her so damn
attractive?*

"I'm sorry," she said again. "I should have been honest
with you from the start, but I guess I've had other things on
my mind and it didn't seem like a big deal."

Mel nodded. "It's okay. Don't worry," she whispered.
"Until you take over, we're just colleagues, nothing else.
We're both having fun so let's continue to do that." Mel
didn't look too sure of herself as she spoke because they
both knew deep inside that they had gone too far and said
too much to make the attraction undone.

## 17

"Ready to get inspired?" Mel asked. She pointed at the Converse on her feet and danced around the breakfast table before she sat down. "I'm wearing my comfy shoes today."

Sophie held up her cup of coffee. "Cheers to comp-shopping. On days like these, we have the best job in the world, right?"

Mel nodded. "I'm excited. Do you have a plan on where we should go? I've done some research online but then I figured you might know the best places, so I didn't print it out."

Sophie smiled. "Leave it with me. I love to be in charge." She laughed. "We're going to Hong Kong Island, across Victoria Harbour. There are competitor flagship stores, some great art galleries, and exhibitions that I think you'll like and there's also a Korean shopping mall with the latest crazy stuff to spot some of the upcoming trends. We don't have any obligations. All we need to do is make sure we know what our competitors are up to and that we're a little bit more inspired for our next range."

The waiter offered them coffee, and they both held up their cups for a refill.

"Would you like some Champagne too, ladies? It's included in our Friday breakfast." Sophie and Mel exchanged glances and looked up at him in surprise.

"Yes, please. That would be fabulous." Sophie grinned and pointed at Mel's plate. "What kind of wonderful concoction of flavours are you having today?"

Mel chuckled, presenting back the food in front of her. "Let's see... I've got some sushi, blueberry pancakes, Greek yogurt with honey and... this... It kind of looks like custard but it's got a different texture."

Sophie leaned over to sniff the tiny bowl. "Mmmm nice. It's almond soup. Good choice." She chuckled. It's actually a dessert but since you're planning on having sushi at nine in the morning, you might as well."

MEL ADJUSTED her cap to protect her eyes from the sun, and Sophie put on a pair of shades as they followed the path along the Victoria Waterfront. The gardens along the way were in full bloom, and the benches facing the harbour were all occupied, providing a peaceful retreat for the road workers, families and shop assistants who were having their breakfast in the shade underneath the banyan trees. It was quiet at first, but the path widened as they reached the Avenue of Stars and suddenly they found themselves in the middle of a crowd. Hundreds of tourists were fighting over a picture with the bronze statue of Bruce Lee or one of the movie star hand prints in the marble tiles on the pavement. Sophie took Mel's hand so they wouldn't lose each other.

"This is the Hong Kong version of the Hollywood Walk of Fame. Four hundred and forty meters of cinematic history. It's popular with Asian tourists, and at night, this is the perfect spot to watch the Symphony of Lights. That's the light show on Hong Kong Island," she explained. "They play music from the speakers here to accompany the laser display, and it's really iconic to Hong Kong."

Mel sighed. "We need some more time here. I don't know if it's the two glasses of Champagne I had with breakfast, but Hong Kong seems like a happy place in daylight." She waved at a little boy who was with a group of Taiwanese tourists, carrying matching parasols. They all waved back. "Maybe we should get one of those if we'll be walking around in the sun all day? We could share?" She batted her eyelashes and Sophie couldn't help but smile. Mel's eyelashes were long and dark, and she knew exactly how to put them to use.

They crossed a square full of busking musicians and dancing seniors before jumping onto an old, rusty looking ferry.

"I'm glad we can see land, or I'd be worried to board this," Mel said, leaning over the balustrade. The engine roared, and the water splashed up high against the hull when the ferry took off. As they came closer to the other side, the Victoria Peak came into clear sight, rising above the skyscrapers and the observation wheel. The cityscape set against the green background was a stark contrast that still fascinated Sophie, even after numerous visits.

"How on earth did they build this?" Mel asked as they crossed the road into town. "It's so steep. And how do people get home from work at night?"

"Well, there's the tube, the tram, and there are taxis all over the island. But today we are taking the escalators." Sophie made a theatrical gesture for Mel to go first and laughed at her stunned face when they turned the corner.

"Welcome to the largest outdoor escalator system in the world. Our first stop is five escalators away, but if you see anything you like on the way, we can jump off."

"Are you serious, Sophie? This is amazing." Mel's eyes widened at the maze of narrow streets they passed on their way up. First, there were colourful markets and tea shops. Then came small restaurants, independent hipster-esque coffee shops, Japanese hairdressers and Korean beauty salons, all built up against each other at different heights like stacked up Lego pieces. In between were private homes with swanky roof terraces and balconies, showing off their premium space. They got off on Hollywood Road, where antique shops and art galleries dominated the street, only broken up by the odd wine bar or convenience store. Sophie took Mel's hand again when they crossed the road. By now, it didn't seem awkward anymore. They had become so intimate over the past week that she simply couldn't do without the physical closeness. Each time they touched, an electric bolt shot through her arm, down into her core, spreading an array of joy and excitement. When she wanted to let go, Mel tightened her grip.

"Don't," she said. "I like holding your hand."

## 18

"Let's get some lunch," Sophie proposed after they had made their way back down. "It's been a long morning, and I'm starting to feel hungry. How about you?"

Mel nodded. "I could eat now." She laughed and wiggled her thumb. "Plus my hand needs some rest. I've taken so many pictures that it's starting to ache. That was great by the way. I had no idea the stores here were so inspiring."

The alleyways turned narrower as they walked further into the maze of stalls and restaurants, squashed in between the skyscrapers. They tried to avoid the steam blowing from the wok-stations on either side, filling the air with the scent of garlic, soy, and ginger. Mel gazed at the ladders of neon-lit signs that bathed the buildings in yellow and orange.

"It's so alien," she said. "Nothing is like how I thought it would be. It's like being in a theme park without the rides, but at the same time, it's like going back in time. When I look around me, it feels like a local market fifty years ago, but when I look up, there's futuristic architecture reaching into the clouds."

"I know. It's fascinating, isn't it?" Sophie pointed at a shabby looking food court in the middle of a mews and led them to the only available table next to a food truck, where two senior chefs were cooking dishes for the crowd from two large woks.

"Don't worry," Sophie reassured her. "You won't get sick, I never have. It's all fresh, and it's cooked so hot, it will kill any bacteria that could possibly harm you." They ordered beers, and Sophie asked for the chef's recommendations. The waiter looked puzzled and tried to convince them to go for some simple rice dishes.

"Please," Sophie said. "Just give us whatever is good today."

Mel laughed. "Feeling brave, are you? I thought that was my thing when it came to food."

They watched the chef throw ingredients into the hot wok. He shook it around before adding sauce and spices to finish off the dishes in under a minute. Within no time, they had a table full of food. Oyster omelette, chicken livers with garlic, steamed greens and fish in black bean sauce, accompanied by white rice and a bowl of chili oil. Mel stared in confusion at the mouth-watering display that seemed to have appeared from out of nowhere.

"Wow. I don't think we need to eat tonight." Mel laughed. "Oh Sophie, I'm having such a good time. I'm going to miss you." Her eyes met Sophie's, and she held her gaze, her face more serious now. Sophie swallowed hard but didn't shy away. Their exchange of glances was so much more than friendship, and Sophie found her eyes wandering down to Mel's mouth once again. She forced herself to concentrate on the food in front of her.

"I'm going to miss you too," she said quietly. "It's

different with you. Different from spending time with other people."

Mel smiled and covered Sophie's hand with her own. "I know."

## 19

The hotel bar was busy on Friday night. Men and women in work attire were gathered around the bar, celebrating the end of the week or perhaps the end of a successful trip. Others were already dressed up, ready for a long night out in one of Hong Kong's swanky nightclubs. Sophie and Mel joined the crowd, determined to get some liquid courage in their system before heading out to Central to meet Aldo and his friend Rick.

"Miss Scott?" Sophie turned around to find the concierge with an envelope.

"Yes, that's me." She smiled at him.

"I have a message from your mother. We tried to get hold of you this morning and left a copy in your room, but you must have missed it."

Sophie took the envelope and opened it. "Thank you." She frowned as she read the note.

SOPHIE DARLING,
    *It seems impossible to get hold of you, but the kind man at*

*reception ensured me this note would reach you in time for your date with Aldo.*

*I have transferred three hundred pounds to your account. Please spend it on a decent dress for tonight and don't forget your manners.*

*Your mother.*

SOPHIE BURST out into laughter and read it again to make sure she wasn't hallucinating. She handed Mel the fax.

"Wow." Mel giggled. "She really is serious about this matchmaking, isn't she?"

"My mother never gives up. It's insulting, and it even feels a bit dirty." Sophie tore the note in half. "I'm transferring that money right back."

"So what are you wearing?" Mel asked.

Sophie shot her a sceptical look. "What do you mean? I'll just stay as I am. I don't need to impress anyone." She knew that wasn't entirely true. She wanted to impress Mel, but she didn't think Mel was the type who got turned on by evening gowns. She hadn't even brought one with her. All she had in her suitcase was a body hugging black satin cocktail number with a low-cut cleavage. She didn't love wearing it but it looked good on her, and it was her 'anytime, anywhere dress'.

"I have a black dress with me. I'll wear that one," she said, after seeing Mel's disappointed look.

"Great!" Mel yelled, clapping her hands. I brought a little something along too. Do you want to get dressed together? We can take this to your room?" She pointed at the bottle in the ice cooler between them. "I mean, we could go to mine, but it's a mess. Seriously, you have no idea how messy my room is."

"Mine too." Sophie laughed. Her heart was jumping at the prospect of having Mel in her room. "But the cleaner will have been in by now so it shouldn't be too bad. I'm in room number fourteen thirty-four." She took the bucket and their glasses and gestured at the waiter to put their drinks on her room tab.

Mel jumped off the bar stool. "I'm excited. It feels like a girls' night out, and I haven't had one of those in a while. I'll be up in no time."

Sophie rushed to her room to inspect the damage. She cleared away her dirty laundry and checked the bathroom for anything embarrassing, but it was spotless. She ran over to the mirror in a nervous frenzy and inspected herself, then suddenly remembered that Mel had seen her only a couple of minutes ago. She shook her head, confused by her irrational behaviour and tried to calm her nerves.

A couple of minutes later, she opened the door to Mel, who immediately walked into the room and dumped her stuff on the bed.

"Do you mind if I have a quick shower here?" she asked.

"Sure," Sophie gestured to the bathroom. "Help yourself to towels; I'll go in after you." She liked the idea of having Mel naked under her steaming hot shower, using her soap and her towels. She felt a flash of heat between her legs when she heard the water running and imagined Mel stripping off. This is crazy. Why is everything about this girl such a turn-on? She tried to stop her thoughts from going in the wrong direction but ever since their tube ride together that had proven close to impossible. She poured herself more wine and took a large gulp. Then she got the hotel steamer out and concentrated on her creased dress. After what seemed like an eternity, Mel came out of the shower with a large fluffy towel wrapped around her.

"Nice dress," she said, pointing at the dress in Sophie's hands. "I bet it looks great on you." Sophie stared at her for just a little bit too long, taking in her bare arms and legs and the cleavage that was the result of the tight towel around her chest. Mel noticed and gave her a curious look. A tiny smile formed around her mouth.

"Are you okay, Sophie?" she asked.

"Eh...Yeah, I'm good," Sophie stammered. "I'm just going to have a quick shower too. Wine's over there. I poured you some more." She pointed at Mel's glass on the nightstand.

Sophie tried to wash away her thoughts under the shower, but now all she could think of was Mel getting dressed in her bedroom. It was incredible that something as simple as two women getting dressed to go out together could be so arousing. It almost felt like some erotic ritual. The shower, the pampering, the dresses, the wine and the compliments.

Mel was dressed when she returned to the bedroom, and she looked stunning. The white backless dress complemented her skin tone and showed off her amazing figure. It was decent enough to wear to a smart dinner, yet the open back gave it a seductive touch.

"Wow," was all Sophie could manage to say.

"You like it?" Mel twirled around a couple of times. It made her hair bounce up and down around her shoulders. "I bought it on sale before I came here. I didn't even have time to try it on. I'm so happy that it fits." She handed Sophie her dress. "Here, I finished the steaming for you. Put it on."

"You look hot," Mel said, when they inspected themselves in the mirror. "I like the cleavage."

Sophie blushed. "Thank you. So do you." They were both feeling slightly tipsy from the wine and Sophie had started to relax a little bit.

"Do you want me to put some make-up on you?" Mel asked. "Not that you need it," she added. "I just enjoy doing it." Sophie rarely wore makeup, but she smiled and nodded anyway. Suddenly, makeup seemed like the best idea in the world, if only for the prospect of Mel touching her face.

"I won't put too much on. Just a little bit to emphasize your amazing features." Mel leaned over Sophie and started working on her eyebrows. Her face was close, and Sophie could feel her breath on her skin. She felt a jolt of arousal and tried to calm herself down so Mel wouldn't notice her erratic breathing.

"Do you look like your mum?" Mel asked. Her lips were moist and inviting as she spoke, her voice husky and sweet, almost whispering. "I bet your mum is stunning, like you." She studied Sophie's face as if she was looking at a work of art. She tilted her head and squinted, taking a step back. Sophie blushed and shifted uncomfortably in her chair. She wasn't used to someone looking at her with such intensity.

"Yeah. I bet you do," Mel continued. "The pale skin, the prominent cheekbones, the dark blue eyes with long lashes and the slender figure... You must get that from someone.

Sophie looked down, shying away from Mel's gaze. "I have my mother's genes. She used to be a model, a long, long time ago. She's still obsessed with her looks to the point where it gets alarmingly out of hand sometimes."

Mel nodded. "I can understand that. It must be hard to grow older when you used to make a living from modelling. Can I see a picture of your mum?"

Sophie smiled. "Are you sure?" She scrolled through her phone, searching for a recent photo. "Here. This was

Christmas last year. She zoomed in on the photo and pointed at her mother in front of the family in a long, black evening gown, awkwardly smiling at the camera with a cocktail in her raised hand."

Mel's eyebrows shot up in surprise. "Wow, she looks like she's had quite a bit of work done... am I right?" Sophie nodded. "I guess quite a bit would be an understatement."

Mel applied some cream underneath Sophie's eyes, and Sophie shivered at the light touch of Mel's fingers on her skin.

"Tell me about her," Mel said, searching for something in her toiletry bag. Sophie sighed, trying to think of ways to describe her mother without putting her down.

"My mother is quite uptight. I guess you could call her a Stepford wife. She wasn't always like that, but over the past couple of years she's been obsessed with being perfect in every single way. It's like she's lost all her natural spontaneity. Until about eight years ago, we were often mistaken for sisters. My mother has always looked naturally younger than her age, but when she turned forty, she finally managed to persuade my father, who's a plastic surgeon, to do some work on her.

"Your dad is a plastic surgeon? Wow, I've never met one of those. Or people who've had plastic surgery. It's fascinating, but it's also quite alien to me. Was it weird for you, your dad operating on your mum?" Mel asked.

Sophie shrugged. "I don't know. It was certainly weird in the beginning. My mother has never been a stranger to Botox, but at least it hadn't done her face any harm. Her best friend Deborah organizes these Botox parties at her house in Wimbledon every three months, and my mother has always been one of her most loyal attendees. But in the end, Botox couldn't preserve her forever, and on the day of her fortieth birthday, she had a minor meltdown. I remember my parents arguing when I came home to have dinner with them. My mother was yelling hysterically, accusing my father of neglecting her feelings. He's given hundreds of women facelifts you see, but he always refused to touch my mother's face because it was sacred to him and he thought she was beautiful the way she was. But my mother was adamant she would get her way." Sophie put on a screechy voice, mimicking her mother.

*"What is wrong with you, David? You know I've been feeling insecure lately. I need this. Do you not understand that? Mark gave Deborah fillers for her fortieth. It's not a big deal. Do you not care about how I feel at all? How am I supposed to go through life looking like this? I swear David, if you don't do it, I'll go to somebody else."*

Mel giggled. "So, he gave in?"

"Yes, he did. She threw herself on the couch and cried until he finally agreed to schedule her in for a breast augmentation, a facelift and lip-and-cheek fillers. I think he lost the will to argue altogether. He's given her what she wants ever since." Sophie pointed at her mother's face again. "And that is how my mother turned out like that. But hey, if it makes her happy, who am I to stop her, right?"

Mel smiled kneeled down in front of Sophie, levelling with her face. "Yeah. Who knows what we'll be up to in a couple of years?" She opened a tube of lip gloss and squeezed a small amount on her finger. "Part your lips," she said, making Sophie's heart jump. Sophie shivered when she felt Mel's finger on her mouth, gently applying the liquid to her lower lip before moving up. Mel's gaze focused on Sophie's mouth with a look that could only be described as desire.

*She wants me.*

Mel stepped back, as if suddenly woken up from a daydream. "There. All done," she said with a flustered look on her face. Sophie got up and walked over to the mirror on the wardrobe door. She looked at her reflection and was relieved to see she still looked like herself. No funny colours and no clumpy lashes either.

"Thanks," she said. "I don't normally bother, but I like it."

Mel studied her intently. She took a strand of Sophie's hair and twirled it around her finger. Then she gently pulled it behind her ear and stroked her cheek.

"There," she said. "Perfect." Sophie tried to ignore the response that this simple action had triggered. Her arms were covered in goose bumps, and her chest was heaving up and down when she followed Mel over to the door.

"Are you ready to go?" Mel asked.

Sophie felt nervous. "It's awkward," she said. "It feels like a date but it's not a date, and I have no desire to impress Aldo."

"But it is a date," Mel said, casting her a flirty glance. "Don't you get that by now? It's our date. The guys are just entertainment. Plus they're paying." She winked and handed Sophie her bag.

## 20

The showstopper that came with the restaurant on the thirty-first floor of a commercial building was its eye-catching, panoramic view over the city. Sophie had to admit that, although it was pretentious as expected, she was quite impressed with Aldo's choice. He had booked a table outside, overlooking Kowloon Harbour. They could see their hotel from where they were sitting. The infinity pool on the rooftop was lit up, and it looked like the water was pouring over the edge of the building. The temperature was pleasant, the sky clear and it was the perfect night for outside dining. Aldo seemed relieved when the waiter showed them to the table where he was waiting with his friend.

"Sophie, darling," he said, kissing her on both cheeks. "Lovely as ever to see you again. How stunning you look tonight. I've never seen you like this; all dressed up." He stared at her cleavage for a moment before he remembered his manners.

"This is my friend Richard, or Rick as I call him." Aldo turned to his friend with a sense of pride that only a mother with a new-born baby would trump. Rick straightened his crisp pale blue shirt as he stood up to greet them. He was blonde and slim with great teeth and a healthy tan, the typical English public schoolboy-look. Sophie spotted his watch and knew he was wealthy. She wondered if Aldo looked up to him, living the high-life in Hong Kong. She kissed Rick on both cheeks and put a hand on Mel's shoulder.

"Gentlemen, this is Mel. My lovely new colleague as of this week." Both men seemed pleasantly surprised by their company for the night and immediately beckoned the waiter to take their drinks order.

"Champagne, ladies?" Aldo suggested.

"Actually, do you mind if I have a Dirty Martini?" Mel asked.

"Make that two please," Sophie said to the immaculately dressed waiter. The men decided on a beer and Aldo took charge, ordering food for everyone, only checking with Rick when he wasn't sure. Sophie shot Mel an amused look as to say, 'I told you so.' The moment the waiter had brought over their drinks, the big bragging began.

"Rick is my friend from Cambridge. He works in private equity, right here in Hong Kong Central. Isn't that right, old chap?" Aldo said.

Rick nodded and raised his hands, gesturing around him. "Yes, I suppose the English weather drove me to more exotic places, shall we say? It's quite extraordinary living here." He grinned and took a large gulp of his drink.

"So was it your first time here when you moved?" Sophie asked. "That can't have been easy, am I right?"

Rick laughed and leaned back in his chair, running a hand through his thick, blonde hair. "Rickie Ricardo can settle in anywhere," he said, and Sophie cringed. "I did take on a local girlfriend for the first month or so. She was great. Helped me find the best supermarkets, restaurants, and clubs. She even got me an accountant, a taxi app and a membership for the local cricket club. They're good at keeping their physique as well, the Asian girls. They very rarely get fat like the English, and they don't complain much either. It didn't work out, of course."

Sophie looked at Mel and could see that she wasn't the only one disgusted by Rick. He didn't seem to notice their exchange and shrugged his shoulders cheerfully.

"Anyway, I don't believe in relationships between people from different social backgrounds. Not that they're not civilized enough per se, they just don't appreciate the finer things in life, and I happen to like someone that I can share those with."

"Right," Sophie mumbled, hiding her balled fists under the table. She felt rage welling up already, and they had only been there ten minutes. She took a deep breath. What on earth were they doing here with these pompous pricks? They could have gone out for a lovely dinner together. Just her and Mel. It would have been a whole lot better than wasting the precious time they had left on Aldo and his cocky companion.

"So, let me rephrase that," she said, raising an eyebrow. "You 'took on' a Chinese girlfriend while you needed her and after you were all settled, you dumped her because she wasn't as 'refined' as you?" She made quote marks with her fingers in the air.

Aldo laughed. "Oh come on Sophie, don't be so sensitive. You've been coming to Hong Kong for years, and we all know how it works here so let's not pretend otherwise, shall we?"

Sophie was fuming. She was about to think of something rude to say when she suddenly felt Mel's hand under the table, searching for hers. It broke off her train of thought entirely, and all she could do was smile in surprise, entwining her fingers with Mel's. She felt goose bumps appear on her arms and shivered. As she watched mouths speaking and hands moving, her insides did somersaults. Sophie knew it wasn't just a comforting touch. She squeezed back and closed her eyes, savouring the moment. When she opened them, Mel winked and smiled at her. It was an unspoken promise that said more than a thousand words. They both wanted more, and they wouldn't be able to fight it much longer. She didn't hear a single word the boys were saying. It felt like she and Mel were the only two people on the roof, overlooking the Hong Kong harbour, with its millions of flickering lights. Sophie was disappointed to let go of Mel's hand when the starters came out.

"I'm sorry," she corrected herself. "I didn't mean to be rude. Let's just agree to disagree, shall we?" Aldo nodded and smiled. Glasses were refilled and clinked, and people around her laughed. Conversations passed her in a haze. Sophie wasn't sure if it was the alcohol or the setting or their terrible company, but Mel looked more beautiful tonight than she could ever have dreamed of.

"So Mel, tell me about yourself," Rick said. "What does your family do?" Mel smiled politely, dabbing her mouth with the napkin.

"What my family does is not important, Rick. Not because I'm ashamed of telling you, but because I don't think this is the right place or time to steer the conversation in that direction." She gave him a challenging look. "Perhaps you would like to know what I do?" Sophie tried to repress a giggle. This girl could hold her own against the likes of Rick and Aldo.

The answer seemed to please Rick, and he gave her an apologetic look with a hand on his heart. "I'm ever so sorry," he said. "Where are my manners? Of course, I'd be much more interested in what you do, Mel. Please tell us."

"Great." Mel smiled as if the sharp exchange of words had meant nothing. "I'm a senior designer for the same brand Sophie works for. I've just had my first week, and I'm really looking forward to working with her in future. She's very talented and fun to hang out with, so I feel like I've won the lottery already." She pulled Sophie in and gave her a playful kiss on the cheek. "I've designed for two other fashion labels before this, mainly in London, but I also spent a year in Berlin with a really cool outerwear brand and six months in Milan as an assistant designer before I graduated. That's where I designed that very shirt you're wearing." She pointed at Rick's shirt.

Rick's eyes widened, and he patted his shirt. "This one?" He said. "Really?" Then he laughed. "This is my favourite shirt. I've been carrying a piece of you with me for years before I even met you." He gestured to Mel. "I think we were meant to meet tonight." When Mel didn't reply, he slapped Aldo on the shoulder. It was something they seemed to do a lot.

"Isn't that fantastic, old chap?" Aldo laughed at Rick's romantic gesture and then turned his attention to Sophie. "So, have you designed anything I might have in my closet, Sophie?" Sophie shook her head, swallowing a piece of fish.

"No. I only design women's wear so unless you're into cross dressing, you wouldn't have anything in your wardrobe attributable to me." That comment brought hysterical laughter from the boys to the table.

"Well it just so happens," Aldo said. "That I only wear Italian brands made to the highest standards. I don't like this 'made in China' rubbish." He leaned forward and gave Sophie an intent look, emphasizing how serious he was about the subject.

Sophie leaned back in an attempt to create more distance, casually resting her elbows on the chair's backrest behind her. "It's all the same," she said. "A lot of Italian brands are made in China. Just because they happen to hand-sew the buttons on in Italy doesn't mean the fabric or the whole garment was made there. So you've probably got a couple of shirts in your wardrobe that have been produced right there over the border." She pointed to the direction of the Chinese border and gave him a self-assured look. "And your phone of course," she said pointing at the device in his chest pocket. "Oh, and let's not forget about your laptop, your toothbrush and any other items you might have in your toiletry bag."

Mel giggled and glanced at Sophie sideways, biting her full bottom lip. "She's right," she said. "Milano, the brand you're wearing now, actually owns a small factory in China." Her hand disappeared under the table again, this time searching for the hem of Sophie's skirt. She pulled it up a bit and let her hand rest on Sophie's thigh. Sophie gasped. The immense pleasure of Mel's hand on her bare skin and the graphic images that were going through her mind would have been enough to keep her bedtime fantasies going for at least the coming months. Flashes of more to come entered her mind and she tried to breathe slowly and focus on the conversation. Mel wanted her. And she wanted Mel to take her any way she pleased. She had never felt so ready for anything before and, as she picked on her main course oppo-site the oblivious Aldo and Rick, she knew this would be the most exciting night of her life. Mel's hand moved towards her inner thigh, squeezed her leg and only let go when the waiter came over to take their plates. Sophie heard a distant mumble that sounded like Mel pretending to be interested.

"Oh gee, Rick! That is so fascinating. Isn't it Sophie?"

Sophie turned to her, trying to keep the look of overwhelming desire hidden from their fellow tablemates.

"Yes, absolutely," she said without a clue what he was talking about. "Tell me more, Rick."

Aldo broke him off. "I'll tell you something, Sophie," he said. By now he'd had quite a bit to drink. Sophie could tell by the way he raised his voice when he spoke, determined to be the centre of attention. "You and I would be perfect together, don't you think?" he slurred. "We'd make a great pair, and our families would be delighted if we got together. Think of it. It's a no brainer." He gestured to Sophie and then placed his palm on his chest. "We're both good-looking, educated and we come from excellent backgrounds." He laughed, but she could tell by the unease in his eyes that he was serious. He shrugged. "Why not? We'd have gorgeous children and proud grandparents. You'd never have to pay another visit to a factory in your life, and you could live comfortably, knowing that everything was taken care of." He winked. "Come on, Sophie. You know you fancy yourself a bit of Aldo." Sophie shot him a cynical look, clearly not very keen on the prospect. Aldo shifted in his chair, taken aback by Sophie's lack of enthusiasm. He tried to save face by saying all the wrong things. "Think of it; it's perfect. You can let your hair grow long again. We all know this is just a phase of rebellion and I like that about you. You're cool Sophie. And if you grow up a little, and start behaving like the beautiful adult that you are, you'll be perfect. So how about we go on another date in London?

Just you and me?" His head was wobbling from side to side, intoxicated and insecure.

Sophie smiled and refilled his glass, determined to make him feel even worse in the morning. "I'm flattered, Aldo. I really am. But I really don't think you and I are a good match if you know what I mean. We've known each other for years, yet there's never been any sign of chemistry between us. That says something, right? I've never fancied you and you've never fancied me so let's just leave this drunken conversation right here."

Aldo laughed it off but Sophie could tell he was mildly upset. The only girl approved of by his parents hadn't thrown herself in front of his feet yet and that was hard for him to digest.

"Well of course Sophie. Don't flatter yourself. I was only joking, my darling." He gestured to the waiter for the bill, steering the conversation back to Rick.

THE NIGHT WAS ALREADY in full swing in the bar of the Dragon nightclub, located on the floor below the restaurant. Sophie and Aldo had managed to secure a high table while Rick ordered drinks. Despite Sophie's desperate attempts to make her stay until Rick was back, Mel had left them alone to find the bathroom. Aldo had his hand on Sophie's back during their conversation and it was already making its way down towards her bottom.

"Isn't this marvellous?" He said. "You and me on the other side of the world with our lovely friends? You should come back to the hotel with me, Sophie. We're both young and single; there's no reason why we shouldn't have a bit of fun together. I've had a nice bottle of bubbly sent up to my suite just in case." He grinned and Sophie felt disgusted by his predictable behaviour. Hadn't she been blunt enough? She looked around, searching for Mel, the only person she really wanted to be close to tonight. She sincerely hoped she wasn't out there flirting with someone because frankly, she didn't think she could handle that. She'd been in the toilet for a long time now. As if Mel had sensed her desperation, Sophie felt a warm hand on her neck and Mel's warm breath against her ear.

"Want me to save you?"

Sophie shivered at the sound of Mel's voice. She nodded slowly. Aldo's lips were moving and his hands were flapping around, ranting on about something to do with the interior of his car. Sophie couldn't hear him. She couldn't even hear the music. Mel's lips against her ear had reduced all sound into a thumping beat in the background. She felt high from the sexual tension that had been hanging between her and Mel all night.

"Here we go ladies," Rick interrupted them. He passed the drinks around while scanning the room for hot bodies.

"Thank you," Sophie said, taking the opportunity to escape from Aldo's grip. She took a sip from her gin and elderflower cordial and turned around to find Mel facing her. Mel held out her hand and Sophie took it as if it was the most natural thing in the world. She looked into Mel's green eyes and then down at her full, luscious lips, still wet from the rhubarb cocktail she held in the other hand. She didn't care about Aldo or Rick in close proximity. She didn't care about manners or etiquette or whatever it was that had held her back in the past. She wanted Mel so badly. Sophie put her drink down on the table before she leaned in, her mouth against Mel's ear.

"I want to kiss you," she said, searching for approval in Mel's eyes.

Mel licked her lips and smiled. "I'm not stopping you. I've wanted to kiss you since we first met at the airport." Sophie was startled by the declaration but Mel didn't give her time to think about it. She pulled her closer, cupping her neck with her hand. Sophie felt Mel's lips on hers. So soft, barely touching at first. The contact made her legs go weak. She was on fire, her body begging to be consumed. She tilted her head and opened her mouth to find Mel's tongue in a warm, slow embrace. She moaned, thankful that no one could hear her over the loud music. Her hands were drawn to the perfect, curvaceous body that was now pressed against her and she wrapped her arms around Mel's waist. She pulled her closer while she tasted and explored the mouth she had been longing for all night. Her lips felt just like she had imagined. They were wonderfully soft. The impact their kiss had on her was something she could have never prepared herself for. It was like a seductive dance, wild and sexual, and Sophie forgot all about her surroundings as she lost herself in the moment, falling deeper and deeper into Mel's embrace.

Mel was the first one to step away. She looked flustered and stared back at Sophie in surprise, the tip of her fingers against her lips. Then she giggled, regarding their audience. Sophie snapped back into reality too. She saw Aldo and Rick's gaping faces, staring at them from their table.

"Shit," was all she could manage to say. Mel seemed equally shocked by their kiss. She had a bewildered look on her face and stared at her drink before downing it in one go.

"I don't think this is the right place for making out," she whispered into Sophie's ear.

Sophie nodded. "I think we need to thank the boys for dinner and tell them we're leaving. I really want to leave." Before they had the chance to apologize, Aldo stormed off, casting Sophie an angry glance over his shoulder. Rick didn't move.

"I'm sorry," Sophie stammered. "I didn't mean to upset him."

Mel held up a hand. "I'm really sorry too. We didn't plan for that to happen. I don't know... maybe we've had too much to drink. Please apologize to Aldo from us and thank him for dinner." She watched him disappear through the door that led into the nightclub. "I don't think he wants to speak to us right now."

Rick shook his head, not in the least fazed by the events. "Yeah sure, no problem. He'll come around. Wait... are you two leaving?"

"Yes, that's probably for the best," Sophie said.

"Well just so you know, in my opinion, there's no need to apologize, ladies. That was one of the sexiest displays I've seen in my lifetime." Rick grinned. "Any chance I can come back to the hotel with you?" They stared at him in disbelief.

"No, you can't," Sophie said. "But thank you so much for a lovely evening. It was great to meet you and we'll take you out next time you're in London. How's that?" Rick looked disappointed but gave them both a drunken goodbye hug and promised to talk to Aldo.


"THANK you for saving me in there," Sophie said as they entered the hotel lobby. She was still blushing.

"It was my pleasure," Mel grinned. "I hope we didn't upset your future husband too much."

Sophie shrugged. "It's okay. He deserved it, the way he was behaving all night. I don't think he'll tell anyone; he's far too proud for that." She laughed nervously and lingered as they passed the bar.

"Do we need to talk about this?" Mel asked as she climbed onto one of the stools. Sophie took a seat next to her and leaned on the bar, cupping her forehead in her hands.

"What the hell is happening, Mel? This thing we have... It's amazing, but as much as I want this, we really shouldn't. We work together." Sophie's worried eyes met Mel's. She tried to read her but all she saw was lust. Pure lust.

"I know," Mel agreed. "How do you think I feel? I'm still in my trial period. I'm in my first week. And I don't want you to think I make a habit of kissing people I work with. Because I've never done that before." She paused and shook her head smiling. "I think the drinks might have had something to do with it. And those two assholes, of course, they needed to be put in their place."

Sophie giggled. "As you can probably guess, I don't normally do this either. It's also very unlike me not to care about what other people think of me. I have no idea why, but I really don't give a shit that they saw us." When Mel didn't say anything, she looked down and took a deep breath before asking the question. "It was good, right? The kiss?" Mel nodded slowly without saying a word, her intense green eyes piercing right through Sophie's. A smile spread across her face.

"I told you that you should give it a try, didn't I?" Mel cocked her head in a smug manner. "And in case you hadn't noticed, it was just as good for me as it was for you and I'd probably do it again, even though it's a really bad idea." She hesitated, studying her trembling hands before continuing. "Look at me; I'm all nervous. It's been a while since someone swept me off my feet, that's for sure."

Sophie shot her a questioning look. "Really? But I thought you had..."

"Not like this, Sophie," Mel interrupted her. "Not like this, with the butterflies and the craving and the all-consuming thoughts about getting you into bed." She put a hand in front of her mouth. "Shit, did I just say that out loud?" Sophie giggled and her heart jumped at Mel's confession. She felt the same craving and the same need to feel Mel's body against hers. She could barely control her actions anymore.

"What are you saying?" she asked. The unsteady voice that came out of her mouth barely sounded like her own. Mel leaned forward, resting her elbow on the shiny surface of the bar.

"What I'm saying is...maybe we shouldn't be so strict with ourselves. We're both having a good time and we can keep this between us, right? We're only here for one more night anyway. After that, it's back to normal." Sophie's insides did summersaults and the excitement that spread across her face must have been visible from miles away. She was so aware of her own body. She could feel every limb, every muscle, in a way she never had before.

"Any drinks, ladies?" The bar manager asked them. Mel got off the stool.

"No, I think I'm good, thanks." She smiled at him and took Sophie's hand. "I'm going upstairs. Are you staying here?" Sophie shook her head and followed Mel into the lift.

A Japanese couple jumped in with them just before the doors closed and they stood there in an awkward silence. Mel glanced at Sophie and held her gaze. She looked aroused. It made Sophie's heart jump with anticipation but she was also terrified. Mel got out on the thirteenth floor. She turned around before the doors closed.

"You know my room number," she said.

## 21

Sophie was shaking under the shower. She had never felt more confused and excited at the same time. "You know my room number," was all Mel had said. *Was it an invitation? Of course it was.* Sophie knew the room number indeed. Room thirteen thirty-four. One floor beneath her. *Is she having a shower too?* Sophie imagined Mel rubbing soap over her full breasts, down to her stomach, and she felt herself getting wet with desire. Will Mel expect me to come down? Is she waiting for me? Naked? She wanted nothing more than to see Mel naked but it was the most stupid thing she could do. They would be working together, and it could make things pretty awkward between them. And she was scared; there was that too. She stepped out of the shower and dried herself off, looking at her reflection in the mirror. Her hair looked good when it was wet, and she ran her fingers through it. She felt sexy. Mel made her feel sexy. In a panic, she rooted around in her suitcase, searching for something suitable to wear. Not too dressy but certainly not too casual. It also had to be flattering and come off easily. She grinned at her own thoughts. *Am I really going to do this?*

Just as she was about to slip into a simple cotton dress, she heard a soft knock. She threw the hotel robe around her and walked towards the door with shaking knees.

"It's me," she heard Mel whisper. Sophie unlocked the door with a trembling hand, and Mel walked in, closing the door behind her. She was wearing a robe too. Drops of water from her recent shower were still glistening in her neck.

"Hi," she said in a soft voice. "I wasn't sure if you were coming and I couldn't stand waiting for another minute."

Sophie couldn't speak. The thick white robe was tied loosely around Mel's shapely waist, showing off a hint of cleavage where the droplets had gathered in a tiny pool between her breasts. She could see Mel's chest heaving up and down. She looked nervous. Under her left eye was a smudge of mascara, a reminder of their evening out. Mel stepped forward, her face so close now that Sophie could feel her breath. Her heart was racing at what felt like a million beats per minute.

"I didn't mean to scare you, barging in like this," Mel said. "And we don't have to do anything you don't want to do. But the kiss we shared tonight has been playing over and over in my mind since we left the bar. It was good. Actually no, it was incredible. I just..." She shuffled nervously from one foot to the other. "I just really want to kiss you again before I go to sleep. Just one more time."

Sophie nodded slowly. "Yeah. Same here," she said. "I want to kiss you too." She kept her eyes on Mel's mouth. It was a perfect mouth, and Sophie had never experienced such an urge to kiss someone. She leaned in, carefully placed her lips on Mel's bottom lip and sighed. The kiss felt even more sensual now, without the loud music and the crowd around them. It was quiet and intimate, and Sophie's senses seemed to be picking up on every move, scent, and sound. Mel tasted like cocktails and mints, and when Sophie parted her lips, she felt an overwhelming craving for more. She moaned when Mel deepened the kiss, sinking into a pool of sexual desire. Encouraged by Sophie's boldness, Mel pulled her in closer and wrapped her arms around her neck and waist. She plunged her tongue into Sophie's mouth, and Sophie felt herself getting wet and wild with hunger. She sunk her hands into Mel's thick hair and pushed her against the wall. She could feel a smile forming on Mel's lips by the way they tightened against hers.

"Told you that you would like it," she whispered again when Sophie pulled away. Sophie was breathing fast, trying to think. It didn't make any sense. She wasn't supposed to be attracted to Mel. She was supposed to ease her into her job, help her with her fittings, sit through some dinners with forced conversation and then fly back to London mildly irritated that she wasn't Maggie. Not this. Not kissing this woman half naked in her hotel room. A woman for God's sake. She shook her head and took a step back. Mel noticed the hesitation and held up her hands.

"I'm sorry," she said. "Maybe it's better if I go now." Sophie sighed in relief but as soon as Mel turned towards the door, she panicked. She didn't want her to go. No one had made her feel this good by just kissing her, and now it was a force she couldn't deny anymore. Before she had the chance to change her mind, she grabbed Mel's wrist and pulled her back. Mel seemed surprised by her action as she turned back slowly, studying Sophie's face for an explanation. Although Sophie couldn't give her one, she leaned in close to Mel's face again.

"I want you," she whispered. Mel said nothing for a

couple of seconds before she nodded and kissed her again, carefully.

"Then let me touch you," she said. "And don't be scared. It's only me." She untied Sophie's robe and let it fall open. Sophie shivered when her hands slipped inside, exploring her waist and her back. Mel's hands were soft and gentle, her fingertips dancing over her skin like magic markers, leaving a trail of ecstasy. Sophie could still feel the sensation everywhere they had been as they moved up towards her shoulder blades.

"You're so fucking beautiful," Mel said softly, her mouth against her lips. Sophie closed her eyes for a brief moment, still trying to process what was happening. She felt the hands move to the front of her body, and her legs almost gave way underneath her as they moved over her breasts, two thumbs caressing her nipples. She gasped, and Mel calmed her down with another careful kiss, pulling her hands away.

"Are you okay?" She whispered.

"Yes." Sophie's hands were shaking as she untied Mel's robe. Just like her, Mel was naked underneath it, and Sophie stared at the flawless caramel-coloured skin and the perfect full breasts that were exposed now. Her hands gained a life of their own as she finally reached out to explore Mel's body. She moaned into Mel's mouth, feeling the firm shape and the hard nipples against her fingertips. She was nervous, her hands lingering as they moved down, tracing her hip bones. Mel noticed her hesitation and turned them around, so Sophie was now standing with her back against the wall, her whole body trembling uncontrollably. She opened her own robe again and pressed her body against Sophie's. Sophie sighed. It felt warm and soft and so right. Her insides were dancing. *Is this what insanity feels like?* By now, she had lost all control over her thoughts and had stopped analysing her actions. It was simply too good to think about. She could feel her own wetness between her legs when Mel placed a thigh between hers. It was warm and firm, leaning against her. She wrapped an arm around Mel's waist and moved her other hand down to her round, perky bottom, pulling her in even closer. She was afraid she might have an orgasm right there and then, the way her pulsating centre reacted to the press of Mel's thigh. She wanted her. She wanted her hands, her mouth... Then she felt fingers tracing her inner thigh, moving upwards so slowly that it left her in agony. The touch of Mel's hand was soft, but it felt like a bullet when it slipped between her legs.

"Oh God,' she moaned when Mel's fingers suddenly pressed against her clit. Her vision became blurry, and she buckled when Mel pushed harder, opening her up with her fingers.

"Does that feel good?" she whispered, smiling. Sophie was unable to answer as the fingers that entered her sent her into an immediate climax she knew she would remember for years to come. Waves of ecstasy washed over her, touching every nerve-end, and she shook helplessly, only held up straight by Mel's arm around her waist. Mel slowly pushed her fingers further with a smug look on her face, making circles with her palm until Sophie finally opened her eyes and looked straight into hers.

"And?" Mel said, now grinning from ear to ear.

Sophie panted heavily, steadying herself against the wall. "Wow," she whispered. "I had no idea anyone could do this to me."

Mel laughed. "And I had no idea you were so into this." She planted her forehead against Sophie's, resting it there. "I'm sorry it was so fast, I couldn't help myself." She stroked

Sophie's face. "I'll make it up to you if you let me stay tonight. Three minutes aren't nearly enough to show you how good it can be." Sophie smiled and sighed. She felt a sense of freedom and relief that was hard to describe. Her nervousness was gone, and all that was left was a screaming curiosity and a raging thirst for more. Her hands reached out to touch Mel's body as she kissed her again, hungrily. Mel moaned softly when she reached her hips and her thighs, stroking inwards towards her centre. Then she pulled out of the kiss. She took a couple of steps backward, dropped her robe to the floor and fell onto the bed, daring Sophie to follow. Sophie didn't need any encouragement. She took off her own robe and lowered herself on top of Mel. They both sighed at the contact and Sophie sank deep into their kiss and Mel's soft, feminine body underneath her. She was eager to touch her, to taste her and to own her but she wanted to take it slowly. She wanted to remember this for the rest of her life. Every single second. She nestled a leg between Mel's and could feel how wet she was. It made her want her even more, and she moved down, kissing her neck and her breasts. Mel closed her eyes and exhaled, throwing her head back.

"You're doing great already," she whispered. "Don't stop. Just do whatever you want to do to me."

Sophie listened to the sound of Mel moaning and her ragged breathing while she parted her lips and took a hard, dark nipple into her mouth. Mel arched her back and cursed when she licked it carefully. Sophie was amazed by how sensitive her breasts were. She took the other nipple into her mouth and pushed her centre against Mel's. It drew another loud cry from Mel's mouth. It was a beautiful sound, and Sophie wanted to make her scream. She kissed and licked her way down to Mel's belly, making sure she didn't miss a single inch of the delicious skin against her mouth. Mel was smooth and firm, yet she had feminine curves in all the right places. Sophie had never admired a man's body like this, and she finally understood why. Mel was perfect. Although she had stopped thinking about what she was doing, everything she had doubted in the past fell into place naturally as she caressed Mel's stomach and her hips, listening to the sounds of pleasure that came from deep within her. Mel opened her legs when she got down to the strip of dark hair between her thighs, giving her a view of her pulsating centre. Sophie felt a flash of heat between her legs, which only grew stronger when she finally traced Mel's sex with her tongue for the first time. She'd had no expectations, and she certainly hadn't anticipated that she would love the taste of her so much. She slowly moved her tongue in circles, kissing her and stroking her thighs. They both moaned as she took Mel's clit into her mouth and sucked it gently until Mel started to buckle underneath her. Sophie's heart skipped a beat. *Could I really make her come?* Sophie wanted to see her face when she did. She kissed her way back up and let her fingers slide through Mel's sex, listening to her accelerated breathing. Mel's eyes were closed, her eyelashes fluttering, and the long, wet hair was spread around her face. She was biting her own knuckle to stop herself from being too loud. Sophie gasped at the sight and slowly entered her with two fingers while she lowered herself on top of her. Mel opened her eyes when she sensed Sophie's mouth close to hers.

"That's so good. That's fucking amazing," she whispered. "Fuck me, Sophie. I want you to make me come." Sophie felt beyond herself and pushed her fingers deeper, slowly penetrating Mel as she kissed her neck and her cheeks and finally her mouth again. She felt Mel's thighs tighten against her own hips.

"Yes," Mel shouted, guiding her hand and pushing it against her clit. Then there was a long, loud moan followed by heavy breathing and silence. Tiny drops of sweat had formed on Mel's forehead and in the crease of her neck. She looked up at Sophie with a mixture of surprise and relief, and Sophie had to blink twice to make sure she wasn't dreaming. Grinning from ear to ear, she wondered who had gotten more pleasure out of it because she could do this all night long, every single day. She laughed out loud, and Mel laughed too.

"Damn," Mel smiled. "That was awesome. I need to step up my game now, or you might think I'm a total loser." She licked her lips in a way that made Sophie weak throughout her whole body.

"God, you're sexy," Sophie said. "I've been longing to touch you for days and you certainly didn't make it easy for me, looking the way you do." Mel kissed her, tracing Sophie's mouth with the tip of her tongue.

"If only you knew what's been going through my mind this week," she whispered. "Just so you know, I have no plans of going back to my room tonight. I'm staying right here, and I'm going to do all the things to you that I've been fantasizing about." She pushed Sophie over and rolled on top of her. Sophie moaned when she felt Mel's weight on her like a warm blanket. She was too turned on to speak, and so she closed her eyes while Mel placed her hands over her head on the pillow. She held them down with a firm grip and used her other hand to caress her face.

"I love your face," Mel whispered.

"You do?" Sophie replied coyly.

Mel grinned. "Haven't you noticed how I've been looking at you?"

Sophie lifted her head and brushed her lips against Mel's. "I did think you were a bit flirtatious," Sophie mumbled against her mouth. "But I didn't know you. A lot of people are naturally flirtatious. It wasn't until we were squashed in the MTR together that I started to realize you might want something more from me than just help with your tech packs." Mel smiled and licked her lips before kissing her slowly. When their tongues met again, Sophie moaned and pulled her in closer to deepen the kiss, tightening her thighs around Mel's hips. She needed to feel her as close as she possibly could. Mel responded by thrusting into her core. She traced Sophie's breast with her free hand and slowly licked her way down her neck. By the time she reached her belly and let go of Sophie's wrists, Sophie was swimming in pleasure and anticipation. She closed her eyes and sunk her fingers into the curly hair that tickled her skin. When she felt Mel's hot breath between her legs, she gasped. It hit her like lightning, and she screamed out when she felt a warm tongue slide down, exploring her most intimate of places. The sensation was almost too much to bear. She arched her back instinctively, grabbing the pillow beneath her head with both hands. Mel was good. Really good. Sophie spread her legs and moaned when Mel's tongue entered her before slowly gliding up towards her clit. She started to tremble again, and her breathing became more rigid with every second that passed. Mel made her way back up and traced her neck and her chin before moving back to her mouth with her tongue.

"Not so fast,' she whispered. "Not this time." She lowered herself back on top of Sophie again and thrust into her, kissing her with hunger and conviction. They only interrupted the kiss to catch their breath

"Please Mel, don't stop," Sophie begged. Mel shifted and pressed her centre hard against Sophie's, regaining the grip on her wrists. She smiled when Sophie moaned in pleasure. Mel was rough, but it felt great, and Sophie gave in to the sensation of being taken in a way she'd never dreamt of. They both moved slowly, finding a rhythm together while kissing passionately. She felt Mel's wet mouth on her neck, kissing down past her collar bone. She felt teeth scrape over her skin until they reached her nipple and she gasped when Mel bit her softly, then harder. Mel let go of Sophie's wrists and lifted her chin with a finger.

"Look at me," she said in a husky voice. Sophie opened her eyes to meet Mel's. Her light green eyes had gone dark and hazy. Her lips were parted, wet and sensual. She looked aroused and determined to give Sophie what she wanted and more. Sophie moaned louder when Mel pushed a hand in between them and thrust two fingers into her. Then she slowly pulled out of her before penetrating her in deep motions, burying Sophie's body underneath her own. Sophie fought to keep her eyes open when she felt the uncontrollable twitching of pleasure building up in her lower abdomen until they both gasped and cried out. Sophie wrapped her legs around Mel, pulling her in as close as she possibly could. She held her there for what seemed an eternity until she finally started to feel her limbs again. The after effects of her orgasm rendered her body useless, as she looked up at Mel. It wasn't just her own pleasure that astounded her. It was the feeling of togetherness and the look of pure delight on Mel's beautiful face that left her captivated and speechless. Was this what it was supposed to be like? What had she been doing, wasting her time all those years, never coming anywhere close to what she felt now? She felt alive and excited and sensual. Their bodies were warm and sweaty. Mel draped herself over Sophie in a state of total relaxation and buried her face in her neck.

"Are you okay?" she asked. She lifted her head to meet Sophie's eyes.

Sophie blinked. "Yeah. I...I think so," she stammered. "I'm just surprised at how right this feels. I feel exhilarated, but it's so much more intense than I thought it would be. I can't believe how much I want you." She sighed. "It's overwhelming."

Mel smiled, stroking her hair. "The first time is always overwhelming if it's with the right person. Even the second time. And the third. I can leave if you want me to. Do you want to be alone?"

Sophie shook her head and laughed. "No, please don't leave. I want you to stay." She paused. "I want more."

## 22

"So...back home tonight." Mel pulled the duvet higher, covering their naked bodies. A sad look spread across her face, making Sophie's stomach churn. Sophie lifted a lock of hair from Mel's forehead and finger-combed it to the back before placing a kiss above her eyebrow.

"I know. I don't want to leave this bed," she whispered.

Mel sighed. "I'm going to miss it too. I'm going to miss this... just you and me in a hotel room. Nobody's business." She took Sophie's head in her hands. "I really like you, Sophie. But I also need this job. There's much more at stake for me. I have my mother to take care of."

Sophie nodded. "Yeah. I understand. We should stop now before it's too late. It's the sensible thing to do." She paused. "But I'm also I'm pretty sure I have a big crush on you. I've never felt like this before, and I'd do anything to spend more time with you, Mel. And to be honest with you, right now, I don't even care about my job."

Mel frowned. "Don't say stuff like that, Sophie. You're great at your job, and you have fantastic career prospects.

You've earned your place. Don't fuck it up because of this."
She gestured from Sophie to herself. Sophie tried to hide
the stab she felt.

"This," she said, making the same gesture Mel just had,
"means something to me."

Mel shifted closer and pulled Sophie into a tight
embrace. "I didn't mean it like that." She sighed. "Look, I
think we both know we're in it deeper than we'd like to
admit but I think it's best if we let it sink in while you're
away and see what the situation is like when we see each
other again." Sophie nodded. She couldn't help but smile
when Mel pressed a thigh between her legs. The all-
consuming lust that had been absent during their short
conversation was back, and she shivered at the contact,
craving more. She laughed.

"Seriously, Mel. Is this how you deal with difficult
conversations? Because if it is, you're very good at problem-
solving."

Mel grinned. "I didn't mean to make light of the topic,
but we'll have all the time in the world to talk when you're
back. Let's not waste our last two hours in this room being
serious when we could be doing much more interesting
things." They sank back into the pillows, and Sophie turned
to Mel. The curtains in the room were thick and dark, but
the small strip of sunlight that fought its way in was bright
enough to highlight Mel's side of the bed.

"You're so pretty in the morning. Your hair... it's all messy
and cute."

Mel smiled, and tiny dimples appeared in her cheeks.
"You think I'm cute?"

Sophie nodded, sinking deeper under the covers to hide
her blush. "Yeah. I think you're super cute." She traced Mel's
neck and collarbone down to her breasts. "And I think I

might be obsessed with your boobs." She laughed. "I'm sorry. I know that sounds weird. It's just such a delight, touching you. You're so soft and smooth."

Mel leaned in and kissed her. "Sophie Scott, discovering the delights of a woman. Well, let me tell you something. I happen to think you're pretty damn cute too. And soft. And smooth. And did I mention sexy as hell?"


"ONE CAPPUCCINO with two sugars for the pretty lady in bed."

Mel handed Sophie one of the coffees she had ordered. Sophie moved up and pressed the button on the wall next to the bed, opening the curtains. Mel covered her face in her hands.

"Oh my God, I'm so stupid. So that's how you open them!" She stared at the window in disbelief. "I swear, I've been yanking at them every morning with my full body weight until I was exhausted and finally gave up. It's a miracle I didn't break the mechanism!"

Sophie burst into laughter. "Are you serious? You haven't used these buttons?" Mel shook her head. "Well then I think it's time for a lesson, Miss Johnson." Sophie pointed at the panel. "So this button is for the curtains, I guess you know that now. And this row..." She pressed the middle button. "This row is for the bathroom. They heat up your toilet seat, run your bath and switch on the speakers." She shot Mel an amused look. "And this button is for turn down service. If you press it, the light next to your door will switch on and cleaners will walk into your room at any given time of the day to fluff up your pillows and put water and fresh fruit on your nightstand." Mel's eyes widened.

"Are you serious? I can't believe I didn't know that. It's

not fair. I've never had turn down service in my life and I've never sat on a heated toilet seat before but now it's too late. Anything else I've been missing out on?"

Sophie laughed. "You've only been here for a week. Of course you've been missing out. Which brings me to the next question. What do you want to do today? Besides spending time in bed with me until they kick us out of the room at noon." Mel chuckled and thought about the question.

"Tell me," she said. "If you could pick a place in Hong Kong right now, anywhere... where would you take me?" She shifted closer, placing her thigh over Sophie's leg.

"I don't know," Sophie whispered against Mel's mouth. "What would you like to see?"

Mel shook her head. "No. It's up to you. Where would you like to take me?" Sophie shivered at the light touch of Mel's lips.

"I know where I'd like to go if I was here on my own, but you might not like it. It's a place I used to visit a lot when I spent four months out here but it's not exactly glamorous." She laughed. "It's actually really uncomfortable."

"Uncomfortable sounds perfect," Mel said. "Take me there."

## 23

"I know you don't want to tell me where we're going," Mel said as they exited the tube in Tai Po. "But I'm getting quite curious now." She looked around the deserted MTR station, surrounded by overgrown mountains that seemed too dense to climb. "Where the hell are we? Please enlighten me."

Sophie shook her head. "No chance." She laughed. "You might back out if I tell you." She inhaled deeply, cherishing the fresh air, and scanned the empty parking spaces beside the tube station. "We could take a taxi, but it doesn't seem like there are any around right now so we might as well walk. It's not too far."

They crossed a footbridge, leading into suburban Hong Kong, passing small brick houses with neatly kept gardens and al fresco community restaurants. There wasn't an English road sign or a neon light in sight. No cars, no traffic lights. Sophie led them up a hill through a sub-tropical forest. It was so steep that they had to stop five times to catch their breath. "Just fifteen more minutes," she said. "Almost there."

"I don't care," Mel panted. "It's beautiful here. Look at those trees. They must be hundreds of years old. And it's so green with vegetation, so untouched." She held up a hand. "Listen to that noise. Are those birds?"

Sophie looked up at the trees. "Yeah. Birds, monkeys, frogs, bats, crickets... I even saw a sounder of wild boar crossing the road here once." They stopped off at a stream to splash some cold water on their faces. It was clear and cold, running down the hill into a small lake. There was a pebbled plateau with a picnic table, surrounded by wooden benches for families to enjoy a day out, but today there was no one. Mel stared at a makeshift warning sign along the winding path.

"Really? Snakes?" She pointed at the snake symbol with the exclamation mark and cautiously scanned the area. "I know I said I didn't mind uncomfortable but we're safe, right?"

Sophie laughed. "We're perfectly safe as long as you don't decide to run into the jungle and step on one while you pee in the bushes. The ones to watch out for are cobras and bamboo snakes, but they usually don't come near the footpath. They're more scared of us than we are of them and they'll only attack if they feel threatened." She took Mel's hand and pulled her closer, pointing at a white building on top of the hill. "Almost there." Mel's face lit up when she heard the barking from afar.

"Dogs?"

Sophie smiled. "More than you can handle."

They climbed the last distance, hand in hand. It felt great, holding Mel's hand now that they didn't have to beat around the bush and look for excuses anymore. Finally, it was okay, to be honest, and hold her just because she felt like it. Or at least for now. Mel looked down at their entwined fingers, and Sophie knew she felt the same. She didn't let go until they reached the gate that said 'HKDR.'

"Hong Kong Dog Rescue," Sophie explained. She knocked on the heavy metal door that led into the large fenced off compound. An old lady who answered the door graced them with a wide toothless grin.

"Sophie!" she yelled in a high-pitched voice.

Sophie gave her a hug. "Kit, it's so nice to see you again." She gestured to Mel. "Kit, this is my friend Mel. Mel, this is Kit. She runs the place on Saturdays." To Mel's surprise, Kit flew around her neck too, before running a hand through her hair, examining the texture. Then she nodded appreciatively and led the way into the open corridor with lockers and washing facilities for the volunteers, all the while talking to Sophie in Cantonese.

"I didn't know you could speak Cantonese," Mel said when Kit ran into the office to get them both a bottle of water.

Sophie laughed. "I don't but she doesn't speak English, so this is how we communicate. She talks, and I pretend to understand and smile." The loud barking started as soon as they passed the first pen and the twenty dogs in there immediately set off the others around them. Mel looked mildly uncomfortable when a German Shepherd jumped up against the fence next to her.

"So you worked here?" Sophie nodded.

"I volunteered every Saturday and Sunday morning for four months. They have quite a lot of volunteers here, but the shifts are all before midday and after five pm. It's technically too hot for both the volunteers and the dogs to go for a walk in the middle of the day."

Mel frowned. "So you walk them? I mean... how? There

must be at least five hundred dogs here, and they're all huge."

"They have a good system going," Sophie said. The aim is to get each dog walked at least once a day. Some go in the morning shift and the others in the evening shift. There are also trainers who work with the traumatized ones. They socialize them and teach them how to walk on a lead so they can be adopted. It's a no-kill shelter, privately funded. That's why they have so much space to run around here."

Kit pointed at one of the pens. "Buba," she said. Sophie smiled at the sight of the overexcited dog and took Mel's hand.

"Come on, let's go in." She opened the door and dragged Mel inside before she had the chance to change her mind. A big, brown Labrador came tearing up to Sophie, wagging his tail. "Buba! My boy, come here. You remember me, don't you?" She got down on her knees to face him and scratched him behind his ears. "Why haven't you been adopted yet? You're such a good boy!" The rest of the pack came closer, barking and growling. They were slowly closing in on them, and Mel didn't look too sure of herself.

"I'm a bit overwhelmed. They're so big, and there are so many. They're not going to kill me, are they? Because they might be able to smell the fear on me."

"It's okay," Sophie said. "The tricky ones are in the pens on the top of the hill. Just let them sniff your hand. Mel bent down and held out her hand. Four of them were brave enough to approach her, and after a while, they were wagging their tails, begging for attention. A Husky snuck up to her and licked her in the face.

"Aww, you're so cute," Mel said in a high-pitched voice. She got comfortable and sat down on one of the stools. "Not so scary after all." She giggled when one of the mongrels ran up to her, bringing her a stuffed animal. She turned to Sophie, who was now sitting in the sand with the happy Labrador between her legs. "So you two know each other, huh?"

Sophie scratched the dog behind his ears. "Buba's my favourite. He was in a terrible state when he came here, but it only took him a month to get used to people and to trust the volunteers. He's such a lovely dog." She kissed him on his head. "I expected him to be gone by now but I guess he's quite old and the old ones aren't that popular when it comes to adoption. He seems happy and well taken care of though." Kit came into the pen with two leads.

"Want to go hiking?" Sophie asked. "It's not too hot today, so it should be fine even though it's out of hours. We'll take some water."

Mel smiled. "I'd love to go hiking with you and these darlings." She looked up at Kit and gestured at the other dogs. "Which one should I take?"

Kit pointed at the Husky. "Stella," she said. Stella understood what was happening and jumped up at her in excitement. A chubby mongrel behind Stella looked disappointed that he wasn't being picked. He stared up at them with his tiny head that was way out of proportion to his body. Mel stroked him. "Oh no, poor thing. He wants to come too. Can we take three?" She held up three fingers to Kit, who seemed to be agreeable to the idea. She laughed and rushed off as quickly as her old legs could carry her to get another lead.

SOPHIE AND MEL sat down on a bench by the stream and let the dogs off the lead. It was the only open area they had encountered so far after an hour's walk. They sprinted towards the water and started splashing around, excited to get the special treatment they so rarely had.

"Don't worry, they'll come back," Sophie said. "Kit wouldn't let us take them this far if they're runners. They've had bad experiences outside the compound, so they'll stay close to us and make sure we take them back." She shifted closer and put her head on Mel's shoulder. Mel sighed, looking out over the towering trees and plants, taking up different levels of the forest. It was warm and humid, and the sun cast thin rays of light through the thick leaf ceiling, leaving a mysterious glow in the air.

"It's been the best week ever," Sophie whispered against Mel's hair, inhaling the sweet scent of her shampoo.

"Yeah, it has." Mel shifted and put an arm around Sophie. "Is it weird for you?" She asked.

Sophie frowned. "What do you mean?"

"Well... I'm not a man, in case you haven't noticed. There must be some internal conflict going on in that pretty head of yours? I mean, it would be strange if there wasn't." They both laughed.

Sophie thought about the question. "I don't know. I guess it's strange. Maybe. It's certainly different. But it feels good and right now, I don't want to think about it."

Mel smiled. "Me too. Right now, I wish we could stay here forever." She ran a hand through Sophie's hair. "You're special; you know that?" When Sophie didn't answer, she continued. "I've had the best time with you, and you keep on surprising me. I mean, look at them." She pointed at the dogs, who were now soaking wet, chasing each other through the forest. "It's so sweet of you to think of them on your day off. You're a good person, Sophie." Sophie smiled at the sight of Buba, who had the biggest grin on his face.

"It's not like that," she said. "I should have taken him

years ago, and I didn't. I assumed someone else would adopt him, but nobody did and now the poor boy is still here. I feel awful about it. There are just so many of them, and at the time, it didn't feel like I could make a difference just by adopting one dog. But now..." She sighed. "Now he's seven, and he's still here. He's never had a loving home, and he only gets a real walk like this occasionally."

Mel shook her head. "Don't act like it's too late. It's never too late. You can still adopt him, right? He loves you, I can tell." She beckoned Buba to come over with her arms spread out wide and he came tearing at her with a stick in his mouth, unsure of what to do with it.

Sophie laughed. "You're right," she said, looking down at him. "Do you want to come back with me, Buba?" She tried to take the stick from him, but he wasn't having any of it. He bounced back each time she tried to snatch it from him. She leaned forward, lowering her head to his level. "Do you want to come to London with us?" Buba cocked his head as if trying to figure out what she was saying. Then he turned back to his friends who were barking at something high up in a tree.

Mel laughed. "With us?" she said. "Are we a family now?"

Sophie's cheeks turned red. "Sorry," she said. "I didn't mean it like that. It's not like I'm hoping for a happily ever after with you." She buried her face in her hands. "Oh fuck, that sounded lame. Please ignore me; I'm such an idiot."

Mel laughed even louder now. "It's okay, Sophie. I'm just teasing you."

She smiled, exposing her dimples. "Look at you, all shy and rosy. It's cute." She got off the bench and walked around it to give Sophie a hug from the back. She sighed.

"So what are we going to do when we see each other in the office?" Mel sounded more serious now.

"I don't know." Sophie turned around, her eyes desperately trying to read Mel's face as she plucked a leaf from her hair. "What do you think we should do?"

Mel shrugged. "I don't think there's much we can do. We can't see each other if we work together. Not like this, anyway. My job is really important to me, and I've only just started." She hesitated. "It won't look good on either of us if they find out." She pulled Sophie's head back against her chest, stroking her forehead with gentle fingers.

"It's not just the gossip we'd have to deal with, you know. You'll be my line-manager soon. It's a recipe for disaster." Sophie nodded. She knew Mel was right, but she had already begun to wonder how much she would be willing to give up for her.

"I think I'll find it hard," she said. "I mean, I know we'll still see each other every day, but it's not the same." Mel laced her fingers through Sophie's hair and pulled it behind her ears.

"I know. It'll be hard for me too." She bent over and placed a kiss on Sophie's forehead. "It's probably for the best that you're going on holiday. At least I won't have to suppress the urge of jumping you every time I see you." She grinned. "Now that I know you don't mind." Mel's hands moved over Sophie's shoulders and into her top and her bra, tracing the side of her breasts. The afternoon felt bitter sweet. The holiday that Sophie had been looking forward to was only hours away. But it didn't seem that enticing anymore. It felt like goodbye, and all she wanted now was to stay in Hong Kong, with Mel. As if Mel could feel her sadness, she changed the subject back to Buba. He was sleeping in the shade under a tree, exhausted from his adventure.

"You're going to do it, right? Adopt him? Seriously, he's so cute. If you don't take him, I will."

"Yeah, I will." Sophie nodded and searched for the bag of boiled chicken in her bag. "My only regret is not doing it sooner." She sighed. Look at him. How can I not? It's just sad that we can't help them all." She held up the bag, and the dogs ran up to her, eagerly waiting for their share of the treats. Buba looked up, stuck his nose in the air and stormed over too. He sat down in front of her and joined the others in the staring competition. Sophie threw him a piece. "It's going to take a couple of months, buddy. But we'll get you home with me no matter what."

## 24

"Thank God for the hotel spa." Mel sighed. "It feels good to be clean. I couldn't believe how dirty I was after that hike." They were soaking in the Jacuzzi in the spa on the top floor of the hotel and had already sampled the sauna and the infrared cabins after a long shower. Candles and incense surrounded the tub in the private room they had splashed out on and, as perfect as it was, the prospect of having to say goodbye made Sophie feel sad. Their time was up, and soon they would pretend that none of it had ever happened.

"Can I call you?" Sophie asked.

Mel shrugged. "I don't know. Maybe better not." She played with a lock of Sophie's hair. "But then again, I can't promise I'll be able to resist texting you either." She splashed some water over Sophie's back. "You are so beautiful. Do you know that? Even your shoulders are a delight to look at."

Sophie smiled and leaned back, turning her face against Mel's breasts. "I feel like we've been away for weeks. It just feels so natural being here with you. I can't imagine never having a bath with you ever again."

"Yeah," Mel said, stroking Sophie's forehead and pulling her closer with her other arm. "I'm not quite ready to let go of you either."

## 25

The yellow hammock, that Sophie had claimed for the week, hung between two large trees over-looking the white-sand beach and the ocean. Its gentle rocking felt like a warm comfort. She tried to read her book, but her mind kept wandering, consumed by daydreams. Behind her, reggae music was playing from the speakers, spreading a happy vibe. She stretched out and lifted her head to listen to the sound of laughter from the beach. A group of holiday makers were trying to navigate a floating bar into the sea, but the tide kept dragging them back onto shore. It was late afternoon, and the light was beautiful this time of day, framing the palm trees along the waterfront and leaving a shimmer on the calm surface of the water. Surfers were making their way back from a long day at the beach, stopping off on the way for a cold beer. A loved-up couple were drinking sundowners on the porch in front of their cabin. The multicoloured one-bedroom huts were either scattered along the beach or built on poles in the ocean, about a meter above sea level and, although they were basic, there was something very charming about them.

Sophie's hut was on the beach, underneath a group of palm trees. Her square room had a large bed in the middle with a pink mosquito net draped over the frames on either side, clashing with the bright orange of the bed sheets. Sophie preferred the hammock though, and more than once had she woken up in the middle of the night to find herself still sleeping in it, surrounded by lizards and mosquitos.

The hippie resort was the perfect place to be alone. Sophie could swim in the sea or lie in her hammock and watch people surfing. If she wanted someone to talk to, she could join the other guests at the long table by the beach, where a bonfire was lit and dinner was served after sunset. She hadn't realized just how tired she was until she was doing nothing at all. She had been working hard the past year, and she could slowly feel her body starting to relax again. The daily yoga classes on the beach were a great way to loosen up her muscles. She could already feel a change in her body. Her stomach felt harder, and her arms and legs seemed more toned. Sophie hadn't been to the gym in a very long time and exercise was something she hated. Here in the sun on the beach, it wasn't all that bad though.

"Sophie?"

Sophie turned around. "Pong! Hey! How are you? Good to see you again." She shielded her face against the sun and squinted while her eyes adjusted to the shade that Pong's broad frame created behind her. The Thai owner of the resort was in his early thirties, tall and lean, with a friendly face and a long ponytail which dangled down his bare, tattoo-covered back. He was wearing his usual costume of board shorts and flip-flops as he walked around her and took a stance next to the hammock, legs wide, hands on his hips. He nodded.

"Welcome back."

"Thank you," Sophie smiled up at him. "Glad to be here again. Where have you been? Haven't seen you around these past couple of days."

He shrugged. "Just some family stuff up north. I drove all night, couldn't wait to get back to my waves." He knocked on one of the surf boards that was leaning against the wall and dusted the sand off. "So, can I finally convince you to take some surfing lessons?" He winked. "My offer still stands. First one is free."

Sophie started to shake her head, but then she hesitated. "Maybe. I'll think about it." She said.

Pong looked surprised. "Feeling braver this time around, are you? What happened?"

"Nothing happened." Sophie laughed. "Actually, a lot has happened, but I'm still sort of processing it." She sat up in the hammock, her legs dangling down on either side. "You know what? Okay. Why not?"

Pong clapped his hands together. "Great. I'll pick you up at nine tomorrow morning. You'd better be ready." He turned around and started walking towards the bar. "Actually, make it ten," he yelled without looking back. "I'm going for a drink!"

Sophie laughed. She opened her book again and tried to remember what it was that she'd been reading for the past couple of hours, but her thoughts had been consumed with flashbacks from the previous week. Whenever she tried to concentrate, she became distracted by visions of Mel's naked body, and memories of how it felt pressed up against hers. It aroused her instantly every time, to the point where she no longer had control over her own body. It was her new favourite pastime, fantasizing about Mel. Her intention had been to try to forget about her during her holiday, but instead, her fascination with Mel had grown to borderline obsessive. The more time passed without Mel, the more Sophie thought about her. It was a lot harder to let go than she had hoped it would be. Her phone beeped, and she jumped up, searching for her bag. Although they had agreed not to be in contact outside of work, Sophie couldn't help but hope that it might be Mel each time a message came in. There was nothing apart from a long text message from her mother.

*'Hi dear, it's your mother. Are you enjoying your holiday? We're busy here. I've hired a flower stylist, and he's done a great job with the dining room, but we're still working through the kitchen, throwing some country flair into the mix. Orange shades are quite the thing right now, but it's hard to find pots and vases that work with such an unusual colour! Genevieve can fit you in for a hair extension appointment in two weeks. Let me know if you've changed your mind. I'll ask her to keep the hour free for you just in case. You still haven't told me how your date with Aldo went. Did you buy yourself a nice dress? Please let me know. Deborah and I are dying to hear all about it.'*

Sophie ignored the question regarding her date like she had in her previous messages. She sent a short reply to let her mother know that she was fine and then started typing another message.

*'Hi Mel.'* She shook her head and erased it. *'Hi there. Just thinking of you. Did you get back okay?'*

Sophie sighed. Of course she had gotten back okay. It sounded like a poor excuse to talk to her, which it was. She tried again after staring at the screen of her phone for at least half an hour.

*'Hi there. How's your first week in the London office going? Hope they're nice to you!'*

She pressed send before she could change her mind and immediately regretted it. Mel hadn't texted her so maybe she shouldn't have reached out either. *Damn it. Now I'm going to look desperate.* She didn't know whether to switch her phone off or to leave it on. Both options were nerve wracking. It was still morning in the UK and Mel would be at work now, probably in a meeting or a fitting. She slammed her phone in the sand, angry with herself for her lack of self-control when it beeped. She held her breath, scared to look.

"Fuck!" she said out loud.

*'Hi Dear. Glad to hear you're having a good time. How did your date go? Why are you ignoring my question? I'm having lunch with Deborah at the Grand later, so please get back to me as soon as you can. Be careful and don't eat any of that foreign food. Your mother.'*

Despite her frustration, Sophie couldn't help but chuckle. Her mother had a fear of anything exotic. She was convinced that eating Asian food would lead to instant food poisoning and that it was dangerous to venture beyond the borders of her SW3 postcode, with the exception of fenced-off resorts with armed guards at the entrance. She shook her head, put her phone in her bag and walked towards the sea, tiptoeing to avoid the hot sand on the soles of her feet. It would do her no good hanging around her phone, waiting for an answer. She passed a shower cabin with a sign that said, *'Please turn off the water after abuse.'* Sophie laughed and wished Mel was there to laugh along with her. She waded in to her waist, jumping when the waves hit her. It felt cold on her skin after the burning heat of the sun. She shivered as she splashed water on her chest and upper arms before lowering herself into the ocean. It was nice, just riding along on the gentle tide. Her hair spread around her face, tickling her neck. Thoughts came and went as she drifted into floating mode, but none of them were able to distract her from the matter that really bothered her. She was in love with Mel. Things that had seemed important to her before, like her promotion or her friends' opinion of her, had faded into the background. If only Mel felt the same way, any obstacle could be overcome, including the work situation. By now, Sophie had had a lot of time to think things through, and she didn't feel uncomfortable with the fact that Mel was a woman. In fact, she cursed herself for having been so blind all those years. Cat had been the first clear sign, but she had dug a very deep hole and buried her feelings so far down that they had only resurfaced now. She tried not to think about her mother. Her parents didn't have to know, or at least not yet. Anyway, she didn't think they would take it too well. Her brother would understand though. He had a lot of gay friends that he went out with on the weekend. According to him, Soho was a much better place to party than Chelsea, and his absence at most Sunday lunches was the clear evidence of that. Stewart had never invited her to come along on one of his nights out. They just didn't have that kind of bond and Sophie had never craved a closer relationship either. They were brother and sister, related by blood. Nothing more. But now, it seemed more important than ever to be closer to him. She tried to wipe the salt water out of her eyes and immediately made it worse with her wet hand. It started to sting, and she made her way back to shore with very limited eyesight, stumbling out of the water.

After cleaning her eyes out and applying another layer of sunscreen, she searched for her phone in her bag. Her heart skipped a beat when she saw the message icon jumping.

*'Hey, sexy. Happy to hear from you. They're lovely here*

*apart from the skinny white girl in the shoe department. She's grumpy as fuck.* ☺ *How's Thailand? Thinking of you.'*

Sophie checked to make sure no one was around to witness the wide smirk on her face when she read the message. Mel had called her sexy. That alone would be enough for her to thrive on for the coming days. Her hands were shaking from excitement while she thought about an answer.

*'Hi, gorgeous. Thinking of you 24-7. All good here in paradise. You would love it!'* Sophie hesitated for a moment, then continued. *'Miss you* ☺.*'*

She thought about deleting that last part. Maybe it was too much. But Mel's text had seemed genuine and so she would be too.

So, what now? What was the protocol? *Is she going to send me another message back?* It didn't matter all that much anymore because Sophie was floating on cloud nine. She subconsciously started humming a Chinese tune she remembered from the elevator in their hotel. It had always annoyed her, the way it played on repeat and that she'd had to listen to it twelve times a day, but now it seemed rather charming. Another message came in, and she pulled her towel over her face to block out the sun from her phone screen.

*'Miss you too* ☺. *Can't help but picture you naked. It's keeping me from my job. What are you wearing?'*

Sophie felt a tingle in her lower abdomen and smiled. Was she sexting now? That would be a first. She read the message over and over again before thinking about a reply. Her heart was thumping in her throat.

*'Tiny bikini. White. Tassels at the side.'* Her phone beeped immediately after she sent it.

*'That sounds hot. Send me a picture.'* Sophie giggled while

she tried to take a selfie. After about ten attempts she was happy with the result and sent a shot taken from the top. Her mouth and breasts were in sharp focus. The rest was blurred by the sunshine. Mel seemed pleased with it.

'OMG. *If only I was there with you...*' Then she received another message.

'*Got to go. Meeting. Will message you later. Send me some more pictures so I can get through this week :)*'

Sophie felt elevated. Her shaking hands hovered over her phone. She tried to think of something to send back but put the phone away eventually. There was no rush. Mel would stay in touch and so would she. And that was all she had been hoping for. She sprinted up to her cabin to put her phone on charge.

THE REST of the afternoon and night passed in a haze. Sophie visited a market to do some shopping. She needed souvenirs and snacks to take back home for her friends and colleagues. She also bought some funny t-shirts and stocked up on the street food on the way back so that she could have a quiet picnic on the beach by herself. She had gathered her towels and spread them out over the sand, creating a comforting base. The food was scattered out on paper plates around her. Occasionally, she would throw something out for the seagulls to pick up. The yellow crab curry, fish cakes, and papaya salad were delicious but spicy, and the white wine went down faster than Sophie had planned. The orange haze on the horizon and the clear sky promised another starry night, and everything was perfect apart from Mel's absence. Feeling slightly braver after three glasses of wine, she took a snapshot of the food with the glowing sunset in the background and added: '*Wish you were here.*'

She didn't wait for a reply, knowing Mel was still at work. She watched the resort staff build a campfire and set up the barbecue for the guests later that evening. In other circumstances, she might have joined in, but tonight, Sophie was happy enough with her own company. By the time her screen lit up again, it was dark, and she had just crawled into bed, tired from the sea breeze.

'*Nice sunset. Are you still awake? Had long meeting, just finished. Almost home now.*'

Sophie wiped her eyes and smiled. Suddenly she felt wide awake. '*I am now. In bed.*' She hesitated for a moment and added: '*Naked.*' Another message came in only seconds after she had sent hers.

'*Picture!*'

Sophie giggled and replied. '*You first. I need something to look at too.*' She waited in anticipation for the picture that would most likely keep her up all night. The ten minutes that followed seemed to last an eternity. She poured herself another glass of wine from the bottle on the floor next to her bed and slipped back under the crisp sheets. Her breath caught when it came in. Mel was in her bedroom, naked as promised. She smiled into the camera above her head, one arm over her breasts covering her nipples.

'*Wow,*' she wrote.

Mel replied straight away. '*Glad you like it. Your turn now.*'

## 26

"**M**elzinha, dinner is ready!" Isabella knocked on Mel's bedroom door until her daughter's sleepy face appeared.

"Sorry, Mum. I must have dozed off. What time is it?" Mel put on a pair of tracksuit bottoms and pulled her messy hair into a top-knot.

"It's almost eight, Melzinha. What's wrong with you? You never sleep after work."

"Nothing. Just tired." Mel yawned and sat down at the table on the patio. Isabella regarded her while she scooped the fish soup into two bowls before topping it off with parsley and chili salt.

"You've been acting strange lately," Isabella commented. "I know we talked about privacy while I live here and I won't get up in your business if you don't want me to. But I need you to know that you can talk to me about anything. You know that, right?"

Mel smiled and nodded. "Don't worry about me, Mum. How's your back today? Any news on the operation yet?"

She closed her eyes after the first spoonful. "Mmm, that's nice." Isabella sat down opposite her.

"Looks like it's going to happen soon," she said. "They're trying to schedule me in six weeks from now."

Mel let out a sigh of relief. "Finally! That's great." She leaned in and placed a hand over her mother's. Imagine, you might be able to walk normally again in a couple of months. Maybe even up the stairs!"

Isabella laughed. "Imagine that! It's a start, Melzinha. There are no guarantees, and I don't expect to be the same as I was before, but I would be so happy if I could walk to the market or the community centre again. I hate having to rely on you or other people to drive me around all the time."

"You know I don't mind," Mel said. "I like helping you out. But I also know you miss your house and your own space. It will be good for you to get your independence back."

Isabella passed the breadbasket after tearing off a piece of flatbread for herself. "So, when is your friend Sophie coming back?" she asked. Mel's heart skipped a beat at the sound of Sophie's name.

"Saturday," she said, trying to sound casual.

"Are you going to see her on the weekend?"

Mel rolled her eyes at the sight of her mother's mischievous smirk. "Maybe. Maybe not. She'll be tired from the flight when she lands. Anyway, you promised to stop prying. Nothing is going on between us."

Isabella let out a sarcastic chuckle. "Fine," she said. "But you're the one who keeps on mentioning her name, not me."

AN HOUR LATER, Mel had returned to the darkness of her bedroom. The T.V. was on, but she wasn't watching. A friend had asked her to join her for drinks, but she didn't feel like going out. Her mother was right. She hadn't been herself all week, and she knew exactly what the root of the problem was. Sophie. She thought about her at work, she thought about her on her way home, and she thought about her at night. All night. It was supposed to be simple, but it wasn't, and nothing could have prepared her for the uncertainty she felt in Sophie's absence. She reached over her nightstand and flipped the switch on the plug socket, turning on the hundreds of tiny fairy lights that were scattered throughout the room. She let herself fall back on the bed and stared up at the twinkling lights. Mel's bedroom was her pride and joy. The exposed brick wall behind the headboard and the high ceiling were in perfect harmony with her light blue walls and dark wooden floor. Tall windows looked out over the street, framed by full-length vintage lace curtains. Mel had spent hours attaching the strings of fairy lights to the beams in the ceiling, and the result was impressive. She turned to her phone lying on the pillow next to her and sighed. If only Sophie were here. She was the one who had proposed they should keep their distance but so far, she had spent every waking hour waiting for Sophie to contact her. Two days had passed since Sophie had sent her the picture she'd spent most of her free time staring at. But even when she wasn't looking at it, the mouth-watering image of Sophie's naked body on top of the orange bed sheets was printed in her memory, and she could remember every curve, every detail.

"Fuck it," she mumbled as she went to her text messages.

*'Hey, you. Are you having a good time? I bet you're not ready to come home yet...xxx.'* She waited. Her body felt paralyzed by nerves as she lay on her bed, hoping for an answer. After a couple of minutes, she checked if the message had been

sent, just to make sure. Four hours went by without an answer. *Why isn't she glued to her phone like I am? She must be sleeping.* Mel turned over and pressed her face into the pillow to stop herself from screaming in frustration. Finally, her phone vibrated.

'*Hey yourself* ☺. *Sorry for the late reply, went surfing yesterday and I couldn't wake up this morning. Definitely lacking talent lol. It's lovely here but happy to come home now.*'

Mel sighed in relief, then jumped up when another message came in.

'*Can't wait to see you.*'

Mel giggled out loud and immediately checked if her door was closed. She quickly replied. '*Can't wait to see you either. When are you landing?*'

'*Saturday. 4 pm. Why? Are you going to surprise me?*' Mel sat straight up in bed. She had to read the message twice to make sure she got the hint. Her hands shook as she started typing.

'*Don't dare me. I might be there. xxx*' She closed her eyes for a moment, savouring the happiness she felt. The ball was back in her court.

## 27

Sophie sucked up one of the large watermelon seeds through the straw of her smoothie, carefully lifting it from her glass before blowing as hard as she could. The seed shot off and hit one of the canoes that were turned upside down in the sand. She had discovered the joys of firing off tiny objects from her hammock when no one was looking. The resort was quiet on Tuesday. Most guests had headed out for a two-day festival on the other side of the island. Sophie had no one to talk to apart from Pong, and therefore all the time in the world to think about Mel. She dropped the straw and the glass in the sand underneath her and covered her face with her t-shirt to stop her cheeks from getting sunburnt. Since their last exchange of messages, she had finally been able to relax a bit. Knowing that Mel missed her too made things a lot easier for her, but it also brought new complications along. *What if it becomes serious?* Although it wasn't something that had to be dealt with right away, she would have to tell her parents at some point. And her friends... She would have to tell them she was gay. *My parents will never understand.* Then another thought occurred to her. *What if someone finds out about us when I'm her manager? Could we get fired? Should I look for another job?* Sophie tried to stop thinking about all the what-ifs, but it was hard to let go of questions she had no answers to. *What if she hates my family and friends?* Looking for a distraction, she lifted a lazy hand and blind-searched for the cocktail menu that was attached to a tree branch dangling somewhere above her face. She missed twice before grabbing hold of the clipboard and pulling it down by its retractable cord. *Don't think about it. Focus on the good stuff for now.* She scanned the menu for anything strong enough to send her to sleep for a couple of hours and decided on a Zombie. If only Maggie were here. Sophie was dying to tell someone about Mel, and she was sure Maggie would understand. She wouldn't judge her like her family and maybe even her friends would. But every time Sophie tried to call her, she was either at work or asleep. Cat wasn't an option. Telling her felt daunting. Sophie's confession might bring up questions about the past, and she didn't want to go there. She sighed. The only person she could discuss her situation with was in a different time zone. *What does that say about my friends?*

## 28

Sophie broke out in cold sweat walking through customs. The meet and greet area at Heathrow Airport was flooded with parents, lovers and tour guides and she tried to steer her luggage cart around the groups of people who were blocking the way, laughing and hugging their loved ones. She had been nervous all the way back and hadn't managed to sleep for a minute.

'Don't dare me; I might be there,' Mel had messaged. Sophie looked around, trying to spot her big hair in the crowd but she didn't see her anywhere. She felt her stomach drop with disappointment. What was she thinking? Of course, Mel wouldn't be here. She was bound to have better things to do on a Saturday than to travel all the way to the airport. Sophie was about to turn left towards the exit when someone slapped her on the back of her head with a bunch of roses.

"Surprise!" Mel shouted. She flew around Sophie's neck and grinned, scrunching up her nose. Sophie's heart jumped at the sight of her. Mel looked great in jeans and a navy shirt that hugged her curves in all the right places. Her hair was tied up in a casual top-knot that bounced from side to side when she moved.

"Mel! I can't believe you're here." Sophie tightened her grip around Mel's neck and sighed. She lifted her head and welcomed the joy that exploded in her stomach when their eyes locked. Mel's face was close, and Sophie could smell chocolate on her breath. God, how she had longed for those lips. She laughed and kissed her. First softly, barely brushing. Then she parted her lips and sank deeper into Mel's mouth. Her body seemed to agree with the kiss and was screaming out for more. They indulged in each other until a group of teenage boys whistled at them. Mel reluctantly took a step back and laughed.

"I was watching you from that table over there," she said, pointing at a cafe. "I had to make sure you really wanted me to be here. I can't tell you how happy I was when I saw you looking out for me."

Sophie smiled and took her hand. "That was mean, and you know it," she said, blushing. She pointed at the flowers. "Are those for me?"

Mel handed her the bunch of red roses. "They are." She shuffled on the spot. "I borrowed my mother's car, so I can take you home if you want? Are you tired?"

Sophie nodded. "I haven't slept at all. I was thinking about you the whole time." She giggled and looked down at her shoes, surprised by her own confession. "But I think I just got a new splurge of energy."

Mel tucked Sophie's hair behind her ear. "Good," she whispered. "Because you're going to need it." Sophie felt Mel's hand disappear underneath her sweater and she almost forgot her suitcase as they walked to the car.

.  .  .

"So, DID YOU MISS ME?" Sophie asked when seated in the front of the old blue Ford. Mel looked surprisingly sexy while she was driving, with her rolled up sleeves and air of casual concentration on her face. It was weird, seeing her in a different context.

"Did I miss you?" Mel repeated the question, still focusing on the road. "Do you remember that conversation we had in Hong Kong right before we left? About keeping it casual?" Sophie nodded. "Well, I've never regretted anything more in my life than that conversation." They both laughed.

"All I could think of," Mel continued, "was you being all 'casual' in Thailand, hooking up with hot surfer chicks to celebrate your newfound sexuality."

Sophie giggled. "Really? You thought I'd do that?"

Mel shrugged. "I was kind of hoping you wouldn't." She held up a hand and grimaced. "By the way, if you did, please don't tell me. I don't want to know. I don't think I could handle it."

"Well I haven't been hooking up with any hot surfer chicks," Sophie said. "I've been thinking about you, mostly. And I've been thinking about whether or not to text you just about every second of the day. I'm telling you, Mel. It's been so bloody stressful thinking about you; I think I might need another holiday." She sank back in her seat and opened the window, enjoying the relief and happiness that washed over her.

"So THIS IS WHERE YOU LIVE." Mel took a step back and looked up at the Victorian building before entering the narrow staircase, leading up to Sophie's apartment. "Fancy location, I'm impressed," she yelled up the stairs. Sophie turned and looked down at Mel while searching for her keys in her bag.

"I hope it's not a mess. I wasn't exactly expecting to have someone over after my trip, but I did ask the cleaner to pop in for a couple of hours." She blushed when she opened the door to the spacious, spotless apartment. As instructed, her mother's cleaner had put fresh roses in a crystal vase on the rustic wooden dining table and aired the rooms that very morning. It was nice to be home again. Mel raised an eyebrow when she stepped into the white, modern kitchen.

"Fancy postcode, fabulous apartment and a cleaner? My God, Sophie. I think we need to get married."

Sophie laughed. "It's not what you think. I usually clean the house myself, but I was secretly hoping you might come over, so I needed some help. Just in case." Now that she was back, she wasn't sure how to behave around Mel anymore. Sophie really just wanted to kiss her again, but she didn't know how to approach her. She stuck her head in the fridge to hide her uncertainty.

"Would you like a drink? I have wine, gin, coffee, tea, sparkling water..."

Mel smiled, walked over to her and silenced her with her lips while she closed the fridge door.

"What I would like," she said, "Is for you to put down your handbag, take off your coat and show me to your bed, couch, carpet or whatever it is you would like me to throw you on after I rip your clothes off." Sophie took in a deep breath. Her heart was pounding so fast now that she could almost hear it, and the wetness that spread between her legs made her ache for Mel's body. She took Mel's hand and led her into the living room because she didn't think she could manage another flight of stairs on her shaking legs. Mel looked from the couch to the thick rug and back.

"Good choice," she said with a grin while she took the hem of Sophie's sweater and pulled it over her head, exposing a black, seamless bra. Then she took off her own shirt in one fluid motion, moved closer and placed a kiss on Sophie's neck, just below her ear. She lingered there and cupped Sophie's cheek with her hand.

"You smell so good."

Sophie gasped and tilted her head. She felt teeth scrape over her neck, and her jawline before Mel's lips met her own, claiming her mouth. They both moaned into the kiss that deepened when their tongues found each other, warm and wet and sensual. Sophie moved her hands up Mel's back and unclipped her bra. She tugged it down without breaking the kiss. Her hands explored Mel's tanned breasts and dark nipples, causing Mel to shiver. Mel's breathing accelerated when Sophie's bra fell to the floor a little later. Her fingers then worked their way around to the waistband of Sophie's leggings and briefs. She kneeled, moving them down slowly until Sophie stepped out of them, exposing her nakedness.

"You're so beautiful," Mel whispered, kissing her way back up over Sophie's thighs, waist, and breasts. "You have no idea how much I've been longing for you." She licked around a nipple with the tip of her tongue. "How much I've been longing for this." Sophie buckled at the sensation of Mel's mouth on her breasts. She fumbled with the button on Mel's jeans, desperate for them to come off.

"Take them off, please. I can't do it...my hands are shaking."

Mel took off her jeans, kicked them to the side and pulled Sophie back in by her waist. Sophie closed her eyes. The feeling of Mel's delicate skin against hers was wonderful and calming.

"Finally," she sighed. "I've been dreaming about this."
Mel leaned forward and before she knew it, Sophie was
lying on her back on the soft rug, Mel's breasts pressed into
her own.

"So, you like it on the floor, do you?" Mel whispered.
"You keep on surprising me, Sophie." Sophie tried to
answer, but she was silenced by Mel's lips once again. She
ached with need and anticipation. Mel kissed her way down
her collarbone and her breasts where she lingered, carefully
biting her. Sophie gasped and threw her head back when
Mel planted a hand between her legs, tracing her sex
upwards until the twitching in her lower abdomen became
almost unbearable. Mel's skilful fingers pressed down and
circled between her legs, almost sending her over the edge.
She felt Mel's tongue and lips move down towards her thigh,
then slowly inwards, releasing warm breath on her centre.
Mel took her time, teasing her until she parted Sophie's legs
further and licked her full length up to her clit before
moving back and slipping her tongue inside of her.

Sophie buckled, crying out. "Oh my God, Mel. Yes! That
feels amazing." She weaved her hands through Mel's hair,
lifting her hips when Mel entered her again.

"You taste so good," Mel whispered. She buried her face
between Sophie's thighs again and sucked until Sophie felt
dangerously close to exploding.

"Stop. Please stop." Sophie pulled her up, so they were
face to face, both heavily panting.

"Come here. I've missed you, and I want to touch you
too." Mel smiled and kissed her. She slipped a hand in
between them, and Sophie did the same, shivering when
she felt how aroused Mel was. She pushed two fingers inside
of her wetness, drawing a loud moan from Mel's mouth.
Sophie looked up at her and felt even more turned on by the

look on Mel's face. Her eyes were closed; her lips parted as if she was about to scream. They found a rhythm together, moving like they were one. Sophie felt her body tensing. She held her breath while the warm glow in her lower belly started to spread outwards, reaching her fingertips and her toes. She could feel Mel was close too by the way she started to move faster. Sophie tightened her grip on Mel's shoulder, exhaled deeply and gave in to the wonderful feeling that washed over her. Mel buried her face in Sophie's neck before she tensed up too and started to tremble. They held each other tight, riding out the last waves of their orgasm, laughing at how perfect it was.

## 29

"Well, good morning to you too. That was kind of hot," Mel said in a sultry voice. She stared up at the ceiling, her arms and legs wrapped around Sophie. The sexual attraction between them had kept them up most of the night, but now Sophie felt a very happy and content sense of tiredness. She gently stroked Mel's face with the palm of her hand. Her other hand was between Mel's legs, two fingers still inside of her. Mel was shivering from the orgasm Sophie had just given her.

"My God, Sophie. You're getting good at this. Really good." Sophie couldn't stop smiling. It felt surreal, having Mel in her apartment and she didn't want her to leave. Mel drove her wild, made her irrational, impulsive and greedy for more. The morning had been blissfully perfect. Sophie had made coffee and toast, and they had talked, kissed and made love all morning in bed.

"This is so nice." Sophie sighed. "Last time I woke up next to someone, I wanted to chew my arm off."

Mel laughed. "Really? That bad?"

"Yeah. It was bad. I'd had too much to drink one night,

and when I opened my eyes the next day, I was staring right into the gaping mouth of one of my exes. He was half on top of me, and I spent about an hour trying to wrangle myself out from underneath him without waking him up. Unfortunately, he did wake up just when I thought I would manage to escape." She grinned. "I then spent the rest of the morning explaining to him why there was no chance of us getting back together, even though I had let him into my bed again."

"So, no urge to escape today?" Mel ran a hand through Sophie's hair.

Sophie kissed her, slowly pulling her fingers out. "Absolutely not. In fact, I've been thinking of tying you to the bed and keeping you here."

Mel smiled and turned on her side, facing her. "Can I take you out on a date tonight?"

Sophie's face lit up. "Really? You want to take me on a date?" She giggled. "I'd love to but unfortunately I can't. My mother is expecting me for dinner at eight. She's called me fifteen times since I landed and I haven't spoken to her in two weeks. She'll be livid if I don't show up today."

"Don't worry," Mel said. The date can wait. I need to take the car back anyway." She planted a kiss on Sophie's cheek. "My mum needs it this afternoon, so I'd better get going soon." Then her face became suddenly serious.

"What are we going to do, Sophie? At work tomorrow? I mean, nobody can know, obviously. We can't risk people finding out."

"Nobody will find out," Sophie said, looking for her robe. "It really shouldn't be that hard. We're both adults, and as long as we act accordingly, we'll be okay. We just need some basic rules for the office. For example, we shouldn't arrive or leave together, and we should avoid bars where we might run into people from work. It doesn't mean we have to hide; we just need to adapt a little bit. Our private life is none of their business as long as it doesn't affect our work, right?" Mel didn't look too convinced, but Sophie carried on anyway. "And when I get the promotion..." She sighed. "I guess we'll just have to take it day by day when the time comes. If anyone is going to get into trouble, it should be me, not you." She rolled her eyes, laughing. "And I'm the last person they'll suspect of having a thing with a woman, so I think we're good. At least for now anyway." She held up her hand and crossed her middle and index finger. "I promise I'll try not to picture you naked in meetings or stare at your boobs." They both laughed, and Mel crossed her fingers too.

"And I promise not to drag you into the toilets during lunch break." Sophie watched her put on her sweater with a mischievous grin on her face.

"What's that smirk for?"

Mel shook her head. "Nothing." She hesitated. "I wanted to ask you something, but I don't want you to think that I'm needy."

Sophie smiled. "Oh come on. Tell me." Mel was finger-combing her hair into a high pony tail.

"I don't think I'm ready to say goodbye yet. Do you want to come with me to my place? We have time, right? " Sophie was unable to hide her excitement at Mel's invitation.

"Yes! I'm so glad you asked. I'd love to come with you. I want to see where you live." She frowned. "Wait. Is your mother going to be there?"

Mel nodded. "She probably will be, but she's cool. Nothing to worry about - apart from her talking your ears off and sniffing out your secrets like a police dog."

"Well, in that case, I'd love to meet my mother-in law."

Sophie bit her lip and buried her face in her hands. "I'm sorry. Was that joke too soon?"

"You sound like you want to be my girlfriend," Mel said in a teasing tone. She raised her eyebrows. "Do you want to be my girlfriend?"

Sophie giggled, her insides doing summersaults. "I thought I already was your girlfriend. Since you missed me so much and all that..."

Mel chuckled and shook her head. "Uh-uh. No. You have to say it. I want to hear you say it." She poked Sophie in the ribs and immediately got a screaming response.

"Don't tickle me, please! I'm your girlfriend." She grabbed hold of Mel's hands and pushed them away from her midriff. "I'm your girlfriend!" she yelled again. "I'm all yours!"

## 30

"Thanks for coming with me," Mel said. Sophie glanced around, taking in Mel's neighbourhood. It was nice. The main high street still belonged to small business owners. There were restaurants and take-aways, very cool looking bars and cafes and scattered in between them were butchers, fishmongers, bakeries, and newsagents. The mix of Jamaican heritage with a young, urban vibe was intriguing. A block of piled up containers covered in graffiti was the home of independent pop-up shops and eclectic barbers and hairdressers. A little further down, Victorian buildings formed the backdrop of the main street, housing art galleries and vintage clothing stores.

"It's cool; I like it. Not sure why I've never been here before." The smell of freshly baked bread welcomed her when she opened the window. "It's funny, isn't it? As a designer, I travel the world for places like this, yet it's never occurred to me to look for it in my own city." Mel stopped to let an old man cross the street.

"Well, aren't we all guilty of that? Apparently, there are lots of great galleries in Southwest London that I've never been to." She waved at him from behind the wheel when he thanked her. "There's no market today so we can park in my street. Normally you have to fight your way through the crowd to get to the front door, but today, we're in luck." She took a left turn into a street where cars were parked on either side, leaving just enough space for them to drive through. "People don't understand how I can live here with all the hustle and bustle and the noise from the bars, but I love it. The food around here is great too. I'll have to take you out for dinner next time you're here." Sophie felt her stomach flutter at those words. 'Next time.' They turned the corner and Mel managed to squeeze the Ford into a tiny space between two other cars. "Here we go. Welcome to Brixton, Miss Chelsea."

Mel's ground floor apartment was squashed in between a record shop and a Jamaican restaurant that she shared the hallway with. Sophie inhaled the mouth-watering scent of jerk chicken and salt fish when they entered.

"Smells amazing in here."

"Told you so." Mel knocked and only seconds later, her mother appeared in the doorway.

"Come in, come in. You must be Sophie. I'm Isabella." Sophie felt an immediate sense of relief at the sight of the lovely lady in front of her with long, grey hair, whose smile was just as wonderful as Mel's. She had dimples too, and the crow's feet around her eyes were clear evidence that she laughed a lot. Isabella put an arm around Sophie and led her inside through the living room and the kitchen out onto the patio in the back.

"Please take a seat, my love. The weather is nice enough to sit outside so why waste the day? I'll get you a drink."

"Make yourself comfortable. I'll be right back," Mel said, before following her mother back into the kitchen. Sophie noticed Isabella was limping and looked like she was in pain. If she was, it didn't affect her mood. Isabella seemed cheerful, positive and quite the opposite to her own mother who spent most of her time worrying about what other people thought of her.

The patio was homely and cosy with two chairs and a wooden bench placed around a rectangular wooden picnic table. Homemade patchwork pillows were tied to the seats with red ribbon that matched the large red lavender-filled buckets that had been hung along the outside wall under the kitchen window. It was sunny and almost warm in the secluded garden, protected by high conifers on either side. Sophie was impressed by Mel's ability to create such a charming and welcoming atmosphere. She turned around to see into the vintage kitchen, eyeing up the blue and white Spanish tiles that covered the walls above the workspace. Plants hung from the ceiling by the door in baskets, and fresh herbs were growing in boxed wall units above a rattan kitchen bench. There was basil, mint, rosemary, chives, and sage, all giving off a lovely smell.

"Here we go," Isabella said. She placed two jugs on the table filled with lemon and mint. "Homemade lemonade. One with rum and one without." She laughed. "I don't drink anymore, you see. I have trouble keeping my balance enough as it is." She poured Mel and Sophie a large glass with the alcoholic mixture and held up her own. "Welcome to our home, Sophie. Or should I say, welcome to my daughter's home." Motherly pride was written all over her face. "I have a bad back, and I can't walk up the stairs in my own house at the moment, so I'm staying here for a while until I've had my operation." She turned to Mel. "And then another couple of weeks until I've recovered."

"Is it bad?" Sophie asked.

Isabella shrugged. "My doctor says it's hard to tell right now. I have a slipped disk, and it's compressing a spinal nerve. They might be able to fix it, but I'll never be able to walk like before. There's already too much damage." Then she smiled and raised her hands. "But hey, I'm no teenager anymore either. It is what it is. As long as I can move back into my own house and walk to the market again, I'll be happy." She looked from Mel to Sophie and back. "Now tell me. Did you girls have fun last night?" Sophie laughed at the word 'girls' as if they were still a couple of teenagers. "When Mel didn't come home last night, I thought to myself 'I bet those two are having a great time together.'" Isabella winked, and Mel shot her a warning look.

"What did we talk about mama? Privacy, remember?"

Isabella patted Sophie on the knee, ignoring her daughter. "I've heard all about what a great colleague and friend you've been to Mel. Thank you for that. My Mel...she works very hard, you know. And she can set her mind to anything if she wants it badly enough. Anything. Right Melzinha?" Mel rolled her eyes and kissed her mother on the forehead. The simple gesture of affection brought a lump to Sophie's throat, but she managed to swallow it down. It was endearing and sweet and just when she though she couldn't possibly admire Mel anymore, she sunk deep into another cloud of adoration. Mel took a sip from her drink and winked at Sophie from behind her glass. It made her blush.

"I love your kitchen," She said, trying to take her mind off of Mel's flirtations.

"Thanks." Mel nodded at the back door. "I did most of it myself. The floor, the tiles, the wall units. The kitchen unit itself was ancient, but I painted it, put new handles on the cupboards and sprayed the work surface with kitchen marble. I'm quite chuffed with it. It's... "

"Mel has done such a great job. I couldn't believe it," Isabella interrupted her. She gestured to the garden, then towards the apartment. "When she showed me this place before she bought it, I begged her not to sign. It looked like a drug den, didn't it, Melzinha?" She glanced at Mel but didn't wait for an answer. "It was dark and dirty. Parts of the floors were missing, the bathroom was ripped apart, and there were rats and cockroaches running around in the kitchen. The garden was overgrown and full of rubbish." Isabella grimaced. "My heart sank at the thought of her living here all by herself. But now... It's so clean, and light and I've been begging her to do my own house up too." She leaned in closer to Sophie. "Mel has two brothers, but they're not nearly as good as her when it comes to DIY."

"They're perfectly capable," Mel said, laughing. "They're just lazy. And you know I don't have time. I had to take a whole month off work to get this place in a semi-presentable state!"

"I know, I know." Isabella waved a hand towards the kitchen. "Melzinha, do you mind getting the tray from the fridge? I made us some snacks when you told me Sophie was coming over. It just needs heating up for a couple of minutes. And get some plates and napkins too, will you?"

Sophie gave her a warm smile. "Isabella, you didn't have to do that! Anyway, I can't stay for very long. I need to go to my parents' house for dinner later."

Isabella shook her head. "It doesn't matter. You're here now, and you're our guest."

As soon as Mel had disappeared into the kitchen, Isabella moved her chair closer to Sophie's. She lowered her voice, making sure Mel couldn't hear her.

"I'm so glad to meet you, Sophie. When Mel said she wanted to borrow my car to pick you up, I couldn't have been more surprised. She has never done anything like that for another girl so I figured she must like you very much. Are you two...close?"

Sophie shifted in her chair. Does she know? "I'm not sure what you mean by that," she stammered. "But Mel is great, and I really enjoy working with her." She could feel her cheeks turning red, and there was nothing she could do about it.

Isabella nodded. A tiny smile formed around her mouth. "So, where do you live? And what do your parents do? Are they still together?"

Mel stuck her head around the corner of the kitchen door. "Mama! Privacy, please! Do you even know what that means?"

Isabella waved it off. "I'm just curious, Melzinha. You never bring anyone home. You don't mind, do you, Sophie?"

Sophie shook her head. "Of course I don't. I live in Chelsea. My parents live there too, only a few streets away."

"Lovely!" Isabella beamed. "It's nice that you decided to stay close to home. Your parents must be so happy."

Sophie chuckled. "Yes, it's nice. I have lunch or dinner with my parents every Sunday unless I'm away for work." She left out the part where her parents, or rather her mother, had refused to buy her an apartment outside their own borough because she was afraid Sophie living in a cheaper area would reflect poorly on her.

Isabella gestured towards Mel in the kitchen. "I'm glad Mel chose to live nearby when she moved out. London can be so hard to get around. I only see my sons every two to three weeks when they come home for dinner. One of them moved in with his girlfriend in Slough, and the other one lives in Croydon because the rent is cheaper there." She laughed. "Or maybe they don't want me all up in their business, begging for grandchildren twenty-four-seven."

Sophie laughed too. "I'm sure that's not the case. And yes, London prices are crazy. Mel and I are very lucky to even have an apartment to ourselves."

"I bet you've never tried this before." Mel appeared with a tray full of exotic looking nibbles and dips. "Pumpkin croquettes, avocado dip, red pepper dip, cheese bread, pastel pies and black-eyed-pea fritters with shrimp," she explained. "My mother cooks the best Brazilian food in the world but only on very rare occasions, so I guess that makes you a guest of honour, Sophie."

"Wow, I do feel honoured indeed!" Sophie said as she picked up a fritter and scooped it through the avocado dip. She closed her eyes when she bit into the crunchy snack. "Mmm. Isabella... That is so good. Did you make these? I'd love to have the recipe."

Isabella smiled approvingly. "Of course. In fact, I'll teach you how to make them. Why don't you come over next weekend and we'll cook together."

Sophie was touched but surprised by the gesture and kept a close eye on Mel to make sure she was comfortable with the offer. Mel rolled her eyes, but she seemed fine, so she nodded, accepting the invitation.

"Really? That would be great. I love cooking. I just don't do it very often because I never have anyone to cook for."

Isabella clapped in excitement. "Great. I have secret recipes going back to my great grandmother. I'll teach you everything about authentic Brazilian food." She nudged Mel. "Her brothers' girlfriends have no interest in cooking. I always worry that they don't eat enough vitamins what with all the junk food they put away after work. One of them is Brazilian too so I thought she might want to learn a bit more about the food from her country, but she isn't remotely interested." She turned back to Sophie. "So, you don't have a husband or a boyfriend you cook for? Or a girlfriend?"

Mel interrupted her. "Mum, that's enough. Stop interrogating her."

Isabella held up her hands in defence. "Melzinha, I'm just making polite conversation here. It's a very standard question."

Sophie laughed. "No, I don't have a boyfriend." She hesitated. "I'm kind of seeing someone, but it's only been a couple of weeks so I'd rather not get into it right now." She knew she was blushing and when she glanced at Mel, she could sense her discomfort too. Isabella studied them both, rested her gaze on Mel and grinned. "Well, there's nothing like young love. You should enjoy every second of it."

"I'M sorry it's so late," Mel said when they were lingering by her front door two hours later. "I hope you'll still make it home in time for dinner. My mother talks too much and she really gets up in people's business. Next time you come over, I'll make sure she sticks to the cooking class."

Sophie laughed. "Are you kidding me? I had a great time. Your mother is so sweet and funny. I think she might be on to us, though."

Mel chuckled. "She's on to everyone. Nothing escapes her. She's become worse since she stopped working as a cleaner. I think she loved snooping around in other people's private lives and now she needs something else to focus on."

Sophie smiled and kissed her. "That's perfectly understandable. And don't worry about the time, I've already ordered a cab."

Mel shook her head and stepped outside. "No, that's way

too expensive. Let me at least walk you to the tube." Sophie stopped her. "Really, it's okay. My mother has a taxi account. I don't use it very often, but she's perfectly happy for me to do so."

"Wow. Your mother has her own taxi account?" Mel raised an eyebrow. " Do you even know how cool that is in a city where it takes forever to get from A to B?"

Sophie shrugged. "She doesn't like to drive, and she doesn't take public transport. As I said, I don't use it very often." She smiled uncomfortably. "I don't want you to think I'm some kind of spoilt brat. Because I'm not. I've always worked, even through university." She paused. "But I do realize that I've been brought up privileged and that I'm very lucky. And I'm grateful for that."

Mel held up a hand. "Stop it right there, Sophie. Just so we're clear, I'm not judging you. Did I ever accuse you of being spoilt?" Sophie shook her head.

"Come on; I know you're not, so please stop defending yourself, okay? Your world is just different to mine, that's all. It makes things interesting for both of us." She pointed at the car that was pulling up and blew Sophie a kiss. "Now get your cute ass into that taxi and enjoy your family dinner."

## 31

I t was distracting having Mel in the office. Although they were seated on different islands, Sophie saw her each time she walked down the corridor to get a coffee. She felt anxious as she waited for her cup to fill and knew it was down to the ten coffees she drank a day, just so she could walk past Mel's desk and catch a glimpse of her. They never had lunch together. As soon as they started speaking, sparks flew, and it would have been impossible to keep it casual.

"More coffee?" Sophie jumped up and turned around.

"Oh, hey Mel. You can have mine if you like. I've already had way too much."

Mel smiled. "Yes. You do seem to drink a lot of coffee. Just like I seem to fill up on water all the time. It's just that the water in the tank behind your desk is really tasty." She grinned and took the cup that Sophie handed to her. "Thank you. That's very kind of you, Sophie." She winked and walked back to her desk. Sophie stared at her behind until she suddenly remembered where she was.

"Sophie, can I talk to you?" Debbie waved at her from

her office. She was supporting her baby bump with the other hand, looking stressed and exhausted. Sophie wandered over and took a seat at her desk.

"How are you feeling, Debbie? Everything okay?"

Debbie nodded, clearly lying. "I'm good, Sophie. Thank you." She rummaged through her drawer. "I have some paperwork for you to sign. That is if you're still interested in being design manager." She smiled. "It's a temporary position, of course. Until I'm back. But who knows what will happen? You've been great to the company, and we appreciate your hard work. There's a generous pay rise in the contract; please take a look." Sophie opened the file. She tried not to flinch at the hefty number on her temporary salary contract. It was more than she had expected.

"Great," she said. "Do you know when your last day will be? It was supposed to be last week, but I guess it's no secret that you're still here." She hesitated. "I didn't want to bother you because I know you're busy, but if I take this offer, we need to do a hand-over before you leave."

Debbie sighed. "I know. I should have done this sooner; it's very unprofessional of me. It's just been so hectic, and quite frankly, I'm nervous to leave." She paused. "Not that I don't trust you, it's just that..." She hesitated. "Well, you know how it goes. It's hard to combine this job with a baby, and I'm not sure what the future holds for me. My last day will be this Friday, and I should have given your contract to you a month prior to my leaving. I could probably get fired for doing this last-minute, and I honestly don't know why I kept on postponing it. If you need time to have a solicitor look it over, please do." She grimaced. "But don't take too long because this baby could pop out any minute and I'll be fucked for failing my successor-planning if we don't have someone in place by then." Sophie read through the list of roles and responsibilities and nodded. She shifted on her seat when it dawned on her that she would have to do Mel's performance reviews. She'd known it all along but seeing it in black and white made her realize how serious the situation was. She looked at Debbie who was sweating behind her desk, praying for Sophie to accept the offer. She couldn't let her down now. It would be cruel.

"Don't worry Debbie," she heard herself say, "I understand. It must be hard to leave ten years of work behind. I'd be nervous too." She handed her back the file and kept the two contract copies. "Looks fine to me." She signed on the dotted line on both the sheets and filled in her name and date. "Thank you for the opportunity."

Debbie sighed in relief and took one of the copies. "No. Thank you, Sophie." She pulled herself out of the chair by the bookshelf next to her desk and put on her coat. "Well, I'd better head off now." She turned around. "Oh, and one more thing. Mel, the new girl. You two are okay, right?"

Sophie's eyes widened. "Yeah, sure. We're okay. Why do you ask?"

Debbie shrugged. "It's just that I never see you two together, the way I've seen you with your other co-workers. You know, laughing, gossiping, having lunch..."

Sophie laughed nervously. "No, you're wrong. Mel and I get along great. But we've both been more focused on our jobs lately. She's just started, and I'm about to take over from you... Hong Kong was hectic, and we haven't had much time to get to know each other better."

"Very well," Debbie said. "That's good to know. But if you think there might be any problems ahead, you'd let me know, right?"

Sophie nodded and handed Debbie her handbag. "Sure. You'll be the first one to know."

## 32

"So are you going to tell me why you've been all mysterious lately? You haven't texted or called me back in three weeks." Cat bit her nails, trying to act like her question was totally casual, giving Sophie her famous 'either way, I-don't-give-a fuck' look. There was something comical in her delivery, and Sophie knew she had rehearsed the question. Despite her childhood dreams, Cat would have made a terrible actress. They were having their usual Monday night catch up, gossiping over cocktails in a private members club in Chelsea, booked on Cat's parent's memberships. Weekends were busy there but Mondays were quiet, and it was the perfect place for them to talk without being interrupted by drunken men or nosy acquaintances. The premises were dark around their candlelit booth, and Cat squinted, trying to read Sophie's face. Live blues music was playing softly in the background, just loud enough to give Sophie an excuse.

"Sorry, what were you saying?" She felt her heart rate accelerate. The conversation had seemed so easy in her mind, but now, it was almost impossible to speak. Cat leaned in closer and opened her mouth, ready to repeat the question louder. Then she rolled her eyes, walked around the table and took a seat next to Sophie. She put an arm around her, taking a sip from her drink.

"There we go. Much easier this way. So my question was... and I'm pretty sure you heard me the first time...What the hell have you been up to? You're acting all weird. Are you okay?"

Sophie felt flushed and turned her head away, staring right ahead." "Yeah. I'm good. Why do you ask?"

"Well, you've been looking at your phone all night. And you smile every time it lights up. It's not rocket science. Let me see. What's so intriguing that you don't want me to know? Come on." Cat extended her arm, but Sophie snatched her phone away before Cat could get hold of it.

Cat laughed. "Really? Okay, now I know for sure something's going on. And if you don't tell me right now, I'll be appropriately offended, and I'll walk off. Seriously, I'll be out of here. I'm your best friend, Sophie!" Her voice was so loud that the people in the booth next to them glanced over curiously. "What are you looking at?" Cat sneered, giving them a warning look.

"Shush," Sophie said. "Cool it." She shifted further away from Cat, desperate to gain some personal space. She glanced at her friend, whose eyes had now widened to the size of duck eggs, waiting for the juicy gossip to descend on her.

"Cat, I know you like gossip," Sophie started carefully. "But you really can't tell anyone about this, okay? It's really important that you keep it to yourself."

Cat nodded, hungry for Sophie to continue. "Pinkie-swear!" she said, her voice again way too loud. She held out her little finger. Sophie hooked her little finger around Cat's and gave it an awkward squeeze. It wasn't something they'd ever done before, but it felt appropriate somehow.

"I have to tell you something," Sophie carefully started. "It's not easy for me, and I'm terrified it will affect our friendship." She looked down at her shaking hands. *Why is it so hard?*

Cat laughed. "Silly. Don't be so dramatic. It's nothing bad, right? Is it? Do you have an STD?" She studied Sophie's breasts and then her face. "Have you had surgery or fillers? Because it's no big deal, Sophie." She bounced on the pink velvet couch, kicked off her high-heeled pumps and pulled a foot underneath her thigh, adjusting the skirt of her red dress.

Sophie shook her head and raised a hand to the waiter for another round. "It's not bad. It's great. For me, at least." She sighed and decided to blurt it out before she could give it a second thought. "I have a girlfriend."

Cat blinked. "You have a boyfriend? Oh my God. Finally."

"No Cat, I have a girlfriend."

Cat stared at her. A frown appeared between her eyebrows. "You have a girlfriend?" she repeated. "What do you mean by that? I don't understand."

"I mean that I have a girlfriend, just like you have a husband." Sophie chewed on her straw impatiently. "Seriously Cat, it's not like I'm telling you I eat babies for breakfast."

"Okay," Cat stuttered, after a couple of seconds. "So what you're telling me is that you have a girlfriend and that means you're... gay?"

Sophie shrugged, "What I'm telling you is that I've fallen in love with a woman and yes, I'm sure... Or as sure as I can be."

"I see." Cat frowned and pulled her long dark hair behind her ears. She seemed uneasy. "Wow. Okay...So who is she? Do I know her? How did you meet her?" Cat had lowered her voice, finally.

"She's my new colleague. Her name is Mel."

"No. Really? Fuck... The new one you told me about?" Cat said.

Sophie nodded. "Please don't judge me, Cat. It's hard enough as it is. I need you to..." She sighed. "I don't know. I just really need you to be supportive. You're the first person I've told, and you have no idea how scary it is."

Cat pulled Sophie towards her in an awkward sideways embrace, resting her face on Sophie's shoulder. "Wait," she said, still clinging on to Sophie. "I just need to process this for a second." She let go of her grip and stared at Sophie in disbelief.

"You? With another woman? Have you always been into girls?"

"I don't think so," Sophie lied. "I've never felt like this before."

Cat's eyes narrowed, hazy from the alcohol. "Are you in love?" she asked.

Sophie smiled. "Yes." There was an awkward silence.

"Okay. Wow." Cat fiddled with her nails, avoiding Sophie's gaze. "I guess I'm a bit surprised but you know I'll always be your friend, right? It's not like it changes things." She giggled. "I'm sorry. I need some time to get used to the idea so don't mind me just now."

Sophie held up her glass in relief. "Thanks, Cat. It means a lot to me that you're not making a big deal out of this because really, it's not."

"No," Cat said absently. "I suppose it's not." She paused. "So... are you going to tell people? Tell our friends? Your parents?" Her eyes widened. "Oh God, your parents are going to have a meltdown, aren't they?"

Sophie shrugged. "They don't need to know. At least not yet. I'm not ready to tell anyone else right now, and I want to see how things go with Mel first. It's difficult. I just had to tell someone, and I guess you're the only person that I trust with my life apart from Maggie. I'll probably tell her too but she's been working non-stop, and it's really hard to get hold of her." Sophie shot Cat a warning look. "As I said, you really can't tell anyone about this."

Cat nodded. "Of course not, darling. I'm just surprised you didn't tell me sooner. You didn't have to avoid me, you know?" She put a hand on Sophie's knee. "Thank you for trusting me, I feel honoured, and I won't tell anyone." She held up her glass and laughed. "Cheers to my best friend finally being in love."

Sophie rolled her eyes. "Thank you, Cat. I promise I'll introduce you to her soon. Just give me some time."

## 33

"Come on, Sophie. I'm curious to know more about you. You know everything about me by now, but I haven't even seen where your parents live or where you grew up. You owe me that after all the time you've spent with my mother. I want to meet your parents, get to know the people who shaped you into the wonderful person that you are." Mel traced a finger down Sophie's leg, then rested it on her knee. "It's great that you told Cat. That was very brave, and I'm proud of you. So why can't I meet her? Why won't you introduce me to the people that matter to you?"

They were lying on Sophie's bed; both stripped down to their underwear after a sunny picnic in Hyde Park. It was warm in the top floor apartment, despite the open windows and the fan on the antique nightstand. Mel wore navy briefs with white polka dots and a white vest top. Sophie noticed she matched the interior of her bedroom, with its heavy blue curtains, white wooden furniture and thick cream carpet. She looked like a dream, and right now Sophie could think of many things she would rather be doing than talking about her parents and her friends. She shifted the strap on her nude lace bra to check out her tan in the mirror by the dressing table.

"I'm not sure I'm comfortable with that, Mel. Besides, I'm nothing like my parents or even like my friends," she mumbled. "You're not missing out, believe me." She stiffened when she saw Mel's expression shift behind her reflection. It was the first time she had seen her like that. Mel looked hurt, and Sophie immediately regretted her reaction. She turned around, and when her eyes met Mel's, she knew she had made a mistake. *Please don't let this be our first fight.* She reached out for Mel's hand, but it was too late. Mel stood up from the bed and moved to the chaise longue in the far corner of the room. She pulled her legs up and rested her chin on a knee. A hint of anger trembled through her voice when she spoke.

"What's your problem, Sophie? It's not like they're going to find out we're together. Are you scared that I'll tell them? That I'll just blurt it out over dinner and out you? Do you really think I'm that dumb?" She cocked her head. "Are you ashamed of me? Am I not good enough for you? Not good enough for your parents? Do I not fit into your perfect little middle-class world? What is it?" She turned her head and stared out of the window.

Sophie shook her head and moved to the end of the bed. "No, of course not! How can you even say that? Mel, I think you're amazing, and I look up to you. I'm in love with you for God's sake. Madly. It has nothing to do with shame or fear or whatever it is that's going through your head right now. I just don't want you to think differently of me after you've met the people in my life. What if you think less of me?" She picked up the wine bottle next to the bed, refilled one of the glasses on her nightstand and offered it to Mel. When Mel declined, she took a large gulp, trying to calm her panic. "My friends... I'm afraid you'd find them dull. Most of our conversations are based around highly insignificant topics like where to get the best personal trainer or the rising price of avocado shakes or the stress of grocery shopping for two houses and a yacht." She sighed. "God, now I sound like some miserable twat who doesn't like her own friends, and that's not true either. It's just that compared to you, they all come across as shallow. But they're still my friends, and I don't want you to hate them." She swallowed hard. "The same goes for my parents. My father is okay actually. He works hard and minds his own business. But my mother's whole life revolves around her appearance and how every-thing she does reflects on the outside world. I don't want you to have to sit through dinner while she's trying to convince me to go on a date with whomever the latest man is that is she's got her mind set on. And I don't want you to dislike her because quite frankly, you might."

"Well, maybe you should let me decide that for myself," Mel sneered. "And does it even matter if I like her or not? That's not the point. I'm in this with you, not with your mother, or your friends or anyone else." She paused and softened her voice. "But I still want to be a part of your life, just like you're a part of mine. Don't you get that?" Sophie nodded, relieved that Mel had decided to calm down. Just the thought that she had said something to hurt her made her feel sick to her stomach.

"You're right. I'm sorry." Sophie got off the bed too and shuffled over to Mel. She held out a hand. "I wasn't thinking. I'm not used to being with someone. Not someone who's important to me, like you are." She sighed. "I don't want you to think that I'm shutting you out. It's just so good between us, and I'm terrified of losing you.

"You won't lose me." Mel finally looked her straight in the eye, and Sophie knew that she meant it.

She nodded. "Okay. I promise I'll introduce you to my parents and my friends." She lifted an eyebrow and shot Mel a hopeful glance. "We can start tomorrow. How about Sunday lunch?" She gestured to her mobile phone on the bed. "I'll call my mother right now to let her know that you're coming."

Mel softened. "Thank you," she said. Then she took Sophie's hand and pulled her onto her lap on the chaise. "Look, I'm not going to dislike anyone. If they're your friends and your family, I'm sure we'll get along. I'm good with people. You told me that yourself. And I can imagine it might be nerve wracking for you because you've never been in a relationship with a woman before but no one is going to find out unless you want them to. There's no rush, and I would never pressure you into telling anyone about us."

"I know." Sophie wrapped her arms around Mel's neck and pulled her into a tight hug.

"You're right. I'm sure you'll get along fine with everyone, and even if you don't, it doesn't matter." She planted a kiss between Mel's eyebrows. "It's not like I don't want to tell my friends about you. They're pretty open-minded. They'd be surprised, sure. But I don't think anyone would be funny about it. It's just that people talk, even when they mean no harm by it. Our families all know each other, and I want my parents to hear it from me, not from their acquaintances at the local tennis club or one of my father's clients." She shot Mel a crooked smile. "I think they'll have a hard time accepting the situation as it is and their whole inner circle talking about it certainly wouldn't help." She draped herself over Mel, straddling her in the window. "But no, I'm not ashamed of you. I'm so proud to have you as my... girlfriend." She giggled at that word. "Forgive me, I'm still getting used to saying it out loud, but I do like the sound of it."

Mel looked up and moved her hands into the back of Sophie's briefs. She cast her a teasing smile and then slipped her hands further under the thin lace.

"Okay then, girlfriend. Sunday lunch it is."

## 34

"Don't be nervous," Sophie said, resting a hand on Mel's leg under the table. She was feeling more at ease after downing a glass of her father's brandy in the restroom.

"Easy for you to say. I didn't see all this coming." Mel shot her a cynical look and gazed over the opulence of the grand dining room. The house was Victorian, and so was the interior. It had been modernized though, showcasing a tasteful mix of contemporary and antique pieces in light shades of cream, duck egg grey, and white, with high gloss black touches. Large artworks decorated the walls, again, a mix of modern and antique paintings, inherited from Sophie's grandparents. The velvet curtains were heavy and rich, draped along the large bay window, facing the street. There were plants and flowers arrangements, styled with great care on top of a black piano, placed against the back wall. Mel traced the edge of the dining table. It was made of heavy teak wood and surrounded by modern chairs with white and grey backrests.

"It's so nice," Mel said. Sophie followed her gaze, unimpressed with her mother's need to show off their wealth.

"I guess it is. I never think about it because I used to live here. My mother gets a decorator in every five years. She's so anal; it's crazy. The last decorator quit after a week, and she had to find someone else who was willing to finish it under her micromanaging supervision."

Mel nudged Sophie to stop talking when her mother walked in with a basket of bread and butter.

"Are you sure you don't want me to help you, Eleanor?" Mel asked. Eleanor shook her head and tried to smile, stretching the corners of her mouth into an uncomfortable smirk. Her lips were even bigger than they looked on the picture Sophie had shown her.

"Don't worry, Mel. That's kind of you to offer, but Marisol is helping me in the kitchen."

"She means Marisol cooked everything but she's going to take the credit," Sophie mumbled after her mother had left the room.

"Do your parents have a chef?" Mel enquired.

Sophie shook her head. "No. Marisol is their full-time cleaner, but she cooks as well. My mother likes to pretend she's a domestic princess, so they have an understanding. We don't speak about the fact that she cheats when there are guests around. Instead, we all pretend that we're impressed with her kitchen skills. It makes her happy and less on edge." Mel laughed and looked into the hallway where a wide staircase, lit up by a crystal chandelier, led up to the second floor.

"You have to show me around; I'd like to see the rest." Sophie moved her chair towards Mel and leaned in closer. She took a deep breath, inhaling the scent of Mel's shampoo.

"I'll show you my old bedroom after dinner if you're up for it."

They both giggled, and Mel shot her a warning look. "Stop it; your mother will notice something!" She said, and she pushed Sophie's chair back, laughing.

"Well, well, you must be Mel." Sophie's father entered the room and grinned at his own rhyme. Mel looked up at his broad-shouldered stature as he approached her. A cigar was hanging from the corner of his mouth. He was tall, sporting a moustache and a neatly trimmed beard. He removed a hand from out of his suit pocket and reached out to squeeze Mel's hand in a firm handshake.

"Nice to meet you, Mr. Scott," Mel said in her most charming tone.

"Please, call me David. I feel old when people 'Mister' me." He sat down opposite them and sighed.

"Long day?" Sophie asked. Her father nodded, and a deep frown appeared between his eyebrows. He looked tired.

"Twelve hours," he said, refilling Mel and Sophie's glasses before pouring himself a glass of red wine. "The ladies nowadays..." He took a drag from his cigar and leaned back." Sophie and Mel both waited for him to continue but nothing happened. Instead, he removed his tie and focused on his wine, savouring the first sip of his Burgundy. He looked up when his wife walked in.

"Deborah and Mark will be here any minute," Eleanor said in a high-pitched voice. She turned to Sophie. "Your brother cancelled again. He must be in over his head at work, the poor sod. He didn't sound too great on the phone." She wiped her perfectly matte forehead with a napkin as if she'd just been standing over a steaming hot pan and leaned against her husband's shoulder. "So tell me, Mel. How was

Sophie's date with Aldo? Or should I say, your double date?"
She winked. "Sophie refuses to talk about it, but I think she's
just shy. He's a fine young man, don't you think?" She looked
from Sophie to Mel and back.

Sophie rolled her eyes. "It wasn't a date, Mum," she said
before Mel had the chance to answer. "I told you I don't like
him. I only went for dinner with him and his friend because
you and Deborah pressured me into it, remember?"

Eleanor cocked her head and squinted, observing her
daughter. "You're blushing, Sophie." She turned to Mel. "I
know my own daughter, and I think I'm on to something
here. I'm telling you, those two are meant to be together.
Deborah and I are already secretly planning their wedding."
She giggled and jumped up when the doorbell rang. Sophie
pinched Mel's hand before they both got up to greet
Deborah and Mark.

"See?" She whispered. "This is exactly what I was talking
about."

Mel smiled. "It's fine. Just let it go."

"Lovely to meet you, Mel," Deborah sang after handing
Eleanor a bottle of Champagne. "What a sight for sore eyes
you are!" She gave Mel an approving glance-over and
complimented her on her black, sleeveless dress. "And look
at your hair. People would pay a hefty price for those curls.
Where did you get them?" Mel opened her mouth to
answer, but Deborah had already turned her back on her.
She was hovering over a set of micro plants that the flower
stylist had placed in an aquarium on top of the piano.

"Oh Eleanor, I love these," she shrieked. "You must give
me the number of your stylist." She winked. "I wouldn't
mind a couple of these darlings in my dining room."

"Micro plants," Eleanor stated. "They're called micro
plants. They're a big trend at the moment. Yoyo had them

flown in from Japan; I'll get you his contact details later."
She gestured to the flower arrangements at the end of the
table and pursed her lips. "We've gone for an orange theme
this time. Elle Decoration featured orange flowers last
month and the colour photographs really well.

"Clever." Deborah looked impressed. "It's a risk, I
guess... But no statement has ever been made without
taking a risk. Don't you think, Mel?" Mel looked puzzled,
staring at the orange flowers, draped over the edge of a
triangular ceramic pot.

"Euh...Yeah," She stammered. "Bold statement, for sure."

Eleanor beamed with pride. "Thank you, Mel. See? The
youngsters love it too, Deborah." She walked back towards
the kitchen. "Let me just get the starters. We can discuss
Yoyo's fees over lunch. I'm telling you, this man will change
your life."

Mark cleared his throat and shot his wife a warning
look. "I'm not paying for someone to put flowers in our
house, Deborah. It's bordering on insane." He turned to
Sophie's father. "I'm sorry David, no offense to your wife."

"No offense taken, Mark." Sophie's father looked
amused. "If I could talk some sense into her, I would, but
unfortunately I don't have much energy left to fight this
flower nonsense."


SOPHIE NOTICED that Mel had started to relax after their
starter. She even seemed to be enjoying herself, if she wasn't
mistaken. There was a lot of speculation around their
double date, and they both tried to steer the conversation
into a different direction. Deborah let it go after a while, but
Sophie's mother was having none of it. She passed the plate
of salmon fillets to Mel, her eyes wide with excitement. "And

his friend... Rick, was it? Was he your type? Or do you have a boyfriend?"

Sophie's father interrupted. "Please, Eleanor. How many times do I have to tell you that you're not a matchmaker?"

"It's okay," Mel said. "He's nice. Very polite and charming." She hesitated. "But I'm afraid men aren't my preference."

Eleanor frowned. "What do you mean by preference?"

"Well," Mel continued, "I'm gay."

Eleanor was clearly taken aback. "Oh well, that's great, Mel." She sounded uncomfortable, looking down, focusing on her food. Deborah stepped in, determined to demonstrate her people's skills.

"It certainly is great, Eleanor. I agree. The younger generation are so much more open minded than we were at that age. And that's a good thing, isn't it?"

Eleanor nodded and refilled their glasses. "So... how does that work nowadays? Is this something you plan to do for a while, this lifestyle? I assume you would want children at some point? You're around Sophie's age, aren't you?"

"Jesus Mum, listen to yourself," Sophie said. "It's not a choice. And it's not limiting either. Mel can have kids if she wants. Anyone can."

Mel shook her head and put a hand on Sophie's arm. "It's okay," she said. "It's not the first time I've heard it."

Eleanor raised her gaze. "I apologize," she said. "Sophie is right of course. It's just that... you don't look like that kind of person. You're beautiful, and you could have the whole world at your feet."

Deborah nodded, trying to get a word in but Sophie's father raised a hand. "That's enough, both of you. I think it's time we change the subject." He directed his attention back to Mel. "Sophie told me you two work closely together. Do your parents work in the creative industry as well?"

Mel smiled politely. "Not really," she said. "Although my mother is very creative. She likes to sew and upcycle furniture. But she's a cleaner, actually. Or rather she was a cleaner. Her back is bad now, so she's not working at the moment. She's living with me. My father passed away a couple of years ago, but he wasn't much of an artist either unless you count gambling as an art." She shook her head casually. "So no, no artists in my family as far as I know." She looked at Sophie's father. "But you David, you could certainly call yourself an artist. I mean... you re-sculpt bodies and you make people feel happy about themselves again. That must be very satisfying."

Sophie could tell that her father appreciated the compliment, but he shrugged it off.

"Well thank you, I suppose," he said. "But it's not always rewarding. Most people will never be happy with the way they look." He made sure not to look into the direction of his wife, who pretended not to listen while she passed round the hollandaise sauce.

Mark laughed. "I'm with you on that, David. It's..." There was a loud bang, then the clinking of glass against a hard surface.

Eleanor looked up, bewildered. "Marisol?" she shouted into the direction of the kitchen. "I really hope that's not my antique crystal gravy boat." When there was no answer, she got up to inspect the damage. "Oh my God. What have you done? I told you to be careful with that, didn't I? Do you have any idea how much this gravy boat is worth? You've just ruined my luncheon." They heard a dramatic cry and shortly after, apologetic whispering.

Deborah got up too. "Eleanor sounds terribly upset. I'll

go and check on her." Sophie's mind was working full speed, but she couldn't think of a single thing to say to lighten the mood. She watched Mel listening in on the conversation in the kitchen. Her eyes turned cold, and her shoulders stiffened.

Sophie's father turned his head towards the kitchen. "Stop shouting and come back to the table for God's sake, Eleanor. It's only a bloody gravy boat. We'll get a new one." Sophie looked at Mel, who's attention was now fixed on the hallway.

"Please don't mind my wife," David said. "She can be a little dramatic sometimes."

Mel nodded and stood up from the table. "Excuse me; I'm not feeling too well. I think I need some fresh air." She turned to Sophie's father. "Thank you for having me. It was nice to meet you."

Sophie followed her into the hallway, but Mel stopped her. "Please," she begged. "Just leave me, okay?"

Sophie ignored her and followed her outside. "No, I'm not going to let you go. We can go for a walk. Anywhere you want. But please don't leave like this." Sophie closed the door behind her and blocked the front gate. "Wait, Mel. I don't care if you want to leave but we need to talk."

Mel cocked her head. "Talk about what? About how your mother treats her staff? About how she just shouted at a senior lady who has worked hard all her life to please her? In front of her guests, no less. It makes me feel sick, Sophie." She pointed at the house. "I don't want to sit at that table anymore and continue the stupid conversations we were having, pretending everything is fine." She pushed Sophie aside and opened the gate.

"I don't want to pretend everything is fine either," Sophie said. "I don't agree with her behaviour, and I'll tell her that."

She took Mel's hand to stop her from walking away. "Let's talk about this."

Mel shook her head. "It's not just that Sophie. I don't think this is going to work out. Your mother, she almost jumped through the roof when I told her I was gay. How do you think they'll react when they find out we're together? Not only am I a woman, my social background is so different from yours, they would never accept it. They're snobs, you know. Nasty, superficial snobs."

Sophie shot Mel a furious look. "You can't just say that, Mel. They might be snobs, but they're still my parents. And don't you dare judge them on what they have. My father works six days a week. It's not like success just fell into his lap."

"Oh yeah? Well, my mother worked six days a week, and all she got was a bad back and a shitty payoff. Two thousand pounds from the last family she served for fifteen years." She sniffed. "You were right. I shouldn't have come here. You privileged people have no idea how lucky you are. Look at you. You've never had to worry about anything. You have an apartment in Chelsea that your parents paid for, and now you're just darting through life like a... I don't know. I can't even fucking describe how easy your life seems to me. But I'm not in the same boat as you, Sophie." She inhaled through her teeth. "I can't risk my job. I have to take care of both myself and my mother. If I lose this job, we'll be in trouble because she won't be able to take care of herself financially. Her pension is close to nothing. Don't you understand? It's not the same for you, and I'm not going to risk what I have for something that's never going to work out in the first place. We're just too different."

Sophie followed her out to the street. "Are you attacking me because I'm wealthy? Are you saying I don't deserve what I have? What do you want me to do, Mel? Give away all my possessions? You can't blame me for being born into this family, that's just ridiculous. And who says they wouldn't understand?" She took a deep breath to continue her defence, but Mel had already turned her back to her and was making her way to the tube station. Sophie gave up when she felt tears welling up. She didn't want Mel to see her cry. She yelled after her. "You know what? Fine. Walk away. I'm done too."

## 35

"Anything else before we close the meeting?" When Debbie didn't get a reply, she started gathering her paperwork from the long table in the conference room. "Sophie, you've been awfully quiet today. Anything you'd like to share?" Despite her size and the fact that her baby was due two days ago, Debbie was still there.

Sophie shook her head. "No I'm good, thanks. Just not feeling too well." She glanced over at Mel who followed the design assistants out of the room with her laptop under her arm and a mug of coffee in her other hand. They hadn't really spoken for three days and the formal politeness they addressed each other with made it almost unbearable for Sophie to be in the office. She tried to make eye contact when Mel passed her seat on the other side of the window, but she got nothing but a blank stare. It hurt.

"Go home if you're not well," Debbie insisted. "Maybe you just need a good night's sleep. You look tired."

Sophie waved it off. "I'm fine. Just a headache. I've taken some painkillers, so I'm sure I'll be okay in an hour." She gathered her own stuff and made her way back to her desk, past Mel. She lingered there until Mel finally looked up.

"Can we talk, please?" Mel scanned the design area to make sure no one was listening in.

"Not here, Sophie. I'm busy. It's not a good time."

Sophie sighed. "Please, I'm begging you. I can't bear being around you like this. It's killing me that you hate me." One of the developers passed, and she pretended to read the notes in her hand until the girl was at a safe distance. "Can we please go outside? Five minutes?" Sophie realized she must have looked pretty desperate because Mel's expression softened.

"I don't hate you, okay? I'm just angry, that's all." Mel picked up a file and turned her chair to Sophie. "I have another meeting right now, but I agree we should talk. Can I call you Friday night? Or maybe we can meet up on Saturday? I didn't want this 'us' thing to affect our jobs, but it seems like it already is."

Sophie nodded. "I miss you," she whispered.

Mel cast her a sad smile. "Look. Maybe I overreacted towards you but my mother means the world to me and what happened on Sunday really hurt me."

Sophie shook her head. "Mel, I understand that you're angry. Maybe even disgusted. But I'm not my mother and I don't condone her behaviour. This isn't fair to me." Mel opened her mouth to speak, but someone called her from the other side of the room.

"Mel, are you ready? Our model is waiting, and she's cold so we need to wrap this up as quickly as we can."

Mel stood up. "Got to go. Not here. This is a private matter."

Sophie's gaze followed Mel as she walked off towards the fitting area where she greeted the model with a smile. Mel seemed less affected by their fight than Sophie was. At least she was perfectly capable of functioning at work. Sophie felt anxious and dizzy. A sudden sense of panic overtook her as she sat down behind her desk, frantically searching for a bottle of water in the mess around her. She closed her eyes and tried to steady her breathing, holding on to her chest. She couldn't bear the thought of losing Mel. *Is this a fight or a breakup?* Until a couple of days ago, Sophie had been over the moon. She'd finally been able to be herself and completely at ease around someone whom she was madly in love with. She was furious with her mother but also with herself. *Why didn't I defend Marisol? Are we going to be okay? Is it my fault?* Everything was such a mess. If only her mother hadn't been so nasty, they would have been fine. But Mel was hurt, and Sophie wasn't sure if she could fix it. She waved at Debbie from behind her desk, indicating that she was leaving. Then she packed her bag and left the office, desperate to be alone.

## 36

"And that's when I lost it," Mel said, blinking away her tears. Her head was resting in her mother's lap on the couch. It was something she hadn't done since she was a little girl. The gentle strokes of Isabella's hands made her feel calmer, but her anger still hadn't receded.

"These things happen," Isabella said. "It's not Sophie's fault."

"I know," Mel sniffed. "But still, it was in her parents' house, and it can't have been the first time that it happened. It made me so furious, thinking that could have been you. "

"Don't worry about me, Melzinha. How many times do I have to tell you? I made my own choices. I can fend for myself, just like Marisol can. And don't take it out on Sophie. It's not fair to her." She giggled. "I know you like her. You can't fool me, no matter how hard you try."

Mel couldn't help but laugh through her tears. "How do you know?"

"How do I know? I'm your mother. Plus you've talked

about her nonstop for the past month. It's not that hard to figure out."

Mel sat back up and took a deep breath. "I really like her, Mum. More than I've ever liked anyone before. But I can't stop thinking about the 'what-ifs.' I'm the first woman she's been with, and I always seem to fall for the straight girls. What if she changes her mind? What if she decides it's easier to spend her life with a man because her family expects her to? What if she needs more than I can give her? Financially, I mean. And what if I'll never be able to set another foot in her parents' house because I can't stand being around them? What if they find out about Sophie and me and I'm not welcome there anymore? Would it change things between us? Is that even important?"

Isabella shook her head. "Since when did you start caring about what other people think of you? You've always been true to yourself, and I'm proud of you for that." She pulled Mel's curls back and kissed her forehead. "One thing is certain. I've only met Sophie on a couple of occasions, but she's one of the nicest, sweetest women I've ever met. She doesn't strike me as the type to care about class or money or her parents' opinions. So why should you?"

Mel shrugged. "Maybe you're right."

Isabella took her mug of tea from the table and cradled it in her hands. "You know what? I'm going to tell you something I've never told you before."

Mel turned to her in surprise. "What could you possibly tell me that I don't already know about you?"

Isabella took a sip from her tea and cleared her throat. "When I first came to the UK, I had nothing. My parents, God bless their souls, had saved up for five years to buy me a ticket in the hope I would get a chance of a better life here. They had arranged a place for me to stay for the first month with friends of friends. They didn't really know them, but it was my only option at the time so we could only hope for the best. I had ten pounds in my pocket and a small suitcase. Paolo, the man of the house I would be staying in, picked me up from the airport." She paused, her mind wandering back many years. "It was all very new for me. I'd never been on a plane. I'd never even travelled outside Brazil. It was overwhelming, to say the least. Paolo put my suitcase in the back of his car and told me to sit in the front, next to him. He was Brazilian too, and although I knew basic English, I was relieved to have someone to talk to in my own language. Then, after about half an hour, when we were driving on a quiet country road, he asked me if I was grateful for his help. He said he had some ideas on how I could thank him. I knew then something wasn't right. He put his hand on my leg and started squeezing my thigh. I was too scared to move, so I just sat there in silence, and I let him touch me." She sighed. "What could I do? I was terrified, but he was much bigger than me, and we were driving."

Mel looked up, facing her mother. "Mum, that's terrible. He didn't hurt you, did he?"

Isabella shook her head. "When we finally stopped off at a petrol station to fill up the tank, I got out of the car while he was paying. I ran and ran as fast as my feet could carry me. I only had my passport and my wallet." Mel tried to say something, but Isabella stopped her. "Wait. Let me finish. This is not the point I'm trying to make." She took a sip of her tea. "Anyway, I ran and then walked for hours and hours until I somehow arrived here, in Brixton. I saw a pub with a sign 'cheap rooms for rent'. I asked the man at the bar how long I could stay for ten pounds and he laughed. Everyone at the bar laughed, apart from one man. Your father."

Mel swallowed hard. "I don't understand. I thought you met him later." She paused. "Did he help you?"

Isabella nodded. "He was quite a handsome man back then. He was a lot older but good-looking, you know. He asked me if I wanted to join him at his table and I did. He bought me dinner and a drink and inquired about my situation. I think he was shocked to hear that I had ended up in a strange country with nothing but ten pounds and a suitcase that was left behind in the boot of a car somewhere. In the end, I think he felt sorry for me, and he offered to help me. I wasn't sure if I could trust him, but I didn't really have any other choice. He told me he was a builder and that I could stay in one of the houses he was working on until the work was completed. He even apologized for the fact that I couldn't stay at his house because he was married and he didn't think his wife would agree." She smiled. "He was kind. The top floor of the building site was nearly finished, and he bought me a blow-up mattress and a sleeping bag that got me through the night. He brought me food, let me shower in the builders' annex after they had finished for the day and warned everyone to leave me alone. I spent my days walking miles, enquiring for a job in every single shop, office, and restaurant. It was a lonely time, but his encouragement kept me going. Within three weeks, I found a cleaning job in a hotel." Isabella's face lit up when she thought back to the moment her life changed for the better. "I was so happy. Finally, I had a goal in life. I had people to talk to and somewhere to go during the day. Your father and I grew close. After he finished work, he would come upstairs, and we would eat together and talk, sometimes for hours." She put a hand on Mel's knee. "I fell in love with him. We fell in love."

"You did?" Mel frowned. "I'm so sorry. I know I've never

asked, but he was so much older... I always assumed you married him because you had no other choice."

Isabella shook her head. "No, we were in love, very much so. Nothing happened, though. He was married, and my mother hadn't raised me to sleep with married men. By the time the building work had finished, I had saved up enough money to move into a shared apartment with some of the other cleaners I had met through work, but your father and I stayed in touch. One day, he was waiting for me after my shift. He told me he couldn't stop thinking about me and that he'd finally left his wife. I couldn't have been happier. We spent our first night together, and you were born nine months later." Mel was too stunned for words. "I know, I know," Isabella said. "It's probably not what you expected. You never asked, and so we only told you the story in broad strokes. You've always been so protective of me growing up, and I didn't want you to know how hard it had been for me back then. It's just not something you tell your children." She sighed. "Nobody is perfect, Melzinha. Although your father was a gambling addict and drank too much, he has and always will be the love of my life, even though he's not around anymore. And I want that for you too. That's why I'm telling you this now. Please don't let your anger stand in the way of something good. When you meet someone special, hold on to her. Because in the end, love is the only thing that matters. All the rest is just white noise."

## 37

"Sophie? Is that you?" Eleanor's trembling voice sounded upset. Sophie rushed into the kitchen to find her mother on one of the chairs at the table, her forehead resting in her hands. She had puffy eyes from crying and looked like she was about to give up on life.

"Mum! What happened? Is Dad okay? Did something happen to Stew? I came as quickly as I could when I got your message." She kneeled down, wiping the tears from her mother's red cheeks. "Please Mum, say something. Are they okay? Are you okay?"

Her mother shook her head. "No one is hurt, Sophie. At least not in the physical sense. Your father is playing golf, and your brother is... Well, I don't know where he is, but I suppose he's fine."

Sophie frowned. "So why are you crying?" She studied her mother's face and suddenly lost her sympathy. "Is it because we had a fight after Mel left last week? Because I meant every word I said and I'm not going to apologize for defending her. Your behaviour was not acceptable. You never yell at Marisol like that. Did you do it on purpose? To show Mel you were better than her?" Her mother glanced up at her with a look Sophie had never seen before. Was it disappointment? Resentment?

"I know," she said.

"What do you know, Mum? I don't get it." An uneasy feeling overtook Sophie, and it made her stomach drop.

"I know about you and Mel." Eleanor sighed. "I can't believe we welcomed her into our home!" She looked angry now. "I knew there was something funny between the two of you, but I kept on telling myself I was being silly. Do you two even work together or was that a lie too? It's disgusting, Sophie. Do you ever consider what people are going to think about us when you pull a stunt like that? Did you do it for attention?" Then her eyes narrowed. "Are you using drugs?"

Sophie stood up and took a step back. She wasn't sure if she was more surprised about her mother's knowledge of the situation or her unexpected reaction. This didn't seem like her mother at all. She looked at her in confusion.

"Aldo told me," Eleanor said. He came by this afternoon. He wasn't planning on telling me, but he'd overheard people talking about it so he figured the word would travel fast and he didn't want me to hear it from someone else. Thank God your father was out playing golf and let's hope he never finds out. Aldo promised it wouldn't go any further so we'll just have to pray for the best, although he couldn't vouch for your friends who all seem to be well informed about your antics." She bit off a fingernail and flicked it into the ashtray on the table. "Why, Sophie? You had a good chance with this boy. He could have given you a stable future and financial security. Not to mention that he's good looking and crazy about you. He waited three weeks before telling me. Imagine the inner conflict he must have felt! The boy is heartbroken, and so am I."

Those last words brought out a roaring rage in Sophie. She was shaking on her legs, contemplating whether to walk out or not. It was probably for the best to leave because right now, she hated her mother. This was about as bad as it could get. Sophie took another step back. She couldn't be near her anymore.

"What?" she shouted. "I can't believe he told you, what a nasty piece of shit! Do you know why he did that? Because he's a bitter, sneaky little turd. I told you I didn't like him then and I still don't like him. Does my happiness mean nothing to you? Nothing at all? Do you want me to get married and spend the rest of my life with someone I don't like? Is that what you want? Do you want me to be miserable? You haven't even asked me about my side of the story. And even if it was true, so what? Would it be so terrible if I had a thing with a girl? Are you really that kind of a person? I mean, look at you! You're obviously open minded enough to reshape your entire face and think nothing about it. But when your own daughter shares something special with someone who happens to be a woman, you act as if the world has come to an end."

Eleanor's face twitched, and she looked away. Sophie waited for a reply but there was only icy silence that cut through the both of them like a knife. Her mother said nothing and that said it all. In any other situation, Sophie would have denied everything, at least until she had figured out a way to discuss it. But right now, she didn't care.

"You know what?" she said, trying to keep her angry voice under control. "I did kiss her. Not because I was trying to provoke Aldo or hurt him or you and dad. I kissed her because I wanted to. I'm in love with her and you ruined it by behaving like an idiot on Sunday. You ruined what mattered most to me." Sophie turned around and walked towards the door. "And in case you were wondering, I've slept with her too," she sneered before she slammed the door.

OUTSIDE, Sophie had to steady herself against the brick wall by the gate. She felt like she was suffocating. Her mother's words hadn't totally settled in during their conversation and now it was reality that struck her hard. What she had always assumed to be unconditional love was nothing but a lie. Did her mother not care about her happiness? Was she really that selfish? And Aldo.... She couldn't believe he'd had the audacity to show up on her family's doorstep and out her to her mother just because he had been turned down.

"Fucking prick," she said to herself. The big issue wasn't even that he had told her but it was still a shitty thing to do. What really bothered her was her mother's reaction to the whole situation. How could it be so terrible? It wasn't as if they lived in the sixteenth century, and this was London for God's sake. It was a free country. Her mother didn't have to worry about Sophie going to jail or being shunned from society. So why was it such an issue? Clearly, all she cared about was herself. Sophie felt a pain in her chest and wasn't sure if it was physical. She burst into tears, searching for her phone in the over-full pockets of her coat. With shaking hands, she tried to call her brother. She needed someone on her side, someone who knew her mother just as well as she did. She needed someone to tell her she wasn't in the wrong. It went straight to voicemail. She sent him a text but got no answer. Her brother was obsessed with his phone and it was very unusual for him not to pick up. She sunk onto the pavement, her knees pulled up under her chin. A tear rolled over her cheek, and she turned her head away when one of the neighbours opened the window to check on her. Sophie had never felt so alone. She missed Mel, but she couldn't call her. They still hadn't spoken after their fight. She couldn't call Cat either. If Aldo was right and her friends knew too, Cat was the only person who could have told them. Her best friend of all people. She pictured Cat waving her hair around, her eyes wide, whispering behind her back while she spilled the juicy gossip in front of everyone she knew. The thought hurt, perhaps even more than her mother's words. Sophie needed her brother.

## 38

"Hey sis," Sophie's brother said, lingering in the doorway. He looked surprised to see her. "You know I love you but now is not a good time." He held the door half shut between them, only poking his head around the corner. His hair was messy, and he looked like he hadn't seen daylight in weeks, the way he was shielding his eyes from the sun.

"I'm sorry, but I need to talk to you," Sophie sniffed. Stewart squinted against the bright sunlight. As soon as he saw her miserable state, he apologized.

"Oh, I didn't mean to... Wait, just give me two minutes, okay?" He locked the door again, leaving Sophie outside in the rain. A little later he opened the door, this time dressed in jogging pants and a shirt. He smelt of freshly sprayed deodorant. Sophie wiped her tears and looked around in concerned suspicion. The curtains were drawn, and there were empty bottles of wine on the table.

"Are you ok, Stew? You're not depressed, are you? It's five in the afternoon." Stewart laced his fingers behind his head and looked up at the ceiling.

"No, I'm fine, believe me," he said matter-of-factly, then gestured at the couch. "Sit down. What's wrong little sis? It's not often that you come knocking on my door unannounced." There was noise coming from the hallway and Sophie turned to find a man peeking around the bedroom door.

"I'm so sorry, Stew. I know you said I should stay in the room but I really, really need a pee." He came out and dramatically hopped from one leg to the other.

Stew rolled his eyes, then buried his face in his hands. "Great," he said. "Well, as you're both here now... Sophie, this is Roberto. Roberto, this is my sister Sophie. You weren't exactly meant to meet, but here you both are."

Roberto graced her with the biggest smile and waved at her as he sprinted towards the toilet, only covered by a towel wrapped around his waist. "Right back," he yelled.

Sophie was speechless, and for a minute, she forgot the whole reason she was there. She stared at the bathroom door in silence, waiting for Roberto to come back out.

"Is this what I think it is?" she asked. "How did I miss it? Is he the reason you never come home anymore?" She looked up at Stewart with a grin, feeling a tiny bit better already.

Stewart shrugged his broad shoulders, looking more than uncomfortable. "Yeah. And now you know," he said.

"He's hot," Sophie remarked. "You didn't need to hide this from me, you know. I can't say I'm not a bit surprised, but I'm happy for you." She poked him in his thigh, and he began to relax. She even saw the signs of a tiny smile forming on his face. "So are you two serious?" She asked.

Stewart looked through the hallway at the closed bathroom door. "Not sure," he whispered. "It's early days."

He jumped up when Roberto yelled from behind the

toilet door. "Hell yeah! He fucking adores me. He just told me just two minutes before you arrived." Then he burst out in laughter and Stewart blushed.

"Hey, it's okay." Sophie laughed. "It's all good. He's funny too, looks like you've hit the jackpot."

Roberto walked in and gave Sophie a kiss on the back of her hand. "I can see that good looks run in the family," he charmed her with a slight Italian accent. He sat down next to her as if they had known each other for years, still only scarcely covered by his towel, a hand resting on her knee.

"You look sad, Sophie. Would you like to talk about it or do you want me to go back into the bedroom?"

Sophie smiled. "No, it's fine. It's really nice to meet you."

Roberto turned to Stewart. "Handsome, why don't you get your sister a drink? She looks like she could do with one. And while you're there, get me a glass of red as well, please?" He fluttered his eyelashes and grinned. Stewart nodded and gave him a lopsided smile. A couple of seconds later, he came back through with a bottle of red wine and three glasses, still not entirely comfortable.

"Right," Stewart said. "Now we've got that awkwardness out of the way, tell me, sis. I've rarely seen you upset. What's happened?" He looked at Sophie intently as she took a sip of wine and leaned back into the sofa.

"It's Mum. She's evil. Believe me; you do not want to tell her about you and Roberto." Both men frowned at her as she fiddled with the hem of her t-shirt. "Do you remember Aldo?" she asked. "Deborah and Mark's son?"

Stewart nodded. "Uh huh. He's a creepy little dude. Don't tell me you're dating him? He didn't hurt you, did he?"

Sophie twirled the wine around in her glass. "Yeah. Well, he's not so little anymore. And no, I'm not dating him. Never in a million years. Mum and Deborah practically cornered me to go on a date with him over Sunday lunch a couple of weeks ago. We were both in Hong Kong at the same time, and it was just one of those situations I couldn't get out of." She sighed. "I brought my new colleague Mel along and I... well I ended up kissing her in front of him." Stewart and Roberto both shot up in surprise and regarded her with growing interest.

"What? You?" Stewart's disbelief was almost comical, and Sophie couldn't suppress a grin, despite the fact that she felt like crying again.

"Yes, well... it wasn't planned or anything. It just happened. But Aldo...I guess he got jealous. He visited Mum and told her, and now she's acting as if I'm putting the whole family to shame. She thinks I'm some kind of sick attention seeker. She was horrible to me, Stew. I didn't know she could be like that." Sophie swallowed away the tears and looked down at her hands in her lap. "I only told Cat, and I think she might have told others, even though she promised me she wouldn't."

Stewart moved to the couch next to Sophie and put an arm around her. "Shush, don't cry" he hushed. "It will be okay. Just forget about them for a little while. What Mum or your friends think is not important. Right now, you have other things to deal with. Do you like this girl? And since when are you into women?"

"I don't know." Sophie shook her head. "I mean, yes I do. I like her a lot. But we work together and I'm her manager now. Plus we just had a fight after Mum behaved like a bitch over lunch, so I don't even know if she still wants to see me." She paused and looked at Roberto, whom she felt strangely comfortable with. "We only just met at the airport on our way to Hong Kong, about six weeks ago."

"Holy shit," Roberto gasped. "That sounds intense. Is

she the first woman you've been with? Did you sleep with her? Can I ask that? Or is that too personal?" He blatantly ignored Stewart's warning look, ordering him to back off. "Well?"

"Yeah, she is. And I did." Sophie gave him a wry smile and blushed.

"And?" Roberto insisted. Sophie didn't say anything. She just grinned, thinking back to the moments she and Mel had spent together. If only she could go back in time. It had been so perfect in Hong Kong, so carefree. Away from the office, from her family and friends. Safely locked away behind closed doors, nobody judging her.

Stewart got up and refilled their glasses. "You know what?" he said. "Mum caught me with a guy once."

Sophie's eyes widened. "Really? How come I never knew about it? Surely she would have made just as much as a fuss over you."

"Well, she did," Stewart said. "But she didn't want anyone else to know either. I don't think she ever told dad. She likes to brush things under the carpet, our mother." He shook his head. "She walked in on Marcel and me in my bedroom when she let herself in one day. Do you remember Marcel? We used to hang out a lot when I was in my early twenties."

Sophie stared at him. "Really? Marcel? The skinny guy with the braces?"

Stewart nodded. "Yes. Not one of my proudest moments but hey, he was sweet, and he had great taste in music. Anyway, I should have never given her the key to my apartment. Mum was livid, and she made me promise to keep it to myself. That was after a month when she finally started speaking to me again. She was scared it would rub off on you." He laughed. "I guess she was right about that after all.

Anyway, the whole situation was too ridiculous for words. So I just kept it outside the family. That was a long time ago. I stopped coming home regularly after that, as you've noticed." He raised a hand. "It's not that I'm ashamed of who I am, I was just not that bothered with seeing her anymore. To be honest, I thought she would get used to the idea and come around or at least apologize at some point, but she never brought the subject up again, ever. If I can't be myself at home, what's the point of being there?" He patted Sophie on the back. "She can do this to me, but I won't let her do it to you, sis. No way. It's not right, and we can't let her get away with it."

Roberto made a fist. "That's the spirit. A united front. I like that." He looked from Stewart to Sophie. "Hey, I think what we need right now is a good night out. How about we all go for cocktails tonight and get to know each other. You should bring your girl. What's her name?" Sophie hesitated. "Come on, it will be fun," Roberto insisted.

"I'm not sure that's a good idea," Sophie protested. "As I said, we've just had a fight because of Mum, and we're not really in a good place right now. I don't even know if she's still speaking to me."

Stewart waved if off. "So what? You're done with Mum too, right? Or at least for now. It's perfect. You'll have one more thing in common. I'd love to meet her, and we haven't had a proper drink together since..." He laughed. "Well, never actually so even more reason to go out. Call her now." Stewart and Roberto both held up their glasses to Sophie, and she couldn't help but laugh as they clinked. Maybe things would be okay after all. She was too scared to call Mel after their fight, so she sent her a text instead.

*I'm sorry if I hurt you. My mother found out, and she didn't take it well. Please meet me for drinks tonight with my brother*

*and his boyfriend (?!) I'll explain later. I promise you; they're
lovely people.'*

LATER THAT NIGHT, Sophie, Stewart and her new brother-in-
law, whom she absolutely adored, were hanging at the bar
of the Mayfair, waiting for Mel. They had ordered Dirty
Martinis, and Roberto was admiring Sophie's silk kimono
dress that she had thrown on in a hurry to make up for her
sorry appearance that afternoon.

"It's so nice to finally meet someone in Stew's family. You
guys have always been a mystery to me. It feels like the next
step in our relationship. Doesn't it, handsome?" He beamed.
"And don't let him fool you into thinking it's casual. He seriously loves me." He laughed and raised his glass, then
looked over at the door. "Holy shit. Is that her?" Sophie
looked over her shoulder and met Mel's green eyes. They
weren't angry or cold anymore. They were sweet and seductive, like before. Mel smiled at her and Sophie felt a spark of
hope that everything would be alright between them. She
put her glass down and turned as Mel approached. She
wasn't sure how to greet her, what with her brother being
right next to her, but Mel took charge and smiled as she
kissed Sophie, just long enough to show that she meant it,
before giving her a hug.

"Thanks for texting me,' she whispered. "I've been
thinking about you all day. I'm so sorry to hear you had a
fight with your mother, and I don't want you to think for a
moment that I feel smug about it." She tightened her grip.
"I'm sorry I was so angry."

"You don't have to be sorry. I'm just glad that you came,"
Sophie said. She gestured to her companions. "This is my
brother Stewart and this handsome guy here is his

boyfriend, Roberto." Both men said hello and gave her a good glance-over.

"Sophie, you've got good taste, girl." Roberto smirked. "Nice to put a pretty face to the name." He took Mel's hand. "Come on, Mel. Let's grab a table; it will be busy here soon."

Sophie told Mel about the happenings of the day, and Stewart filled her in about his own history with their mother. Mel listened but didn't say very much. She had an arm around Sophie, comforting her when she replayed the painful fight she'd had earlier that day. After they had finished, they looked at her, fishing for her opinion on the matter.

"Hey, don't ask me," Mel said. I know I had a rant last Sunday but I've calmed down now, and I'm done saying bad things about your family. I don't know them like you do so it's way too easy for me to judge." She leaned in and looked at Sophie and Stewart. "But I do want you to know that I'm sorry this has happened to the both of you." She smiled apologetically. "Listen, "I know it hurts. And I know it must seem like she doesn't care about you the way you thought she did. But I think you're wrong. I think she cares a lot and she's desperate because she's convinced you've made a big mistake and that the decisions you've made will ruin your future. She might come around if you both talk to her." She shrugged. "I can't be sure of course, but if she's never been a terrible mother, I'd say she'll probably try to understand eventually. In my case, my father was old. And I mean really old compared to my mother. It took him five years to get over the fact that I liked girls, but two years before he passed away he told me that in the end, he just wanted me to be happy. It wasn't much, but it was something, and it was enough for me. In your case Sophie, be grateful that you have your brother on your side to get you through this because I know how hard it can be when you're on your own."

"I know," Sophie said. "I'm lucky not to be alone in this." She rested her head on Mel's shoulder. Mel had made her forget all about her brother sitting right next to her. How was it possible that this girl, who she hadn't even trusted with the job just over six weeks ago, had turned out to be one of the wisest, most amazing people she knew?

Stewart to Sophie. "You know I love you, right? I know we don't get to see each other much and that's ridiculous because we live so close." He paused. "But it's actually quite fun hanging out with you. We should do this more often." He laughed. "I love your new haircut by the way. Is this your lesbian look?" He messed up her hair with his hand, only to receive a smack on the head back. "Let's talk to them," he said. "But not yet. Let it sink in for a couple of weeks. If we're together, it might not be that bad. Imagine their faces when we both bring up the subject." His eyes widened. "Wait, I have a great idea. How about we do it during one of those lovely Sunday luncheons with Deborah and Mark?"

Sophie chuckled. "That's all very funny, Stew but I'm actually terrified. Mum will probably throw a tantrum and brush it under the carpet again. She's pretty predictable like that. But how's Dad going to react?"

Stewart shrugged. "There's only one way to find out. Now, shall we have another round?"

## 39

"Your brother seems lovely. He reminds me of you," Mel said as they waited in line for the toilets. "His boyfriend is great fun too; I'm having an excellent night." She poked one of the cubicle doors to check if it was occupied and laughed. "How could you not know that about Stewart? My gaydar went off as soon as I saw him. I mean, it's pretty obvious."

Sophie laughed. "I don't know... I just never thought of it as an option. I guess I'm oblivious to stuff like this." Her eyes wandered down to Mel's lips, and Mel glanced back at her, nodding towards the cubicles.

"Why don't you come in with me? Nobody will notice." Mel arched an eyebrow and shot Sophie a flirty look. It was getting late, and by now, the clientele was loud and cheerful. Two girls were singing along with the song that was playing on the dance floor, and a group of women were clearly celebrating the night with something other than just alcohol, talking non-stop at each other. The cleaning lady was blissfully asleep in her chair with a bag of toilet paper in her arms.

"I don't think that's a good idea," Sophie whispered back, her cheeks bright red. She looked around cautiously, checking the line for anyone she knew. She couldn't wait to get her hands on Mel, but she was terrified that one of her friends might see her. It wasn't their usual hangout, but it was a popular spot for a late night dance and a nightcap. "I don't think I need the toilet after all. Maybe we should go home."

Mel laughed. "Sure, little miss good girl. We can go home, but first, I want you in one of those cubicles with me. We haven't made out in almost a week, and I've been lusting after you all night." Sophie's heart jumped in her chest. Mel looked aroused. She was wearing a low cut white top underneath her black blazer and Sophie could see the outline of her breasts through the thin fabric. She wanted to feel them. She licked her lips and traced Mel's waistline down to her hips, then grabbed her ass for a brief moment. One of the toilet doors opened, and two girls came out together, laughing.

"See?" Mel said. "There's nothing weird about it." She grinned, suddenly looking like she was up to no good. She took Sophie's hand and dragged her into the toilet. Within seconds, she had locked the door and pinned Sophie against the wall, holding her arms up by her wrists.

"God, I've missed you, Sophie." Sophie wanted to protest, but the exquisite feeling of Mel's breasts pressing against her own made her willpower melt away like snow. She found Mel's mouth, hungry for her kiss. First slow and sensual, then deep and possessive. She felt Mel's nipples harden against her chest and it made her ache with desire.

"Turn around and face the wall," Mel whispered in her ear. Sophie's eyes widened in surprise, but she did as she was told. She gasped when Mel slipped a hand underneath her skirt from behind, cupping her ass. She felt hot breath in her ear and against her neck, growing heavier when Mel's fingers moved between her legs, stroking her inner thigh. She moaned quietly. Mel moved up, massaging her centre through her thong. She grabbed Sophie from behind with an arm around her waist before moving a finger underneath the elasticated edge of the lace material. Sophie gasped and arched her back, pressing her behind against Mel's thighs. One finger entered her. Then another. Mel penetrated her slowly.

"I love being inside you." Mel whispered as Sophie bit into her hand against the wall to stop herself from making any more noise whilst Mel's other hand moved down into her thong from the front, stroking her. She moved deeper inside, faster and more determined now. Sophie threw her head back and held her breath, amazed by how Mel knew exactly what to do to send her over the edge in no time. Mel bit into her earlobe and whispered again when she felt Sophie's body tighten. "Is that good?" Sophie didn't dare open her mouth for fear of making too much noise, so she nodded, moving her hips to Mel's rhythm.

"I didn't hear you," Mel said. "Does that feel good?"

"Yes," Sophie panted. "That's so good. Don't stop, please." She kept her eyes shut tight and her hand over her mouth before a hot tingle moved up her legs and spread through her core, exploding into a release that made her legs go weak and her head dizzy. She gasped and leaned back against Mel, who was still inside of her, kissing the back of her neck. She rested a cheek against Mel's face and closed her eyes, taking long, steady breaths, shivering at the aftershocks.

"See? Best idea ever, right?" Mel smiled when Sophie turned around, still stunned.

"That was..." She laughed. "That was amazing."

"I'm glad." Mel smiled and winked. "For the record, I'm not done with you yet." She hesitated and watched the door handle turn. "But I think we need to get out of here before they start banging on the door." Sophie nodded and pulled herself together, straightening her outfit. She felt a familiar presence as they came out of the cubicle, still giggling and holding hands, but it was too late. Her stomach dropped when she saw Marnie in the corridor. Her mouth was gaping and her eyes wide as if she'd just witnessed a six-legged talking monkey appear from out of nowhere. Marnie was one of Cat's friends whom Sophie tried to avoid as much as she could. They had nothing in common, and Sophie didn't like her negative attitude. Marnie looked like she had been so grumpy throughout her life that the corners of her mouth had fixed themselves permanently downwards, her thin lips forming a perfect arch of misery. Except for when there was gossip going around. The moment she heard something juicy, her face lit up immediately. And by the look on her face right now, they had given her enough entertainment for at least a month. Sophie saw her nudging her friend in the ribs before waving at her and panic struck when she couldn't think of anything to say that would explain the situation. She walked up to her and tried to act casual.

"Oh hey, Marnie. How are you?" Marnie's tiny smile told them that they were busted.

"I'm good, thank you. This is Estelle, but I think you two have met before, right?" Sophie nodded and smiled at the girl whose face she vaguely remembered, still blushing. Marnie glanced at Mel, curiosity written all over her face. "And who's your friend?" Sophie looked from Mel to Marnie and back as if she had forgotten her name. Mel came to the rescue.

"I'm Mel," she said, holding out a hand. "Sophie and I work together." That answer didn't seem to satisfy Marnie.

"Ah. So you're the famous Mel. That's great. Cat told me you two have been spending a lot of time together. In fact, word going around is that you might be a bit more than just colleagues. Maybe even more than friends. Is that true?" She looked Mel up and down. Sophie sighed and cocked her head, angry and annoyed. First her mother, then Cat and now this. She couldn't take it anymore. Who was this grown woman to judge her? They weren't teenagers anymore. Marnie didn't even know her well enough to pry. It was simply rude. She took a step forward and regained her grip on Mel's hand.

"Well Marnie," Sophie said in a passive aggressive tone, "not that it's any of your business but if you must know, yes. We are more than just colleagues. Mel's my girlfriend."

"Right," Marnie said, rolling her eyes. "No need to be rude, I was only asking. Not that it wasn't obvious, the way you two came out of that cubicle together. Let me give you some advice, Sophie. If you don't want people to know, don't flaunt it, because word travels fast."

Sophie laughed. "Really? Are you threatening me? I don't care, Marnie. So please go ahead and tell everyone because frankly, I don't give a shit about what people like you think about me anymore." She turned to Mel. "Come on, let's go home."

## 40

"There's my girl," Maggie's voice crackled before her face appeared on Sophie's screen. "I've missed your face, loser. Why haven't you called me back?"

Sophie laughed. "Don't be dramatic, Maggie. You've only called me once, and that was last night. Before that, I couldn't get hold of you." She squinted, focusing on Maggie's background. "Wow, is that your apartment?" Maggie nodded and turned her phone to show the bright white loft with exposed beams and a modern cooking island in the middle of the room.

"It's great, isn't it? Expensive but worth it. We even have a spare bedroom and a roof terrace, so you need to get yourself over here as soon as you can before it gets unbearably hot." She smiled. "I miss you."

"I miss you too." Sophie sighed. "How's the new job? Are they nice to you? Are you nice to them?"

Maggie laughed. "It's good. Everyone is friendly. Quite reserved but friendly nevertheless. I can't say I've made many friends yet, but Dan's introduced me to his friends and family and they're all very nice." She paused. "I really want you to come over. Can't you take a couple of days off? Just for a long weekend? I need some girl time. Just you and me."

Sophie smiled. "Of course I'll come. I can't wait to see you again." She paused. "Just not right now. I have some things to take care of, but maybe next month?"

Maggie frowned and leaned closer into her phone. "What do you need to take care of, your childless, petless, mortgageless free spirit? Did you get yourself into trouble?"

"No, not exactly." Sophie grinned. She didn't feel nervous confiding in Maggie. Not like she had with Cat. "I'm dating a girl. My new colleague, Mel. We fell in love in Hong Kong." Maggie gasped. Then she moved further away from the screen again, studying Sophie's face.

"You're not joking are you?" She chuckled. "That's cool, Sophie. It was about time you met someone who knocked you off your feet. No man has ever been able to do that to you so yeah... it makes sense." She laughed. "Mel, huh? I know I've never met her, but I feel like I know her anyway. I looked her up on social media after I found out she had my job. Went through all of her pictures and her posts." She shot Sophie an apologetic look. "I know it sounds disturbing, but it's not like my social life is booming here in New York, so I spend a lot of time stalking people online. She's very good looking... she's kind of hot. And you know what? I tried, and I tried, but I couldn't really find anything that annoyed me about her."

Sophie nodded. "She's certainly hot. But she's also smart, funny, kind and talented. I feel so lucky." She grinned. "And I will also tell her to switch her account to private." They both laughed, and Sophie sat down on the couch, pulling her legs up underneath her. "But it's all a bit of a mess. I told Cat about Mel in confidence, and now everyone knows about us. She obviously wasn't able to keep it to herself."

Sophie rolled her eyes. "It really upset me. Do you have any idea how scary it is to tell someone you're gay for the first time?" Maggie shook her head before Sophie continued. "But she just had to, didn't she? I've had about twenty missed calls and voicemails from her but the thought of listening to her voice makes me sick right now, so I'm ignoring her." And then on top of that, there was my mother. She found out, and she didn't take it very well. She thinks I'm putting our family to shame and that I'm just looking for attention." She sighed. "I'm furious with her. I haven't spoken to her in weeks. My father doesn't know yet, but I'm going to tell them both next weekend. I'll tell them that I'm serious about Mel." She laughed. "Together with Stew. I recently found out that he's gay too."

Maggie burst out into laughter, snorting wine through her nose. "Stewart? I knew it! Didn't I tell you? Remember that one time we had to pick up the keys at his house? We had a coffee with him in his spotless kitchen with the fancy espresso maker. And you told me I was crazy." She laughed again. "I'm sorry. I know this is a serious matter, but I can't stop picturing your parents' faces when you both tell them you're gay!"

Sophie laughed too. "I know. That should be interesting." She paused. "And to make matters even worse, I've signed to take over from Debbie, so Mel reports into me now." She saw Maggie's puzzled face. "I know. It's kind of fucked up. When I thought about it last minute, I didn't really want the job anymore. Not now my situation has changed with Mel. But Debbie was so desperate, and she literally looked like she was about to give birth on the spot, so I couldn't say no."

Maggie laughed even harder now. "Good Lord. You really did get yourself into trouble, didn't you? Talk of the town and sleeping with your direct report? I leave you on your own for two months and look what happens." She shrugged. "Hey, but at least you're happy, huh? Must be exciting, being in love, having amazing sex. I remember what it was like for me when I first met Dan. Don't get me wrong, I'm still happy with him but that first year was the best time ever."

Sophie smiled. "Yeah. It's great. I just wish it wasn't so complicated. We already had our first fight because she thinks my mother is a nasty piece of work but I guess we're kind of on the same page about that now."

"So what are you going to do about the work situation?" Maggie asked.

Sophie shrugged. "I don't know. Next month I'll have my first performance review with her." She sighed. "That's just wrong. Maybe I should look for another job. Do you think I should look for another job?"

Maggie nodded. "That's probably not a bad idea. And I think you should do it sooner rather than later if you're serious about Mel."

"Thanks, Maggie. I wish you were here. Do you know you're the only sane person in my life apart from Mel right now?"

Maggie laughed. "Wasn't I always?"

## 41

Mel was on her way home when she received a text message from her mother.

*Please come straight home, Mel. We have a visitor.* She read the message again, puzzled by the fact that her mother even knew how to send a text. She usually just called. The tube was crammed with people, and Mel squeezed her way through the crowd, trying to reach the doors before they closed again. She managed to jump out last minute and cursed at a group of tourists, blocking the exit with their suitcases.

After crossing the high street, she passed a Turkish bakery and stopped off to get some Baklava. If they had guests, her mother would expect her to feed them, so she ordered eight pieces with extra honey and pistachio. It was a mild evening and sitting outside on the patio seemed like the perfect way to unwind from her hectic day.

"Hey Mum, what's going on?" Mel entered cheerfully with the bakery bag in one hand and her laptop bag in the other, to find a woman crying in her mother's arms. Isabella waved and held up a hand to greet her, while stroking the woman's back with the other. She seemed relieved that Mel had arrived.

"Melzinha. There you are." Isabella patted the woman who was still sobbing on her shoulder. "Honey, this is Mel. She's here now if you want to talk to her." Mel stared blankly at the lady who, when she finally removed herself from Isabella's embrace, turned out to be roughly her own age. She looked up at Mel.

"Hey," the woman said. "I'm Cat." Her eyes were red from crying. She straightened her hair before getting up to greet Mel. "Glad to meet you." Mel glanced at the immaculately dressed girl who seemed to have stepped straight out of a commercial for household products.

"Hi," Mel stammered, still taken aback by the impromptu visit. "Nice to meet you too, Cat. I didn't expect you here."

Cat looked from Isabella to Mel and back. "I'm sorry for barging in like this." She shuffled on the spot. "I need to talk to you." She regarded Mel with begging eyes.

"You're upset," Mel said, stating the obvious. "Please sit down." She looked at her mother, who pointed at the patio. "Or shall we go outside? Maybe some fresh air will do you good."

Cat nodded. "Outside is fine with me. I just need ten minutes."

"Great idea," Isabella said, leading Cat through the kitchen and into the garden. "I'll get you girls a drink and leave you to it."

Cat sat down on the bench and accepted a glass of the rum mixture, which to Mel smelt stronger than usual. She poured herself a glass too, confused by the drama she had walked into.

Cat took a sip and then another. "I'm sorry to bother

you," she said. "But I didn't know who else to talk to." She started crying again. Mel looked to her mother for help, but Isabella had already disappeared back inside. She took a deep breath and another sip of her drink.

"I assume you're here because of Sophie?" Mel said.

Cat nodded. "I made a big mistake, Mel."

## 42

S ophie opened the door to find Mel with a huge bunch of white roses.

"Could you be any more perfect?" she asked, giving Mel a good glance-over. "I love going on dates with you." Mel wore ripped jeans and her black blazer over a denim shirt, and her hair was held back by a jersey hairband, tied at the top.

Mel smiled and handed her the flowers. "You don't look so bad yourself."

Sophie blushed. She had spent over an hour getting ready, changing from one outfit into another. Even after two months, she was still nervous each time they went on a date. She ran up to put the flowers in a vase and adjusted her blue shirtdress in the antique mirror in her living room before joining Mel in the cab.

"So where are you taking me? I thought we were going somewhere around your house tonight." The cabbie was driving towards Fulham, clearly familiar with the streets as he took numerous back roads to avoid the traffic.

Mel shook her head. "I thought it would be fun to try

something new. Besides, I'm in the mood for some French bistro food. What about you?"

Sophie shrugged. "Sounds good to me. It's just not what I expected, that's all."

Mel sighed. "Okay, here's the thing. Ever since that bloody incident with Marnie at Mayfair, you've been avoiding the places you used to hang out. It's not right. You should feel comfortable where you live." Sophie opened her mouth to speak, but Mel held up a hand. "Wait. Let me finish. Everyone knows about us by now so why would you still go through the trouble of hiding it? I'm sure most of your friends won't care. They just want you to be happy." She shifted in the back seat and turned to Sophie. "But you'll never find out if you ignore them. You haven't answered your phone in weeks. You're avoiding your parents and your friends. I don't want you to cut yourself off from the people you love because of me. It feels wrong."

"But I prefer spending time with you," Sophie protested. "I can't be bothered with the small talk anymore, tip-toeing around the subject."

Mel smiled and took her hand. "And I prefer spending time with you. But that doesn't mean you should forget about everyone else. I still see my friends every week."

The cab stopped in front of a cosy French restaurant with a green-tiled façade and an art-deco sign that said, Chez Patrick.

"How do you know about this place?" Sophie asked as they followed the waiter through the restaurant into the courtyard. "I used to come here a lot, but I haven't been in a while." Sophie sat down when the waiter pulled back a chair for her at one of the enamelled tables under a red parasol.

Mel sat down too and looked at the menu. "I heard it was good. Never been here myself." She looked up. "Wine?"

"Sure." Sophie frowned. "Wait. Is that..." Her heart jumped in her throat when she saw Cat entering the courtyard. "Fuck. It's Cat," she whispered, hiding her face behind the menu.

Mel pulled the leather binder down. "I know. I invited her."

Sophie shot her an angry look. "How could you? You know I don't want to speak to her!" Mel ignored her and stood up to greet Cat as if they had known each other for years. Then she turned to Sophie.

"Don't leave, Sophie. Please. Just hear her out, okay?"

Sophie sighed and glanced up at Cat. She looked terrified. Her eyes were bigger than Sophie had ever seen them, and she shifted nervously from one foot to another before she sat down.

"I can't tell you how sorry I am, Sophie. I made a big mistake, and you have every right to be angry." She sighed. "If you never want to speak to me again, I understand. I just want you to know that I'll always regret what I did."

Sophie flinched. "Sorry for what? Sorry for telling everyone the only secret I ever asked you to keep? I wanted to tell people myself, Cat. When I was ready. How could you do this to me?" Sophie's vision was blurred by anger but not enough to miss the tears running down Cat's cheeks.

"I only told Marnie," she sniffled. "She drove me home after a game of bridge one night. I was drunk, and it was stupid. I regretted it straight away, but she promised to keep it to herself." She cradled her forehead in her hands. "I'm so very sorry, Sophie. I understand if you can't trust me anymore, but I can't lose you as a friend. You're the only real friend I have."

Sophie shook her head. "Then you should have thought of that before you blurted."

"I was jealous," Cat cried. "I was jealous that you had another woman in your life who was special to you. I felt like I was being replaced."

Although Sophie was ready to leave the table, there was something about Cat's words that caught her attention. "What do you mean, Cat?" She lowered her gaze to meet Cat's eyes.

"I know I meant something to you once, Sophie. When we were younger. I still remember it like it was yesterday. The way you used to look at me... I saw that look in your eyes when you told me about Mel. And all of a sudden, I understood. It wasn't me anymore. It was her." Cat removed the cutlery from her napkin and blew her nose on it. "I felt the same way about you back then, but I never told you. Just like you never told me, and I guess I always liked the fact that you were available. That you were mine somehow, even though nothing would ever happen between us. Oh God, I've been so selfish." Sophie was too stunned by the confession to think of anything to say, but her anger made place for pity when Cat started sobbing again. She turned to Mel, begging for help.

Mel shook her head and nodded towards Cat, who was now in floods of tears. "Talk to her," she whispered.

Sophie moved her chair and put a hand on Cat's shoulder. "Please stop crying, Cat. I didn't know you felt like this. I had no idea." She sighed. "The fact that I'm with Mel doesn't change our friendship. It has nothing to do with us. I might be angry, but I still love you. You're my oldest and dearest friend. You're just a bit... stupid sometimes."

Cat looked up, a glance of hope sparkling in her eyes. "Really? You don't hate me?"

"Of course I don't hate you, Cat. I'm angry. But I guess what's done is done and if you regret it as much as you say you do, there's no point in holding grudges. I'll get over it eventually so let's try to move forward from here." Sophie smiled at her, and she meant it. Cat was a mess, and she hated seeing her this way. "So just to be clear, Cat. You're not gay, are you?"

Cat shook her head, and finally, she laughed. "No, I'm not. It was just a phase, a silly crush." She paused. "But you're still the most special person to me in this world. I admire your courage and your strength to make your own decisions, to live your own life the way you want to. You know, I used to be jealous of Maggie too. The way the two of you were so careless and free, going out, traveling together, both doing whatever the hell you wanted. When she came into the picture, I felt like I was your boring friend. Nothing ever happens in my life. I'm settled, quite miserable and I always complain about my situation, but I never do anything about it. I was kind of happy when you told me she was moving away and I'm sorry for that too. I should have been more supportive." She shrugged. "I thought I might as well dish up and tell you everything now."

Sophie fought back the tears. She stood up, walked around Cat's chair and gave her a hug from the back. Cat embraced her forearms and sighed in relief. "Thank you." She chuckled. "I hope you both don't think I'm a psycho after what I've told you."

"Absolutely not," Mel said. "I like you, and I appreciate that you came to me." She laughed. "And I haven't even seen you on a good day."

Sophie looked from Mel to Cat and back. "So when did you two meet behind my back?"

Cat bit her lip. "You didn't pick up your phone, and you

didn't reply to my messages. I tried your parents, but they told me they hadn't seen you in weeks either. So I tracked Mel down, and I showed up at her door last week. I was hoping she could help me. Mel wasn't home, but her mother was, and she let me in. She was so kind to me, and before I knew it, I had poured my heart out to her. I feel embarrassed about that, Mel. I really do."

Mel laughed. "Don't be. My mother has a way of drawing information out of people. She would have done a great job in the secret service." She turned back to Sophie. "So anyway, I came home, and there was Cat, crying in my mother's arms. I can't even begin to tell you how surprised I was when she introduced herself."

Cat blushed. "Mel was just as lovely as her mother, and I immediately understood what you saw in her. She promised me she would try to get us together so we could talk. You've hit the jackpot with her, Sophie."

Sophie smiled and looked at Mel, who leaned back and seemed completely relaxed in the chaos of the moment. "I know. She's one of a kind." She put a hand on Mel's thigh. "And look at those dimples! How sexy are they?"

Now it was Mel's turn to blush. "I'm glad you're not angry with me," she said. "I wasn't sure if you would kill me when I invited Cat without telling you."

"I'm not angry." Sophie held up a hand for the waiter, who had been discreetly waiting in the back of the garden, to take their drinks order. "I'm glad you did."

They ordered a bottle of Chablis and Sophie waited until they were alone again. "I'm going to talk to my parents on Sunday, tell them everything. Stew is coming with me so let's hope for the best." She took Mel's hand and then Cat's. "Even if it's a disaster, I'll still have the best two people in the world on my side."

## 43

"Oh, come in my darlings," Eleanor said as she opened the door to Sophie and Stewart. She gave them both a hug. "It seems like a million years since both our children were here at the same time, doesn't it David?" Their father looked genuinely happy to see them both, and he greeted them with a broad smile - a rare phenomenon for him.

Stewart nudged Sophie as they hung up their coats in the hallway. "She seems suspiciously chirpy today, don't you think?"

Sophie shrugged. "Maybe it's her way of saying she's sorry," she whispered. "Or maybe she's actually happy that I'm here after ignoring her for three weeks. Who knows?"

"Or," Stewart jumped in, "Maybe her friends have started questioning why we haven't been over lately, and now she's relieved that she doesn't have to make up excuses anymore." Sophie giggled and gestured for him to stop talking. Stewart seemed nervous. He was fidgeting with his keys as he walked into the living room where the dining table had been set for eight people.

"It's just us today, isn't it Mum?" Sophie asked, staring at the display. "That's what we agreed on."

"Well..." Her mother pulled a painful face. "I know you wanted a quiet one, but I'm afraid it's not just us. I bumped into Lauren a couple of days ago at Partridges. You know, Allan's new wife. She said she would love to meet you. She works in fashion as well. I'm not exactly sure what she does, but I think she has some kind of swimwear label and she's looking for designers because her business is booming at the moment. So that should be interesting, right?" She didn't wait for Sophie's reply. "And then," she continued nervously, "of course I had to invite Deborah and Mark as well. It would just be rude not to, considering Deborah and Lauren know each other from yoga class and I don't want her to think I'm stealing her friend from her or that they're not welcome. You know how word gets around, don't you dear?" She attempted to raise her eyebrows in a cheerful manner, but one of them didn't move.

Stewart sighed. "Ok Mum, but we need to discuss something important, whether it's now or after they've left. It's up to you."

Their father looked up in curiosity. "What do we need to discuss?"

Before anyone could answer, Eleanor had thrown herself in between them. "David, I'm sure it can wait for a bit. I need Sophie to help me in the kitchen right now, or we won't be ready before our guests arrive. Stewart, could you get the condiments, please? They're on the kitchen table." It was more a command than a question. Sophie and Stewart exchanged annoyed glances before getting to work on the preparations for Sunday lunch.

"She's going to regret this," Stewart whispered. "It's so typically her. Anything to avoid discussing the elephant in the room." Sophie felt a nervous pang in her stomach. Although Stewart was usually quite calm and composed, Sophie had witnessed his outbursts several times over the years. She felt the same anger in him today, and it worried her.

"Maybe it's not such a bad thing," she whispered, trying to calm him down. "At least they'll have had a couple of drinks before we tell them." She went to work in the kitchen, searching for the right serving trays. Sophie was still furious with her mother, but she tried to stay calm. *Don't shout at her. Not now. It's not going to make things better.*

"Darling, not that one," her mother pulled her out of her thoughts. "The asparagus goes on the white tray so I can heat them up later." She studied Sophie as if she was trying to read her current state of mind. She had obviously not anticipated both her children wanting to have 'the talk' so badly, and it was the one thing she truly dreaded. She desperately tried to change the mood in the kitchen.

"Would you like to see my new boudoir later? We used your father's old office. There's lots of really nice skincare products and makeup in there if you'd like to borrow some?"

Sophie stared back at her blankly. "You want me to put on makeup? Do I look that bad?" She squinted. "Have you invited Aldo around again? Because if you have, you'll wish you never did in about twenty minutes from now."

Her mother raised her hands in defence. "No, of course I haven't, dear. I just thought you might like to see it. We had an interior designer around yesterday. I'm trying to get the house up to standard for when London Living Magazine come over to do a spread on 'Modern Victorian'. There are a couple of things we need to change but no major refurbishments. The master bedroom will need a makeover, and the kitchen needs some TLC." She pointed at the fridge as if it was a virus. "We'll have to replace that one too; the designer says it doesn't go with the style of a traditional Victorian kitchen."

Sophie looked at the fridge. "What's wrong with it? You only bought it last year and you'd been eyeing it up for God knows how long. It was two thousand pounds. Is dad okay paying for all of this? I bet he doesn't know, does he?" Eleanor wasn't prepared for that question and looked relieved when the bell rang. She sprinted towards the hallway, straightening her cashmere dress on the way. Sophie heard excited screams and false compliments flying around like there was no tomorrow. Someone telling her mother she looked better than ever was like telling a homeless person he'd just won the lottery. Some of Sophie's old friends had started to act in the same way lately, doing the squeaky thing like their mothers. It kind of annoyed her, but she never said anything about it. Deborah and Lauren came to greet her in the kitchen. Lauren was a lot younger than she had expected and she looked immaculate. She was tall and slender and had long, blonde, sleek hair and full red lips that looked like they might have had a bit of work done. Her simple black dress was by an exclusive designer label and fitted perfectly around her amazing figure. Suddenly, Sophie felt very under-groomed, and she wished she'd gone through a bit more effort before she'd left.

"Lovely to meet you," Lauren said, smiling. It was an honest smile, and Sophie liked her immediately. *What the hell is she doing with Allan? Surely she could do better than him? Is she with him for the money?*

"I'm sorry to get right to the point, but I heard you're an excellent designer," Lauren said in a confident tone. "And I happen to need one urgently, so maybe we could talk over lunch? I'm not trying to pressure you into anything but I think you should at least hear me out, it might be interesting to you."

Sophie nodded and smiled. "Of course we can," she said. "No harm in talking. I just need to help my mother prepare lunch, and I'll be out there in ten minutes. Wine?" She held up a glass and a cool bottle of Pinot Grigio from the fridge. Lauren gratefully accepted it and left Sophie to prepare the hors d'oeuvres of salmon and quails eggs. She certainly didn't beat around the bush, this lady. Sophie watched her shake hands with Stewart, who looked like he was about to explode and start pooping rainbows any minute now but he managed to pull his face into a polite smile and complimented her on her dress. Sophie would be lying to herself if she said she wasn't at least a bit curious about the job. It was difficult, being around Mel in the office and pretending they were just mere colleagues. But she hadn't actively started looking for another job and hadn't called any head-hunters yet. She'd been too consumed spending time with Mel, not to mention stressing about how she would tell her parents. If it were up to Stewart, the whole table would know within the hour. By the time they sat down, he was chewing his food slowly, passing shifty looks to both their parents while trying to participate in the conversation about buying second-hand cars versus new ones. Mark was thinking about buying a vintage car now that the children had moved out and Deborah was passionately against the Jaguar Oldtimer he'd been drooling over on eBay.

"Eleanor, please tell him he's being ridiculous," she pleaded. "We'll look like a bunch of idiots, driving through Wimbledon in that car." She turned to Mark. "How do you even know you can trust the seller when you buy it online? We've always bought our cars from the BMW dealer around the corner. How on earth are we going to explain this to him? And what if it breaks down? You can't even change a lightbulb, let alone fix a car!" Deborah dramatically shook her head and massaged her temples. "Never mind. I'll just drive my own car. I don't even want to be seen in that thing. It's blue for goodness' sake." Mark ignored her and passed his phone around with a boyish grin, showing the picture of the bright blue monster he was planning to bid on whether his wife agreed or not.

When the conversation was flowing, and the food was being passed around the table, Lauren turned to Sophie.

"So let me tell you a little bit about myself and my brand if you don't mind." She kept her voice down, trying to have a more private conversation around the crowded table.

"Sure," Sophie said. "I'm all ears. You have a swimwear label, right?"

Lauren nodded. "That's right. I started it about five years ago, after quitting my job in fashion P.R. It wasn't my passion, just something I was good at. Besides that, it paid well, and you know how important that is in London." She laughed. "I actually graduated in design and always dreamed about having my own brand, but I never had the courage to give up my job. Besides that, I didn't have the capital." She rolled her eyes and laughed nervously. Sophie nodded, waiting for her to continue. "Anyway, one day I was so incredibly frustrated with my job that I quit. I panicked at first, but during the third day at home I needed something to do so I started sketching and designed a small swimwear range." She winked at Sophie and whispered: "I used to be a swimwear model to finance my student bills. Best years of my life."

"I'm not surprised," Sophie said. "You have a great body for it."

Lauren smiled at the compliment. "Thank you. I'm way

too old for that now, unfortunately. So as I was saying, I designed the range, and I had no clue what I was doing. I found a small manufacturer in Turkey, and they gave me a reasonable deal for my initial samples. I had some savings and managed to make it work."

"That's so brave," Sophie raised an eyebrow. "I don't think I'd have had the courage to do that." Lauren shrugged.

"Well, I can't say I wasn't scared. I put everything I had into it, and that wasn't enough by a long chalk. But I got lucky and found an investor." She pointed to Allan who blew her a kiss over the table.

Sophie's eyes widened. "So that's how you two met?"

Lauren shook her head. "It's not what you think. And believe me, I know what people think of me. He's older, so everyone assumes that I'm a gold digger and that I'm just after his money. It wasn't like that at all. Allan helped me get my business off the ground because he believed in me." She laughed. "Okay, maybe not at first. He was looking for start-ups to invest in to protect his capital in case his wife spent all their money before the divorce went through. But he saw that I was a hard worker and passionate about the brand so he was happy to help me under the strict rule that he would keep a close watch on the financial side of it. We were just acquaintances and business partners at first, and we had a great working relationship for four years. Allan was going through a difficult time with his divorce, and I was focusing on growing the business. It wasn't until about a year ago that we discovered we had feelings for each other." She smiled at the memory.

"We were celebrating the five million mark of Laurelai and got quite drunk together. I think that's when I started to find him attractive. He was flirting with me shamelessly, and we discovered we had a lot in common. I'd never witnessed him drunk, but then our relationship had always been strictly business. Not long after that, we were sharing a bed too." She grinned at Sophie's shocked expression.

"That's a sweet story," Sophie said. "But I'm also really impressed by the fact that your brand is Laurelai. I love that brand. I have one of your bikinis in my wardrobe. The one with the tassels, from two years ago. Why didn't you tell me straight away?" Sophie felt excited now. How did she get so lucky? The founder of one of her favourite brands was sitting right next to her, practically offering her an interview on a plate.

Lauren raised her glass and clinked with Sophie's. "You didn't ask. And I can't assume that everyone knows my brand, we're not that big yet. We sell in small boutiques and in a lot of high-end department stores, but that's about it. It's booming though. We have some capital to invest now, and I've just hired someone to expand our brand into online channels and create our own online flagship store. I've noticed I enjoy the business side of it just as much as the designing. Alan taught me a lot over the years, and I think I can manage on my own now, so I'm planning on hiring a designer to take over that part from me. It's getting too hectic trying to juggle everything by myself, and I want to spend more time with Allan now that he's close to early retirement, traveling and enjoying life together." She glanced over at him lovingly and then turned her attention back to Sophie. "I need someone I can trust," she said. When your mother told me about you and what you do, I wanted to meet you and perhaps get together so you can show me some of your work or some ideas? You might be happy where you are now, but I can assure you that you won't get any grief from anyone if you work for me. If I like your work, and you manage to stay on brand, I'll leave it all to you, and you'll have full autonomy over the range." She raised a questioning eyebrow and cocked her head. "So, what do you think? Shall we meet up to go through your portfolio?"

Sophie laughed nervously. "You mean you're giving me an interview?" she stammered. "I'm flattered. In fact, it's perfect timing. I've got some issues at work at the moment that I'm trying to work through. Nothing serious," she hastily added. "But yes, I'd love to meet up to show you some sketches and prints." Lauren seemed pleased with the answer and cheerfully passed their empty plates on to Eleanor, who apparently had been eavesdropping on their conversation all along. Sophie could tell by the smirk on her face.

"Care to tell me what your problems were about?" Lauren asked. "Not that it's any of my business, but I might be able to give you some advice?" Sophie glanced over at her mother, and Lauren detected the cautiousness in her eyes.

"I'm going for a cigarette in the garden," she said matter-of-factly. "I know smoking is frowned upon by our fellow table companions, but I always love to have one after dinner. Join me? We can talk there."

Any excuse to get away from the table was a good excuse as far as Sophie was concerned and she felt herself warming to Lauren. She seemed honest, straightforward and surprisingly bright. And somehow, Sophie felt like she could trust her. Maybe it wasn't the smartest move, opening up to a potential employer but it felt like the right thing to do, and so she told Lauren about her current situation. She even told her about the announcement to her parents that was supposed to happen that afternoon. Lauren listened attentively as she took long drags from her thin menthol cigarette and nodded in an understanding manner after Sophie had finished.

"I'm so happy for you," she said. "You might have found the love of your life, and that's beautiful." She flicked the stub into a bucket under the drain pipe and put a hand on Sophie's shoulder. "You have to be strong now and tell them. The sooner you do, the sooner they'll adjust to the idea." She paused, searching for the right words. "I like your parents. They've been very kind to me today. I've had quite different social experiences since Allan and I got together. People assume things about me and judge me, but your mother has made me feel very welcome. My own friends are quite different from Allan's friends. They're more open-minded, I guess. Maybe it's because I'm younger, I don't know. I was quite nervous coming here today but I'm trying to make it work so we can have a life together. I want that for us, to be together as much as we can. Share things. And I want that for you too. Your parents don't seem unreasonable. Just give them some time and they'll come around." She smiled. "I'm willing to bet a thousand pounds that if your relationship works out, we'll all be around the table together six months from now, including Mel."

"Thanks," Sophie said. "I appreciate that. My mother already knows of course but she needs to understand that it's not a phase. And my father... well, I have no idea how he's going to react but I just want to get it over with." She'd left Stewart out of the conversation. It was his decision to tell people, not hers.

"Thanks for telling me," Lauren grinned. "I wouldn't have asked if I didn't think it was strictly work related and I certainly don't want you to think I'm nosey. But it's inspiring. You're inspiring. And I'm looking forward to our next meeting."

.  .  .

A COUPLE OF HOURS LATER, Sophie, Stewart, Eleanor, and
David were sitting alone at the end of the long dining table.
Eleanor was trying to make out that she was tired but their
father wasn't having any of it.

"Nonsense Eleanor. It's not often we have both our children around the table. Let's have a coffee and a brandy
together so we can finally have a quiet family conversation
without that bloody Deborah and her opinions interrupting us
every five seconds." Stewart couldn't help but chuckle, despite
his nervousness. Their father didn't seem to be joking though.

"I'm serious, Eleanor. I've begged you not to invite that
woman over every single Sunday but you just can't help
yourself. I have women like her in my chair and on my table
all day long. I don't need to deal with them on my precious
time off." Eleanor shot him an angry look but he ignored
her. "I'm telling you, that woman is not mentally stable
enough to have a glass of wine. She gets intrusive and opin-
ionated and Mark poor old chap... well, frankly I think he
suffers." He refilled his brandy glass and offered one to
Sophie and Stewart too, before clearing his throat.

"Now, I'm not an idiot like some of you may think. Something's been going on here. You've all been acting strange
and I want to know what you've been keeping from me.
Come on, spill it."

Stewart, who had been planning this moment for most
of his life, looked him straight in the eyes. There was no fear
in them anymore. Sophie could tell he wanted to get it out
of the way, whatever the outcome may be. He could live with
their reaction either way, he had told her.

"I'm gay, dad. And I have a boyfriend. His name is

Roberto. He's Italian and we've been seeing each other for six months." Their father stared at him, expressionless. It was the same look he gave their mother each time he told her she looked great after yet another round of fillers and injections and it was impossible to read his thoughts. Tiny drops of sweat trickled down his neck and nestled in the collar of his crisp white shirt. He opened the top two buttons and removed his tie. He said nothing.

Stewart sighed, relieved that the words were out. When no one spoke, he nudged Sophie, urging her to say something too. Sophie felt her face go bright red. She wanted to run out of the front door, escape from her father's blank stare. But Stewart had done his part and now it was her turn.

"Okay, so I'm gay too," she blurted. "I have a girlfriend. Her name is Mel. You met her; she's the girl I work with." Her heart was racing, and she held her breath, waiting for the moment they would be kicked out of the house. Then, at least, they would both have a reason to hate their parents and wouldn't have to worry about what they thought of them anymore.

Their father shuffled in his chair uncomfortably, avoiding eye contact. It was very out of character for him. Her mother looked nervously from her children to her husband and back. They sat there in eerie silence, waiting for someone to react. It was their mother who spoke after clearing her throat numerous times.

"Despite what you may think of me, you're my children and I love you." Both Sophie and Stewart sighed in relief. They waited for their mother to continue but she couldn't seem to find the words. Eleanor looked like a deer in the headlights. Her eyes were wide, her upper lip trembled and there was a nervous twitch in her left cheek, the only muscle that still seemed to be functioning.

Sophie felt a tear of relief rolling down her cheek and she smiled. "Thank you, Mum. We love you too." She swallowed hard, grasping the opportunity to speak for them both. She had practiced this in her mind over and over again in preparation.

"We know this may not be the ideal situation for you or the future you had planned for us, but I can assure you that we're both very happy. And that's what counts, right?" Stewart nodded and Eleanor tried to force a tiny smile, leaving her mouth slightly crooked. She looked at her husband, begging him with her eyes to speak. David downed his brandy and poured himself another one, finally looking up.

"I knew about Stewart," he said. "I've always known." He turned to Stewart. "At least since you were in your teens. I found some magazines in your room when you were about fifteen. I was searching your room for drugs because you'd been behaving strangely and I was worried about you. When I found them, I was shocked but also relieved to know you didn't have a drug problem. I realized you were struggling with your identity and I'm sorry I didn't help you through that. I had no idea how. For that, I owe you an apology." He sighed. "I suppose I was hoping it would pass one day. Thought maybe it was a phase. I've been waiting for you to tell me for a long time." His eyes shifted to Sophie while he fiddled with his napkin.

"But Sophie, I must say... I didn't see that coming from you." He opened another button on his shirt, clearly uncomfortable with the topic. "It's just a surprise, that's all." He folded his hands on the table, usually a sign that he was done speaking, especially in a difficult conversation.

Stewart looked surprised. There was a shift in his demeanour, going from standby fight mode to a more passive Stewart. He leaned back in his chair and his shoulders dropped. The vein in his neck had stopped pumping vigorously.

"Wow. Okay." He said. "I guess that makes it a bit easier. Thank you, both, for being so understanding. We know it will take some time to get used to it but I'm glad we've taken the first step."

There was another awkward silence and Sophie got up from the table. "Thank you for lunch. I'm glad we had this talk." She turned to Stewart. "Stew, I think it might be best if we go now. I can imagine Mum and Dad have a lot to talk about."

## 44

"Well, well. You certainly know how to charm a woman," Mel laughed. Sophie was at her door with a bottle of wine and an Italian takeaway. She took the bottle while brushing her lips against Sophie's. "Thank you. For being so amazing." She sighed. "I wish we were alone right now." Sophie grinned and followed Mel into the living room, staring at her behind. Mel was wearing an oversized sweater and a pair of tiny shorts. She was one of the very few people Sophie knew who could wear just about anything and get away with it. She looked casually sexy, and it was terribly distracting.

Sophie almost forgot that Isabella was on the couch. When she saw her, she bent down, levelling with her. "Hi, Isabella. These are for you," she said, taking a box of chocolates out of her bag.

Isabella sat up and adjusted the pillow behind her back. "Thank you, Sophie. You're a darling. Come here and give me a hug." She reached for Sophie and grinned in Mel's direction. "Did you hear that, Melzinha? These are for me, not you."

"Just wait until you've had your next pain killer," Mel shouted from the kitchen. "You'll be zoned out, and by the time you wake up, they'll be gone." She came back in with three plates, two wine glasses, and cutlery.

"So, how's the patient?" Sophie asked. "I'm glad the operation went well."

Isabella pulled a painful grimace while she shifted on the couch. "Not too bad. I'm relieved I came out on the other end. It's a scary thing you know, putting your life in someone else's hands. I'm terrified of hospitals.

"She was declaring her dying love for the surgeon when she woke up," Mel said, laughing.

"Don't make fun of me, Melzinha," her mother said. She rolled her eyes. "I might have said something about him being handsome but he complimented me on my kimono, and I was confused from the medication they gave me." She giggled. "The surgeon did a good job though; I'm grateful to him. I just need to keep taking the painkillers until the worst of the post-op bruising is healed. But in general, I feel good." She lifted her shirt, revealing a medical corset. "Apart from this thing. It's too tight, and I have to wear it for five weeks." She sighed. "I don't like to complain, but every time I eat, I feel like I'm about to burst. And you know how much I like to eat, don't you, Sophie?"

Sophie laughed and patted her on the shoulder. "I know. But it's probably tight for a reason. Just do what the doctor tells you to, and you'll be able to eat whatever you want, wherever you want in no time."

Isabella nodded and put a hand on Sophie's wrist. "Enough about me. I heard you got the job. Congratulations, that's great!"

"Thanks," Sophie said. "It's exciting. I've already handed in my resignation, and I've got the feeling Mel will have my job soon." She looked at Mel, who smiled back at her. Isabella's eyes widened.

"Really, Melzinha? Are they giving Sophie's job to you? Why didn't you tell me?"

Mel shrugged and smiled, showing off her dimples. "Maybe, yes. I didn't want you to get all worked up before your operation, so I kept it quiet. Let's wait and see before we celebrate, but it looks like it." Mel handed out the plates and opened the boxes of antipasti on the table.

"Mmm, let's see, what have we got here... Artichokes, tomato and buffalo mozzarella, Parma ham, fennel and blood orange salad..." She opened the final box with a big smile. "And lots and lots of garlic bread. Good choice, Sophie. I'm proud of you." She winked and scooped up some salad before taking a seat on the armrest of Sophie's chair.

"Something strange happened today," she said.

Sophie raised an eyebrow. "Good strange or bad strange?"

"Good strange." Mel paused. "Your mother called me. At work." Sophie leaned back in her chair and stared up at Mel in disbelief. Isabella's mouth was gaping. For once, she was speechless too.

"My mother? I don't believe that." Sophie looked stunned.

Mel nodded. "She sure did." She giggled at Sophie's confused expression. "I can't say I wasn't surprised myself. She was nice to me. A bit strange maybe, but kind. She kept blabbing on about the refurbishment of her bedroom for some magazine spread as if she had no idea how to start the conversation or what to say to me in general. Anyway, we're both invited for dinner tomorrow night. Your brother and Roberto will be there too."

Sophie stared at her before she burst into laughter, almost spilling the wine in her lap. "Really? You're serious, aren't you? I can't believe it. It doesn't sound like my mother at all." She frowned. "That must have been one awkward conversation."

"A little bit," Mel admitted. "But she's making an effort and if she's willing to try again, then so am I."

Sophie put her plate on the table and hugged her. "Thanks, Mel. I appreciate it, but you don't have to do that. I know she's not your favourite person in the world."

"No, Sophie. I want to do this. I'm determined for your mother to like me and I'm determined to like her back. Even if it's just a little bit," Mel said, stacking tomato and mozzarella onto her fork.

Isabella smiled. "You have no idea how happy I am to hear that, Melzinha. See? I told you Sophie's mother would come around, didn't I? It was only a matter of time." She smiled at Sophie, who was attacking the garlic bread. "Never underestimate a mother. They can be full of surprises."

## 45

"Thanks for having me, Eleanor. I can imagine this might be as strange for you as it is for me." Eleanor smiled, and Mel reminded herself not to stare at her. She was still getting used to Eleanor's face that started leading a life of its own each time she tried to express her mood.

"Well, I thought it would only be appropriate to celebrate Sophie's new job at Laurelai." Eleanor yanked at the white cotton tablecloth, then rearranged it, pulling on either side until it was perfectly symmetric. Mel could tell she was nervous.

"Can I help you with anything?" Mel tried to make eye contact, but Eleanor looked down, avoiding her. "No, thank you, dear. I think I can manage." She sighed and sat down at the end of the table, resting her chin on her folded hands. She gestured for Mel to take a seat opposite her. "Can we talk for a moment?"

Mel nodded. "Sure, no problem."

Eleanor rolled up her sleeves and sighed, bracing herself for a difficult conversation. "I believe I owe you an apology for last time you were here. I'm so very sorry if I made you feel uncomfortable. That was never my intention. Sophie told me you were upset because of me and I've thought about it a lot." She looked up, finally meeting Mel's eyes. "You may not believe me, but I don't usually speak to Marisol in that way. It was insensitive and rude, and I regret it." She sighed. "I sensed this energy between the two of you. The way you both looked at each other, the way Sophie acted around you... A mother knows, you know. It made me feel uneasy. I think that deep down, I knew something was going on, and I wasn't myself that day. I want you to know that I've apologized to Marisol."

Mel nodded. "And now? Are you still uncomfortable?"

Eleanor thought about the question. "I suppose so," she answered honestly. "But I know I will get used to the idea eventually." She nodded towards the sofa where Sophie's father was reading his newspaper. "I expected David to have a meltdown, but he's handled this situation a whole lot better than me." She paused. "I'm trying, Mel."

Mel took her hand over the table. "Fine. Then let's forget about it and move on. I can imagine it might be over-whelming when both your children suddenly come out." She smiled at her. "Thank you for trying."

Eleanor looked away. Her upper lip was trembling. Mel could tell she was getting emotional and stood up from the table to make it easier for both of them.


"THIS LOOKS GREAT." Roberto passed the potato puree to Sophie's father, who seemed strangely at ease in the company of Roberto and Mel. Sophie regarded him from across the table. He scooped up a generous amount and passed it on with a content look on his face.

"Yes," he said. "It certainly does. Eleanor is a great chef." He winked at Marisol, who was just getting ready to go home for the day. "And it tastes even better without Deborah yapping in my ear."

"Mmm, how do you get it so flavoursome?" Roberto asked, looking at Eleanor. "I can taste truffle and something perhaps a little herbier." He lifted a finger. "Wait... I think I know. Is it tarragon butter?" Sophie and Mel watched his performance in amusement. They knew exactly what he was doing after informing him about Eleanor's fake status as the master chef.

But Eleanor held her own like she always did. "Yes, I believe it is," she lied. "I don't do recipes, Roberto. I'd rather cook with my gut. Isn't that what the Italians do?"

Roberto nodded as he dabbed his mouth with his napkin. "Some do. But only the great chefs in my family know how to cook fantastic food on intuition alone. My mother still follows my grandmother's recipes to the T and treats them like science. He winked at Eleanor. "So compliments to you."

Eleanor beamed, and Sophie noticed how she was able to look him straight in the eyes. "Thank you," she said. "I'll take that.' Sophie started to relax. Despite the fact that she was lying through her teeth, her mother hadn't said anything to insult Mel or Roberto yet. And maybe she wouldn't. She tried to divert the subject back to her mother again to keep it that way.

"So Mum, what did you do today?" Eleanor looked at her suspiciously. It was a question Sophie rarely asked her mother because quite frankly, Eleanor's life was as predictable as a wasp on speed and she always knew exactly what her mother was up to.

"Well," Eleanor started. "It's Friday, so I went to

Partridges get some groceries for the weekend. It's been ever so busy there lately, so I went early this morning. After that, I met Deborah for lunch at Nola in Fulham. They serve lovely diet friendly dishes there, all fresh and organic. Deborah couldn't believe her luck when she realized the whole menu was gluten free." She cleared her throat and passed a shifty look from Mel to Sophie and back. "She was very pleased to tell me that Aldo had finally brought a young lady home. Her name is Estelle, and he's quite smitten with her. She's a friend of Cat, apparently, so you might know her."

Sophie grinned. "Great," she said. "I'm happy for him."

Mel nodded. "Yes. Good for him. He seems like a ..." She hesitated. "He seems like a nice guy."

Eleanor rolled her eyes. "No need to play polite, girls. I know how you both feel about him." She made an attempt to fold her lips around a bite of salad but missed and sighed in frustration. "We also talked about the two of you. And about Stewart and Roberto. I told her you were all coming for dinner tonight." She glanced around the table and settled on her husband, who gave her an encouraging nod to continue. "Deborah said she was very impressed by Mel and that she would love to meet Roberto too, but I told her that tonight was just for us."

Sophie's jaw dropped, and she turned to Stewart, who looked every bit as surprised. He bent over the table and put a hand on his mother's. "Thank you," he said sincerely. "For not sticking your head in the sand again. I'll be honest, I had little hope this day would ever come, but I'm so glad we're all here now." He squeezed her hand. "I'm proud of you, Mum."

Eleanor looked down at her plate. "Don't say that," she sniffed. "I haven't handled this well. I..."

"It's okay, Mum," Stewart interrupted her. "We know you're sorry and we know you were just doing what you thought was right. Let's talk about this another time and enjoy the evening."

Eleanor nodded and straightened her dress, suddenly snapping back into her role. "Fine," She said. "Another time would be better, I suppose." She turned to Mel. "So tell me, Mel, how is your mother after her operation? Sophie told me she came home a couple of days ago."

Mel held her wine glass up for Sophie's father to refill it. "She's doing alright, thank you for asking. It will take a while before she's recovered, but she's starting her physio next week, and hopefully, she'll be able to move back to her apartment or even do her own grocery shopping again in a couple of months' time."

Eleanor smiled. "That's good to hear, Mel. Please send her our regards."

Sophie squeezed Mel's thigh under the table. Although they were all still on edge, it was going better than expected.

"And what about your parents, Roberto?" Sophie's father asked. "Do they live in the U.K.?"

Roberto shook his head. "No, they live in Italy. I visit them twice a year, but they've never been over here." He laughed. "But that's okay. Italian families can be quite full-on, and I'm not sure if I could handle having them in my tiny apartment." He bent forward and lowered his voice. "I suspect they might not be human. I don't remember a time I've ever seen them go to sleep. They're still up when I go to bed, drinking and gossiping, and they're up when I wake up, complaining that I'm the last one to join them for breakfast." He made wild hand gestures while he was talking. "My uncles and aunties and their children all live in the same street, and they gather in my parents' garden on weekends. I'm always exhausted after my holiday." They all laughed.

Sophie's father cleared his throat. "And your parents, how do they feel about..." He wiggled his finger from Stewart to Roberto and back. "The eh... the situation?"

Roberto cocked his head. "You mean about the fact that I'm gay?"

David Scott blushed. "Yes, exactly that," he stammered.

Roberto sighed dramatically. "Well, I'm not going to lie, it hasn't been easy growing up gay in an Italian Catholic family. Especially in a small village. It was always quite obvious with me, so I was teased a lot at school. People aren't as accepting in my hometown as they are here in London, although that was a long time ago. Things might have changed now with the younger generation. My mother knows, and she chooses to ignore it. She never asks me about my love life, but at least she has stopped trying to set me up with women. We get along well though." He winked at Eleanor, who winced at the remark. "But my father, he doesn't really speak to me. I've tried to rekindle our relationship after I told him I would never settle down with a woman but he's still very uncomfortable with it. It's like he doesn't know how to behave around me anymore." He shrugged. "I don't expect it to change. I'm his only son, and he's an Italian working class man. What can I say? To him, I'm a disappointment, and I've learned to live with that."

Eleanor and David nodded, looking down at their plates. There was an awkward silence and an uncomfortable exchange of glances. Sophie was glad when her father took charge.

"I'm sorry to hear that, Roberto. I haven't exactly handled this in the best way either, but I promise you that I'll do my best to make you feel welcome here and I really hope your father comes around eventually." He pushed his chair back and stood up with his wine glass raised. Stewart and Sophie both stared at him. He looked vulnerable and nervous. The sweat marks under his armpits had spread into two large stains on his white shirt, and his neck was red and blotchy.

He cleared his throat. "For now," he looked around the table, "I would like to thank you all for being here tonight, to celebrate Sophie's new job." He turned to Sophie. "Sophie, I know I don't say it very often, but I'm very proud of you." Sophie swallowed and tried to hold back her tears. Her father shook his head. "I must admit, I wasn't supportive of your career choice initially. I always hoped at least one of my children would study medicine and take over my practice." He paused and looked from Stewart to Sophie and back. "But you both chose to work in fields where your passion lies. I respect that, and I'm glad you have fun in what you do." He laughed. "I wish I could say the same thing for myself, but I'm afraid I did exactly what I always expected the two of you to do. I followed in my father's footsteps." He grinned. "Even though I really wanted to be a jazz musician."

Mel laughed, lightening the mood. "You can still do that, David. It's never too late."

David smiled at her, clearly amused. "Thank you, Mel. I've been thinking about it, but unfortunately, my wife won't let me retire." Eleanor shot him a fierce look, but she raised her glass too, along with the rest of them. They all clinked glasses. "To Sophie's new job."

Sophie smiled and tried not to get emotional. Words of praise were rare, coming from her father. "Thank you," she said. "You have no idea what it means to me that we can all sit here around this table and be civilized." She paused. "I have some more good news." She took a letter out of her back pocket and folded it out. "This arrived today." She turned to Mel and showed her the letter.

Mel took it, glanced over it and gasped. "Oh my God, you did it!" She gave Sophie a kiss on her cheek. "I can't believe you did it. He's going to be so happy!" She handed the letter to Eleanor, who looked slightly concerned with the upheaval.

"I adopted a dog from Hong Kong," Sophie explained. Do you remember Buba, the dog I wouldn't stop talking about two years ago?"

Stewart nodded and rolled his eyes, laughing. "How could I forget? You were like a new mother pestering me about her baby."

Sophie grinned. "Shut up Stewart. He's mine now, so you haven't heard the end of it yet. The letter confirming his adoption arrived this morning. He's a very sweet seven-year-old boy in case you've forgotten. He'll be here in six weeks so you'd better get ready for dog-sitting during my business trips." She winked at Roberto, who seemed genuinely excited about the prospect.

"I love dogs!" He shouted. "If Stewart's not up for it, I am."

Eleanor's eye twitched. She handed the letter to her husband. "Are you sure it's safe to adopt a dog from a country like that? I mean, he might have a disease or fleas, or he might be aggressive or..."

David nudged her. "Stop worrying, Eleanor. I'm sure Sophie knows what she's doing." He put the letter down. "Congratulations Sophie. I suppose that makes me some kind of Grandfather." Then he laughed and turned to his wife. "And you know what that makes you, right Eleanor?"

. . .

"Do you want to come home with me?" Mel asked after they'd left and had said their goodbyes.

"I just need to get my mother a takeaway on the way home." She stated. "I'll understand if you need some time for yourself." Sophie shook her head.

"Absolutely not. In fact, I think I prefer your place to mine. I mean, there's you, of course. I love waking up next to you. But it's also really nice to have a coffee on your patio in the morning. And I like the sound of the market from your bedroom window." She laughed. "And your cuter-than-cute fairy light ceiling."

Mel smiled and took her hand as they walked towards the tube station. "Well, I happen to like your place too."

Sophie raised an eyebrow. "What do you like about it?"

"Well, first of all, I like your fancy coffee machine." Mel giggled. "And your Jacuzzi bath and your view. Not to mention that it's only twenty minutes from work and it gives me an extra hour in bed in the morning. I guess together we've got the best of both worlds." She tightened her grip on Sophie's hand and sighed. "That went really well, didn't it?"

Sophie nodded. "It did. My parents surprised me." She planted a fleeting kiss on Mel's cheek. "You know, I feel like it's all going to be all right."

"Me too. I had a good time." Mel's face turned more serious. "I don't want to freak you out, but I need you to know that I love you, Sophie." She looked down and shook her head. "I'm sorry, I just had to say it. I hope it…"

"I love you too," Sophie whispered. Mel's words had not surprised her, but they had left a warm glow and a feeling of peace and happiness on her mind that was entirely new to her. She pulled Mel closer and smiled, trying to capture the moment. The warm summer breeze felt soothing on her skin, and it carried the scent of freshly cut grass, chip shops and stale ale from the pubs. The sun was setting over Sloan Square, highlighting the Venus Fountain and the War Memorial. There was laughter coming from the local restaurants where people were enjoying a late dinner with generous amounts of wine. And then there was Mel, beside her. And she wasn't going anywhere.

# EPILOGUE

Sophie waited by the harbour, leaning over the railing facing the Hong Kong skyline. In front of her, hundreds of coloured laser lights were dancing to the rhythm of classical music. They parted in different directions, lighting up the sky in an array of dreamy rainbow shades. It was eight o'clock in the evening, and the Symphony of Lights had just started.

"Sweets! Here!" That familiar voice still made Sophie go weak in the knees. She turned around, searching for Mel in the crowd. Her heart jumped when she spotted her, wading through the sea of people watching the light show. Mel approached her with the biggest grin on her face.

Sophie closed her eyes at the touch of Mel's arms around her waist and smiled. "Finally." She hugged Mel back and sighed, savouring the contact. "Two weeks is so long without you." She took a step back and studied Mel's face, running her hand through the thick, curly hair. It felt surreal. "I can't believe we're both here again."

"I've missed you," Mel said, kissing her lightly on the lips. "I was going mad at home without you. It's so quiet."

"I've missed you more." Sophie was surprised at her own soppy reaction. "And Buba of course. How is my good boy doing?"

"Not too pleased with the fact that we're both gone, but he'll be okay. He slept in front of the door for the first two days waiting for you, but he eventually decided that the bed was more comfortable." Mel held out her phone. "I've just spoken to the dog sitter, and he said Buba's been a total diva so far, refusing to eat anything other than cooked chicken." They both laughed and turned to the harbour. The sky lit up each time the music went staccato, drawing gasps from the audience around them.

Mel put an arm around Sophie. "So, here we are again. How's your trip been so far?"

Sophie shook her head. "Nothing like last time we were here together, but it's been okay. What about you? How's the new designer? Did you guys bond on the flight?"

Mel shrugged. "Just like the last one. He's lovely, but I don't think he'll be able to handle the workload." She rolled her eyes. "I'm trying to help him out as much as I can though. I think it's become apparent to everyone that you were quite the trooper." She laughed. "I'm thinking of hiring a part-time designer to help him out, so he won't take off too. But the good thing is, he's got a love interest here so at least I won't have to entertain him. We've got three full nights all to ourselves."

"Sounds like a dream," Sophie said. "I'll take you out for dinner tonight. How's your hotel? It's not too far from here, right?"

Mel shook her head and pointed at a building a couple of blocks from the harbour.

"I did some research," Sophie continued. "I believe my hotel has the biggest pool and yours has the biggest roof garden. They both have endless opportunities for making out in all the wrong places." She laughed. "So where do you want to go?"

Mel had a mischievous look on her face as she searched for something in her pocket. "How about neither?" she said. "I happen to have a fabulous penthouse suite for the coming two nights because we might have something to celebrate."

Sophie frowned at the enticing offer. "Silly, you didn't have to do that." She glanced at Mel who was now holding a box in her hand. It was too dark in the crowd to work out what it was, but when she opened it, everything around her came to a halt at the sight of something glistening. A ring. Mel went down on one knee, and as the people around them started to realize what was going on, they moved over, giving her space. Sophie's legs turned to jelly, and she stared at Mel in disbelief.

Mel sighed. "I'm so nervous." She giggled, looking up at Sophie. "Sorry for laughing but I can't help it. It's too nerve wracking." She held up the box. "Sophie. I love you so much, and I've wanted to do this for a while now. I think it's only right to do it in the place where it all began and I don't care if the whole world is watching. I'm so proud to be your girlfriend. I've never felt a connection like I have with you." She swallowed hard and took a deep breath. "I want to be with you forever, and I can only hope that you want that too. Please don't feel pressured. If it's too soon, I'll understand, and we can carry on having a great time together... But you'd make me so happy if you say yes to being my wife." She blinked away a tear and paused before she continued. "Sophie will you please marry me?"

Sophie was shaking all over, but a big smile spread across her face. She wasn't sure what she was supposed to do so she sank to the floor too, facing Mel. They were surrounded by people, but the noise had subsided. The music was building up to an epic finale, raising the volume with each violin solo. Sophie looked up at the strangers around them, holding their breath for her to answer. Tears rolled over her cheeks when she looked into Mel's eyes.

"Yes," she said, reaching out her hand. "Of course I'll marry you." The excitement on Mel's face was just as explosive as the music. She took Sophie's hand and kissed it, before sliding the ring on her finger. She was laughing, her eyes filled with tears. The crowd burst into joyous cries, clapping and cheering. When they kissed, the cheering became louder, along with the trombones playing the last bars of the finale. Sophie broke the kiss and smiled, swallowing down the lump in her throat.

"I'm all yours." She barely managed to speak, but it was enough.

"I'm all yours."

# ACKNOWLEDGMENTS

First and foremost, I'd like to say a very special thank you to my wife, for helping me out in the early stages of this book and for being patient with me when I'm so engrossed in a project that I forget everything else around me. You've been supportive and helpful and I don't like to admit it, but you always outsmart me :) Also, a huge thank you to Claire and Laure for being so flexible throughout the editing process. I really appreciate what you do.

# ABOUT THE AUTHOR

Lise Gold is an author of lesbian romance. Her romantic attitude, enthusiasm for travel and love for feel good stories form the heartland of her writing. Born in London to a Norwegian mother and English father, and growing up between the UK, Norway, Zambia and the Netherlands, she feels at home pretty much everywhere and has an unending curiosity for new destinations. She goes by 'write what you know' and is often found in exotic locations doing research or getting inspired for her next novel.

Working as a designer for fifteen years and singing semi-professionally, Lise has always been a creative at heart. Her novels are the result of a quest for a new passion after resigning from her design job in 2018. Since the launch of Lily's Fire in 2017, she has written several romantic novels and is currently working on 'The Compass Series'.

When not writing from her kitchen table, Lise can be found cooking, at the gym or singing her heart out somewhere, preferably country or blues. After living in Amsterdam and Hong Kong together and getting married in Spain, she and her wife have finally settled in the UK with their dogs El Comandante and Bubba, and their cats Kanye and Lil' Tittie (who also has his own clothing line).

## ALSO BY LISE GOLD

Printed in Great Britain
by Amazon

26220682R00172